THE LAIRD OF DRUMLYCHTOUN

IAN SKAIR: PRIVATE INVESTIGATOR

HILARY PUGH

1

L*ottie, you're a barking cliché.* Ian pulled the duvet over his head and tried to ignore his dog's manic yapping and the sound of her claws skidding across the wooden floorboards. Dogs and postmen, a stereotype well overdue an update. 'Be quiet, Lottie,' he mumbled, adding a pillow to the duvet to try to muffle the sound. Lottie should have learnt by now. The postman came most days, although Ian couldn't imagine why. He never brought anything interesting, and he always got barked at. Ian paid all his bills online. His clients paid him the same way, unless they didn't want to be discovered, in which case they tapped on his door in the dead of night and handed over envelopes of used twenty-pound notes. But that didn't happen often. Most of his clients were defiant about using his services. They felt it was their right to know what their nearest and dearest got up to. All that left for the postman were flyers for pizza delivery, flashy adverts for new housing developments complete with photos of happy residents - always devoted couples - and heart-breaking circulars begging him for money to help earthquake victims or local donkey sanctuaries. He did occasionally respond to some of those, proving once again what people kept telling him - he was too soft-hearted.

The barking died down. The postman had left and Ian could go back to sleep. But the departure of the postman meant just one thing to Lottie, who now arrived at his bedside with a lead in her mouth. Ian groaned, but she was right. It was time he got out of bed and took her for a walk. He reached for yesterday's clothes and pulled them on: socks, jeans and his usual shirt/sweater combo. He took them off as one piece and put them on again the same way. It saved time. Although time wasn't really an issue. He had very little to do today. A bit of paperwork, walking Lottie, a meal at the pub.

Another glorious day, he thought, pulling back the shutters and looking at the sun, which was just beginning to break through a light layer of mist that wafted over the Tay. He padded into the hall to look for his boots and that was when he saw it. The letter lying on his doormat. Who wrote letters these days? It was probably something sent out to look like a real letter but actually just another device to part him from his money. He'd been caught out like that before, usually by people who wanted him to make a will or who had elaborate plans for his retirement. These were decoy letters. They arrived in white envelopes with his name and address apparently handwritten but in reality carefully generated by a computer to *look* handwritten. The letters themselves always addressed him by his first name. He wasn't one for uncalled-for deference but, probably the result of his upbringing and his mother's ideas of what was right and proper, he resented being addressed by people he had never met, or had any intention of meeting, as *Ian*. What was wrong with a respectful *Mr Skair*?

He laced up his boots, then bent down to pick up the letter with every intention of throwing it into the recycling bin on his way out. But he'd been wrong. This was a real letter with his name and address handwritten in black ink. Better still, it used his professional name – *Ian Skair: Private Investigator*. Turning the envelope over, he noticed a tiny, embossed seal where the point of the flap was stuck down to the body of the envelope. He carried it to the window to examine it. The lettering was too small to read, but in the centre of the seal was the outline of a castle.

He felt that a letter like this should be treated with respect, so instead of tearing it open as he would normally have done, he carried into the kitchen, found a knife and slit it open at the top. He unfolded the letter and noted the same embossed heading. A little larger than the seal on the envelope, it was easier to read. It had the same picture and round the edge were the words *Drumlychtoun Castle*. Below that an address in a village also called Drumlychtoun. He had never heard of it.

It was a brief letter:

Dear Mr Skair

I would like to engage your services on a matter that is of some delicacy, and personal to myself and my family.

Please advise me of your terms and availability.

Sincerely yours

Alexander Lyton

Laird of Drumlychtoun

Ian left it on his desk as Lottie was pestering him for a walk. He would reply when he got back. He put on his jacket, found his wallet and clipped on Lottie's lead. His neighbour, Lainie, was hanging out her washing. 'Lovely morning for a walk,' she said, waving cheerfully. She was always hanging out washing. For someone who lived alone she had a lot of it. He supposed it might be some kind of cottage industry. Taking in washing had gone out of fashion since the arrival of domestic washing machines and launderettes. It was something his mother regretted. She'd always expected *people* to do stuff for her, not machines. He didn't stop to examine what Lainie was hanging out. He didn't want to seem nosy.

Ian agreed that it was a lovely morning. He wondered if he actually needed his jacket, but didn't return inside to take it off. This was Scotland. No one went outside jacketless in early May.

'We're off to the village,' he said. 'Can I get you anything?'

'No thanks. I did a big supermarket shop yesterday.'

He always offered and she nearly always refused. These offers were just neighbourly politeness. Neither expected the other to stagger up the hill from the village with heavy shopping. As neighbours went, Lainie was perfect. She was always happy to look after Lottie when he had to go out and couldn't take her with him. She liked to gossip over a cup of coffee, and they took in parcels for each other. Lainie's parcels were usually packs of wool, which she bought in huge quantities from internet suppliers. His were smaller and heavier: his packs of painkillers or books.

The best thing about Lainie was that she didn't try to pair him off with every unattached woman she knew. Everyone else seemed hell bent on putting an end to his solitary lifestyle. Jeanie, the wife of his closest friend and ex-colleague Duncan Clyde, was always having him over for meals to which she invariably invited some single, divorced or even widowed lady of roughly his own age. All perfectly nice women. He might even consider dating one or two of them if only to keep Jeanie quiet. But none of them so far had struck him as a life partner. Or perhaps he didn't really want a life partner. He'd messed up one marriage and he didn't relish the idea of doing it all over again. Since Lottie's kidnap a month ago, he'd been seeing a woman called Caroline Gillespie now and then. She was good company, sometimes a little more than that. But neither of them wanted to become *an item*. They knew they could call each other for occasional walks or meals out that wouldn't lead to any kind of commitment. And as far as he was concerned that was perfect. No expectations – no failures.

Arriving at the bottom of the hill and the village shop, Ian tied Lottie to a lamp post and went inside for a newspaper and some croissants. While he was in there it occurred to him that the Laird's letter hadn't mentioned a telephone number or an email. He was going to have to reply with a letter of his own. He bought a pack of envelopes and some stamps.

The walk back up the hill to his house had made him hungry. He popped the croissants into the oven and turned on the coffee machine. Then he went into his study and re-read the Laird's letter, formulating a reply in his head and trying to remember when he'd last written an actual letter. How did you address a laird? He turned on his computer and started a Google search for Drumlychtoun Castle. A beep from the kitchen reminded him that his breakfast was ready and, anxious to know more, he collected his coffee and croissants and decided to eat breakfast at his desk.

The castle and surrounding estate, he discovered, had been in the Lyton family for centuries. The Drumlychtoun Estate of several hundred acres was a tenant run co-operative which produced organic food for local marketplaces. After getting side-tracked by links, as one invariably does when using Google, Ian knew a lot more about sustainable food production than he had known before, but very little about the Laird himself. He returned to his search for the castle. The original fortress was built some time in the thirteenth century on a remote part of the Angus coast about fifteen miles from Montrose, but in around 1600 it had been washed into the sea and replaced by a more modern castle built further inland. This, with a few additions over the centuries must, from the address on the letter, be where the Laird now lived. He found photographs of the castle, a dour looking stone building perched on a small hill on the far side of a lake and approached by an arched bridge. He found no information about the current Laird who, from the tone of his letter, didn't sound like a very young man. So why, Ian wondered, did he need the services of a private investigator? His usual cases concerned workplace dishonesty or marital infidelity. As the landlord of a large estate the former sounded more likely and the sort of case he would prefer. Ian hoped that this wasn't going to be yet another case of spying on marital infidelity. It was not much fun in places like Edinburgh or Dundee. It would be a nightmare in a remote coastal village. It would involve sitting in his car, camera poised, parked in windy bits of rural Scotland or outside seedy hotels. Although perhaps someone with connections to a laird would be able to afford less seedy establishments for his or her trysts. It made very little difference. Ian would still have to be parked outside it. Cold winds didn't discriminate between cheap and expensive hotels. On the east coast of Scotland it was windy and wind had no respect for the size of one's wallet.

Ian turned to his reply to the Laird. He had never written to one before, or even spoken to one as far as he could remember. How did they like to be addressed? He clicked into Google again and found a site that dealt with Scottish etiquette. Momentarily distracted by a page that addressed the problem of whether to wear one's kilt belt above or below a sporran chain, not something he had ever worried about before but might just lead to sleepless nights in the future, he found information about the correct way of dealing with lairds. In a letter, it said, a laird should be addressed by his full name and on the envelope he should write the name followed by Laird of_. He trusted Google enough to assume he would get the protocol right and not fall at the first hurdle by upsetting a promising client.

Dear Alexander Lyton, he wrote.

Thank you for your enquiry.

I am enclosing a list of my terms and fees.

I am unable to confirm my availability until I know more about the type and scale of the work involved. I would be happy to discuss this with you further if you find the enclosed agreeable.

Yours sincerely

Ian Skair

Private Investigator

He added his phone number and email just in case someone in the Drumlychtoun household had decided to join the twenty-first century and make his life easier. Then he addressed the envelope to Alexander Lyton, Laird of Drumlychtoun and put it aside to post on his next visit to the village.

2

Ian spent the rest of the morning catching up on paperwork; not his favourite occupation but it was as well to keep on top of it. Particularly after the achingly dull case he had just finished. He needed to get that done with as soon as possible. The only upside was the hefty invoice he was about to submit. He clicked on send and hoped it wouldn't be too long before they paid him. Not that it mattered because right now he was feeling quite flush. A new experience for him. Downsizing had been a good idea. He liked where he lived now, and he had a nice little nest egg in the bank from the sale of Grandad's house.

He was beginning to think it must be nearly lunchtime when there was a knock at the door and the almost simultaneous sound of Lottie barking. He picked her up and went to see who was calling on him. Very few people did. Clients contacted him by phone or email and neighbours like Lainie tapped on his window or called through the kitchen door. For the case that had just ended there had been regular deliveries by a motorcycle courier. A young man whom Lottie had taken an irrational dislike to. So much so that she had to be shut in the kitchen before Ian felt safe opening the door. Perhaps it was the leathers and helmet she hated. Anyway, he'd finished that now.

The final package had been collected yesterday and the case was done. Thank goodness. Not only had it set Lottie off into paroxysms of barking, it was going to top his list of most boring cases ever.

It was now mid-week and school term-time, so this probably wasn't Caroline. That would have been nice. They could have walked down to the village for lunch. But even when she wasn't working, he had never known Caroline to call round without phoning him first. He heaved himself out of his chair, rubbed his aching leg and went to open the door, hefting Lottie under his arm as he went. It was a pleasant surprise to find Duncan on his doorstep. Why hadn't he thought of that? They had seen each other quite a lot recently.

'Working in Greyport?' Ian asked as he held to door open with Lottie wriggling in his arms. Duncan liked to keep an eye on his patch, which stretched from Cupar to St Andrews and across the Tay to Dundee. Now an inspector, Duncan preferred to be hands-on rather than sitting behind a desk giving orders. After the recent discovery that packages of drugs were being delivered in the village, Greyport was high on the surveillance list. It was possible that Duncan might be about to offer Ian a contract to do just that, although Ian would prefer not to have to spy on his neighbours. It would make his evenings in the pub uncomfortable.

'Day off,' Duncan said, indicating his casual get-up of jeans and navy blue Guernsey. 'I hoped you wouldn't be working today. I've something to show you.'

Last time Duncan had something to show him it had been a ransom note for a stolen dog, so this might not be altogether good news.

'Get your jacket and don't look so worried,' Duncan said, laughing and patting Lottie on the head.

This wasn't such good news either. People had a way of telling him not to worry when that was exactly what he should be doing.

Duncan slapped him on the back. 'Bring Lottie. You'll like this.'

Ian slung his jacket over one arm while still holding Lottie under the other and walked with Duncan down his steep garden path to the road.

'There you go.' Duncan spread his arms out towards the pavement where a number of cars were parked.

'There I go where?'

'That one over there. The silver one. Come on, laddie. Where're your brains today? You said you were after a new car.'

'Oh, I thought you'd forgotten.'

Duncan made an exaggerated hurt face. 'As if I would. Do you like it?'

'That one? The silver Touareg?' Ian stepped out into the lane and walked round the car. Then he turned and walked around it in the other direction. It was spotlessly clean and with not so much as a scratch in the paintwork. Only a discreet patch on the roof where he assumed there had once been a blue light. He peered through the windows at pristine black seats and dark grey carpet. It even had a built-in satnav screen and a metal guard to stop dogs, or he supposed, any other kind of animal, jumping into the passenger seats. It was way better than anything he'd expected.

Duncan stood on the pavement looking pleased with himself. 'Two years old, reasonable mileage, used as a traffic patrol car. All fully adapted back to regular civilian vehicle. Harry's prepared to do you a special price after I told him about the Hamilton business.'

Harry, that's right. He remembered now. The guy who dealt in ex-police cars and sold them on. 'Wow,' was all he could think of to say. He knew he'd done well to track down Hamilton and his drug dealing cronies, but it was mostly lucky coincidence. He wasn't sure it justified this, although of course, he didn't know yet how special Harry's price would be.

'Don't just stand there staring at it,' said Duncan. 'How about taking it for a wee test drive? Jeanie's packed up a picnic. I thought we could go for a run up the coast. Get a bit of fresh air in us. What do you think?'

It sounded like an offer no one would refuse. He opened up his old car – a car that definitely lowered the tone of the neighbourhood – and reached into the back for Lottie's blanket. Duncan tossed him the keys and he clicked to unlock the doors, opened up the tailgate and unfolded the blanket. Then he lifted Lottie in. She sniffed around and scuffed at the blanket with her paws. After making a few turns, rather as Ian had done when looking at the car, she settled down with her head on her paws and looked up at Ian expectantly. Cars usually meant trips to interesting places for walks.

Compared to his old heap of a car this one was a joy to drive. Ian drove across the bridge into Dundee and then took the Arbroath road. They considered stopping for a picnic at Broughty Ferry, a small village of upmarket wine bars and craft shops. But Ian was enjoying the drive too much and they decided to carry on through Arbroath and up to Lunan Bay where they could let Lottie run along the coast walk. Ian glanced at the petrol gauge and noticed that Harry had also contributed a full tank of petrol, or perhaps Duncan had filled it up for him. Either way he appreciated the gesture.

An hour's drive up the coast, Ian pulled into a parking space outside a café and let Lottie out to scamper around in the long grass and sand dunes. There was a fresh breeze which ruffled her fur and made her skittish. He pulled his jacket around him and noticed Duncan doing the same. They could see the ruins of a reddish stone castle and looking northward up the coast Ian realised that they must be close to Drumlychtoun. He tapped the postcode into his phone. It was only another nine miles from where they were now but if he took this case, it would involve lengthy round trips. A long way to go day after day to spy on adulterers. But of course, he had no details of the case yet. It could be something entirely different. It could even be something he could work on from home. But he hoped it would involve at least one or two visits to Drumlychtoun, which sounded like something from a nineteenth century romantic novel and might involve raven-haired maidens locked up in granite towers awaiting heroic rescue.

'A penny for them,' said Duncan, dragging him out of his daydream. 'You were miles away.'

'About nine miles. I was thinking about a case I might or might not take.'

'Nine miles from here? A bit out of your way, isn't it?'

'Not as far as visiting the family.'

'Oh aye, and how often do you do that?'

He had a point. On the other hand, Aberdeen was twice as far as they had come today and even with a new car, he wasn't going to make that trip more than was absolutely necessary. Travelling for a case was different. A pleasure if he bought this car. 'It's a place called Drumlychtoun,' he said. 'Do you know it?'

'I've heard of it. Large-ish estate with good farming land and fishing rights. What have they been up to?'

'I don't know yet. I had a letter from the Laird. He said it was personal.'

'Extramarital?'

'No idea. I hope not. You're right. It's a bit of a trek from Greyport and it would need to be more interesting than that. But I haven't accepted it yet, just sent my list of fees.' He still had the letter in his pocket. He must remember to post it on the way home. It would be worth finding out what it was all about. No need to commit himself yet.

Duncan opened a flask of soup and poured it into a couple of mugs. He handed one to Ian, who wrapped his hands around it. There was a fresh wind and they had chosen a draughty bench for their picnic. Lottie was still rushing around enjoying the breeze from the sea. It was good to see her running free up here. When they walked along the beach at Greyport he had to keep her on the lead.

'She does a good picnic, your Jeanie,' Ian said, finishing his soup and tucking into a slice of apple pie.

'You know Jeanie, never happier than when she's filling people with food. She said it would do us both good to get out and blow away the cobwebs.'

She was right. He didn't know about Duncan, but *he*'d not been out much in the last month. A morning in Dundee collating evidence after the Hamilton case, which of course involved Duncan as well.

Then a couple of weeks trawling through company records for a possible breach of data security. These had been couriered to him so apart from walking Lottie, he'd barely been out of the house. And in spite of the cold wind here on the dunes, the weather was beginning to feel like spring. If he bought this car, and unless Harry's price was way above what he expected, he would buy it, he resolved to get out a lot more. He could leave his house and after a few minutes driving in any direction he chose, he and Lottie could be out in unspoilt countryside. He'd not done that when he lived in Edinburgh. Caring for an elderly grandfather hadn't given him much freedom. And he'd not really done much of it since leaving Edinburgh. He'd meant to. It was one of the attractions of moving out of the city, but he'd been too busy, or too lazy. But now he had a dog, a new car (probably) and flexible working hours, not to mention more daylight, he had no excuse. And work in Drumlychtoun could be just what he needed. Out of the house and away from his desk. What were a few extra miles when they meant driving on glorious empty roads with stunning coastal views? Good God, he was beginning to sound like an advert for the Scottish Tourist Board.

Duncan rubbed his hands and looked at his watch. 'It's getting a bit chilly,' he said. 'We'd better be getting back.'

Ian called Lottie and she hopped back into the car and settled happily on her blanket.

'So you like the car?' Duncan asked, as Ian started the engine.

'Definitely.'

'Great. We'll drop in on Harry on the way back and you can sort out the money and the paperwork. Then it's all yours.'

'As long as his price is manageable.'

'It will be. Trust me,' said Duncan, winking.

What was going on here? He suspected Jeanie had expressed an opinion. She always said she thought Ian had got a raw deal from the Edinburgh Police after his injury. Had they had some kind of fundraiser for him? After ten years it wasn't likely, but who was he to argue?

.   .   .

The drive back to Dundee was just as enjoyable as the drive out to Arbroath. Harry's office was on the outskirts of Dundee. Harry himself was a plump, red-faced ex copper and as unlike the stereotypical second-hand car salesman as one could imagine. After some winks and nudges between him and Duncan, he presented Ian with an invoice. Ian looked at it. High enough not to be insulting but well within his budget. 'Fine,' he said, handing over his bank card.

'You're covered by my insurance for a week,' said Harry, handing over a form. 'Send that off to DVLC, transfer your own insurance and you're all set.'

Ian took the papers, folded them up and put them in his pocket, finding his letter to the Laird as he did so. *Mustn't forget that,* he thought, the idea of a case at Drumlychtoun becoming more interesting the more he thought about it.

They chatted for a while about the best way to get rid of his old car. It was worthless, he knew that. So he accepted Harry's offer to take it away for fifty pounds. A bargain under the circumstances and, he was sure, a relief to his neighbours. Then he drove home stopping at the post office in Greyport to post his letter to the Laird.

3

Two days later, Ian logged on and checked his bank account. The fee for his last case had been paid and so had Harry's payment for the car. He spent some time switching sums of money around his accounts. An unfamiliar and not unenjoyable activity. He'd always lived from hand to mouth in the past. Stephanie had mopped up most of his police salary and in the early days after his accident he'd survived, with Grandad's help, on a small police pension. Small because they'd offered him a desk job which he'd refused. After which they more or less washed their hands of him. But it had been enough. He had no debts and very few expenses. And since then, there had been a slow drip-feed of fees from his cases. He should do something with the rest of Grandad's legacy. The new car had made only a small dent in it. Should he start thinking about his retirement? It seemed a long way off. He was just setting out on a new life after seeing Grandad through his final years. He didn't much want to think about his own old age. He'd leave the money where it was for the moment. There were just two things he wanted to buy right now: a new sofa and a large box of crayons for a little girl called Jessie, who had helped him solve what he now thought of as the

'Lottie kidnap case'. He would need Caroline's help with both of them. A nice thought. He might call her later.

Right now, he needed to keep to his new resolution to have his business accounts ready for next year without the aid of his usual cardboard box. He opened the app he had just bought and entered the amount he'd been paid this morning, along with a copy of the invoice. Then he had an idea. Something he'd probably have forgotten about if he'd left all his papers in a box for a year. He needed a car for his work. He could claim it as a business expense, so he entered the amount he'd paid for it and scanned in Harry's receipt. Strange how something as dull as sorting out his finances made him feel he'd joined the real world again.

He spent a few moments searching for sofas online but found the choices baffling. He could pay anything from a couple of hundred pounds to ten or eleven thousand. Did he really need a ten-thousand-pound sofa? Did anyone? His mother, possibly, and Stephanie. On the other hand, if he only paid a couple of hundred would it fall apart in weeks? He definitely needed Caroline's help.

Having probably set himself up for months of online stalking by sofa companies, he turned to his email. Not much of interest. He clicked through, unsubscribing to any that were trying to sell him things. There were a couple for sofas. How did that happen so fast? Then an email from his insurance company with a link to his updated policy. There was one from his mother asking if he'd remembered it was his brother's birthday in a few days. He had remembered but had done nothing about it. He quickly found his way to a site where he discovered a singing birthday greeting with some particularly horrible pink cats warbling in an annoying falsetto and typed in his brother's email.

He had cleared everything out of his inbox and felt the same kind of satisfaction as when he'd scrubbed the kitchen floor, when a new one pinged in. He read the sender's address, *bridget@drumlychtounestates.com*, and clicked it open enthusiastically.

· · ·

Dear Mr Skair,

Many thanks for your reply to my husband's letter and thank you for including your email. I'm afraid my husband is not very good with technology.

Thank you also for including details of your fees etc.

We would like to suggest that you come here and discuss the matter further. We will pay you for one day's work after which we can decide whether or not we want to take things further.

Would you be able to come on either Tuesday or Thursday of next week? If this is not convenient, please offer some alternative dates.

We both look forward to meeting you.

With best regards

Bridget Lyton

Ian checked his diary; a local head teacher wanting him to check out what he thought could be a false CV, a visit to yet another woman who suspected an unfaithful husband, and a curious request from a man who suspected his dog's pedigree was not genuine. Shouldn't he be more concerned with the dog itself? He wouldn't care in the least if he discovered that Lottie had some dubious ancestry. Probably to do with money. Most things were, and if the man had paid an exorbitant amount for his dog, then Ian supposed he would care about the genuineness or otherwise of its pedigree. It felt like a lot of fruitless visits to breeding kennels and he might decide not to do it, although he suffered the ever-present curse of the self-employed – the inability to turn down work. He didn't need to decide now. These were all initial enquiries that he could fit into the second half of next week.

He clicked to reply to Bridget Lyton and said that next Tuesday would suit him very well. He would arrive at nine in the morning and would be at their disposal until five in the evening. He asked if they would mind if he brought his dog, who was small and well-behaved.

Then he sent an email to Caroline asking for advice about sofas and hoping she'd offer to come with him and hold his hand, so to speak.

A rapid reply from Bridget included a map and the assurance that his dog would be very welcome. They would give him lunch, and could he let them know if he was a vegetarian.

So, he thought, communicating with the wife of the Laird suggested that this wasn't about an extra-marital affair. He tried to think of what else might need investigating on an isolated estate in rural Angus, but nothing came to mind. He would just have to wait and see.

Caroline's reply came a few minutes later.

Oh Ian, have you never heard of John Lewis? He didn't think he had. *There's one in Edinburgh. Free on Saturday? I'll buy you lunch. Pick you up around 11?*

Didn't they sell sofas in Dundee? Well, a drive to Edinburgh would be nice. He could show off his new car.

Thanks Caroline, he wrote. *I'll pick you up at 11. I've got a new car!!!!!*

After that he spent some time on the John Lewis website checking out sofas – he'd still need help. But then he discovered that they also carried a range of stationery and art materials so they could buy a thank you present for Jessie at the same time. He rather fancied a selection of sparkling gel pens in gaudy colours and a drawing pad with unicorns on the front.

On Tuesday Ian was woken by his alarm at six-thirty. *Why?* he wondered sleepily and then remembered he had to be at Drumlychtoun by nine. He took Lottie for a quick walk around the garden, swallowed a cup of coffee and gulped down a bowl of cereal. He would be given lunch, but he packed a bag of dog biscuits and chews for Lottie. He tended to travel light when working on cases. He found a notebook and some pencils, but his phone would do most of the work making recordings and taking photographs. He rounded up his phone charger, a warm jacket and his keys. Clipping on Lottie's lead, they made their way down the path to his car. His new car. That still gave him a thrill. He'd had it less than a week so going anywhere in it

- supermarket, a visit to Duncan and Jeanie in St Andrews, giving Lainie a lift to the dentist, driving out of town to walk Lottie, was still exciting. His longest trip had been to Edinburgh at the weekend with Caroline. He had thought he would take Lottie and Caroline's dog, Angus, with them. They could walk them on the way back. But Caroline said they wouldn't be able to take the dogs into the shop and they shouldn't be left in the car. He agreed about the car although he didn't see why they shouldn't take them shopping. They'd only be a few minutes. Caroline had laughed at that. And buying a sofa turned out to be a whole lot more complicated than he'd expected. He thought it would simply be a matter of sitting on a few, choosing the most comfortable, handing over his bank card and arranging for them to deliver it. He was wrong. He lost count of the number of designs he looked at, all coming in a variety of sizes. 'Narrow it down by price,' Caroline suggested and that had helped. He settled for mid-range. Sturdy but not mortgage inducing. 'Two or three-seater?' he was asked.

'Three,' said Caroline firmly. 'You need to be able to stretch out on it.'

He wanted squashy cushions which also narrowed things down. But the only three-seater, mid-price sofa with squashy cushions they had to show him came in a shade of Stephanie mauve and he couldn't live with that.

The salesman laughed. Apparently, this actual sofa was only the showroom model. His would be made for him. He could choose the colour and it would be delivered to him in eight weeks. He was then shown swatches of fabric in about one hundred and fifty different colours. Probably best to choose something neutral, he was told. Go for some bright accessories. Fine by him. He picked out a colour in a shade that was a mixture of mud and Lottie's fur. It would be a thankless job trying to stop her sitting on it, so something that wouldn't show paw marks was sensible. Colourful accessories could wait. Caroline was up for it, but he needed to sit down with a cup of tea, not to mention the lunch she had promised him. Both available without setting foot outside John Lewis.

After a good lunch, choosing something for Jessie was a whole lot easier. In the stationery department you paid for what you wanted, and they put it in a bag for you to take with you. They had monster boxes packed with everything a young artist could wish for; crayons, pastels, gel pens, paints and brushes. Caroline picked a 'thank you' card and offered to parcel it all up and post it to Jessie.

With Jessie thanked and a new sofa on the way, Ian turned his attention to Drumlychtoun. It was another lovely morning and he opened the windows a crack to let in some fresh air. In his mirror he watched Lottie, on her hind legs and with her nose in the air, sniffing appreciatively. He cleared Dundee before the morning traffic build-up and headed up towards Montrose on a pleasantly empty road. He turned on the radio and listened to music on Classic FM. His old car did have a radio, but the engine was too noisy for him to hear very much so he didn't usually bother with it. He wasn't sure about Classic FM. He liked the music. Piano music reminded him with affection of Rosalie. Occasionally there were songs which reminded him of Piers, Rosalie's long-distance lover, for whom he felt a little less affection. A shame really. He'd got on well with Piers and they could have been friends if he hadn't been the love of Rosalie's life. Living in New Zealand didn't help either. Suddenly Ian was irritated and turned the radio off. He didn't like the adverts and all the banter between pieces of music. When he had a bit of spare time, he must work out how to connect up his phone and play music he had chosen himself. He probably wouldn't choose piano music or lieder songs.

By eight-thirty he had turned off the main road into a series of lanes and through villages of little white bungalows and farm buildings. Lottie started jumping up and whining excitedly. She could smell the sea. The lanes began to twist and narrow, his view restricted by high hedges. Tufts of grass appeared in the middle of the road and Ian felt as if he would end up in a field. But then a final bend in the lane and the road opened out again as it ran along the side of a lake. As the road followed the curve of the lake, he caught his first sight of

Drumlychtoun Castle. A picture postcard view of the granite grey building with four round towers and slits of windows, sitting in the lee of a small mound, the drum. The final drive up to the castle took him along a spit of land - a lake on one side, on the other a quarter mile of scrubby grassland and then a rocky beach and finally, over an arched stone bridge. Here he had two choices. He could either follow the road round the outside of the castle or drive through an archway between the castle walls. He chose the latter and found himself in a courtyard, where the building seemed more homely and less menacing. It was, he guessed, a modern addition with large windows, plants in pots and an entrance with double doors.

The courtyard was empty. Should he have continued round to the back of the building and parked at the rear of the castle? Near a tradesman's entrance perhaps. What was his status? Employee or guest? His problem was solved when the door of the castle was opened, and a woman appeared on the steps. She was in her late fifties or early sixties, dressed in corduroy trousers, a Fair Isle jumper and thick socks rolled over the hem of the trousers. He guessed she had recently discarded a pair of wellies. Her brown hair was streaked with grey and held back with a velvet headband. She walked towards Ian and held out her hand as he pressed the button to open the window.

'Good morning,' she said, smiling. 'And welcome to Drumlychtoun. I'm Bridget Lyton, and you must be Mr Skair.'

He nodded. 'Where would you like me to park?' he asked.

'You're fine here. No need to stand on ceremony.'

He climbed out of the car and opened the door for Lottie. 'You said it was okay to bring my dog?'

'Absolutely,' she said, bending down to stroke Lottie. 'We've two of our own somewhere. We don't shut them in. They can't go very far and they'll turn up when they're hungry. Come in, both of you.'

She led them into an enormous entrance hall. *Baronial* was the word that came to mind. It was what he had always imagined the interior of a Scottish castle to be: antlered deer heads, enormous oak dining table, and an open fireplace stacked high with logs, over which was a shield with a coat of arms. On the walls was a selection of weapons; their purpose he could only guess but whatever it was made him flinch. On the far side of the room was a gallery, for minstrels he thought, wondering when minstrels had gone out of favour and been replaced with the more mundane sounding musicians. He couldn't see a way into the gallery and assumed there must a staircase somewhere hidden from view so that musicians could come and go without disturbing the revelry in the hall below. At one end of the hall was a wide staircase hung with portraits.

'Impressive, isn't it?' said Bridget.

He couldn't argue with that. It resonated with generations of Scottish aristocracy.

'We don't use it often,' she said. 'Too big to heat and all those weapons are enough to give one nightmares.'

They'd certainly give him nightmares. But after being shot, any kind of weapon did that. It was quite comforting to know they gave other people nightmares as well. It made him feel less of a wimp.

Bridget led him into a smaller, more comfortable, and definitely warmer room with a view of the gardens, where a path led down to the beach. This was much more like a normal house. There was an armchair facing the window and Ian could see the top of a man's head.

'Xander, darling,' said Bridget. 'Mr Skair has arrived.'

Xander — the Laird, Ian presumed — put his newspaper to one side and pulled himself out of his chair.

He shook Ian's hand. 'Very pleased you decided to come,' he said. He was tall and grey-haired. Around sixty, Ian thought, and dressed similarly to his wife. Thick socks seemed to be standard footwear here. Should he have brought some? It was what he usually wore in his own house. He looked down at the floor. Unlike the stone floor in the hall, this one was wooden like his own floors. Socks were comfortable on floors like these; warm, polished and probably the same vintage as the floors in his own house. The outer part of the castle was old, and Ian couldn't begin to guess when it was built. The part he was in now, he thought, was nineteenth century with doors and windows very similar to houses in Greyport.

The Laird bent down to stroke Lottie, who licked his hand and wagged her tail. 'Have a seat,' he said, indicating a chair.

'I'll go and make coffee,' said Bridget.

'Any of Maggie's shortbread left? Delicious,' he said, turning to Ian. 'Baked by one of our tenants.'

'I'll have a look,' said Bridget. 'Anything for the wee dog?'

'A bowl of water?' Ian suggested. 'She's brought her own snack,' he said, waving her bag of dog biscuits. 'A lovely spot you have here...' He wasn't sure what to call the Laird.

'Call me Xander, everyone else does. And it is a lovely spot. Best place in the world. Nothing nicer than sitting right here watching all the changes in the weather. It's beautiful today with the sun and all the spring flowers, but it's just as beautiful in a winter storm when we get the massive rollers coming in from the North Sea. There's nothing between here and Denmark, Sweden if you go a little more to the North, as many of my ancestors did. Ran out of money you see, in around 1650. Lost everything when the old castle washed into the sea.'

Bridget returned with a tray of coffee, which she set down on a small table. A little too close to Lottie's nose level, Ian thought as he pulled her closer to his chair. Bridget poured them all a cup of coffee and handed round shortbread, breaking off a small piece which she gave to Lottie. 'Is that okay?'

'You'll have made a friend for life,' said Ian laughing. 'Tell me more about the castle. It's an interesting mixture of different styles.' He took a sip of coffee. 'And your ancestors,' Ian added.

'I'll be telling you a lot more as soon as we've finished coffee. But that will mostly be more recent history. Before the seventeenth century it's all a bit more confused. There've been Lytons in this area for centuries. The problem is that it's a very common name in these parts, with variations in spelling of course. Our own name came from Lychtoun as you've probably guessed, but you'll also find records of Litons, Lightons, Leightons, Leichtons and probably more. There's no way of knowing who was related to who. This wasn't made any easier by the two generations who decamped to Sweden. The records become clearer towards the end of the eighteenth century when family fortunes were restored by Robert Lyton who was able to claim a right to the land. He'd made a fortune trading in the early days of the East India Company which probably had a degree of influence with the authorities, who no doubt backed his claim to be a genuine Lychtoun. He was granted the right to the coat of arms in 1780 and no one has questioned it since then.'

'That's fascinating,' said Ian. 'My own name is local as well. I grew up in Aberdeen, but there are quite a few Skairs dotted around Angus.'

'I believe we have a record of a Lyton marriage to a Skair, so perhaps we're related. I'll look it out for you.'

Bridget started to clear away the coffee cups. 'Ian is here to work,' she reminded them.

'Quite right,' said Xander. He stood up and indicated a table where he had laid out a collection of photograph albums. 'We'll come back to these, but first we need to take a look at some portraits.' He pulled on a second jumper and led Ian through the hall to the staircase. About halfway up, he stopped in front of a portrait of a dour looking man with a goatee beard who was dressed in black with a white collar and what Ian took to be a seventeenth century version of a beanie hat.

'Another Alexander Lyton,' Xander explained. 'He was a doctor and puritan pamphleteer best known for his 1630 rant against the Anglican church, for which he was tortured and harshly punished. He lived in London at the time and when he knew the trouble he was likely to be in, he sent his son back here to be brought up in safety.'

Xander moved up a step and stood in front of another portrait. 'This is his son - Robert Lyton. You'll notice that the names Alexander and Robert are used in alternating generations of Lytons. My father was Robert and if I'd had a son, he would also have been called Robert.'

Ian studied the painting. Dressed in black with a similar white collar, the son was hatless and had long hair and a small moustache. But their faces were strikingly alike.

'Unlike his father,' Xander continued, 'Robert was a studious, pious man. He studied at Edinburgh University and eventually became Bishop of Dunblane. You'll notice that he is holding his hand against his heart and if you look carefully, you can make out the ring he is wearing. It's a traditional bishop's ring and the source of the problem I am asking you to solve.'

Ian got out his phone. 'Do you mind if I photograph these?' he asked.

Xander nodded. 'It's important that you do, particularly Robert and the ring.'

Ian took his photos, zooming in for a close-up of the ring.

'I'm intrigued by the architecture,' said Ian, looking around at the stone walls of the hall and the more modern staircase.

'Don't be misled by the hall,' Xander said. 'The old castle was rebuilt by various Lytons who could scrape together enough money. The first stones were laid quite soon after the old castle was washed away. As I said, they were short of cash, so it was added to over the next couple of centuries. From the records I have it seems to have been a bit of a mash up of styles chosen by whichever Lyton had enough cash to add on to it. After Robert took over, he had the whole place gutted. He kept the outer walls and restored the hall to what he thought was its medieval glory and surrounded it with modern rooms – modern by Georgian standards anyway. His great grandson, Alexander, updated it further in around 1870 with inside plumbing. Electricity was added in the 1920s by my grandfather, who also enlarged the windows on the east wall to improve the view of the sea.'

They returned to the living room and sat down at the table. Ian had his notebook at the ready and wondered if he should be making notes about the castle's history. Whatever this case was about, he was being drawn into it. Xander pushed the books aside, reached for a small wooden box and opened it. Inside, on a bed of green velvet, was a gold ring with an amethyst in the centre.

'The ring in the portrait?' Ian asked, comparing it with the photo on his phone.

Xander shook his head. 'I always assumed it was, but I discovered recently that this is a copy. I was asked to lend it for an exhibition in Glasgow of ecclesiastical treasure and they told me it was a fake. They had several experts in to look at it, but they all agreed. The box is likely to be original. The ring itself is a copy, probably made in the 1960s. It was well made and could only have been copied from the original. It was made by someone who knew what they were doing – hallmarked and distressed to suggest its age. They agreed to display it labelled as a copy. I got it back last week.'

Bridget had joined them. 'Have you told Ian the legend?' she asked.

'It's just a stupid story.'

'All the same, it might have some connection.'

'Well,' Xander continued. 'It is believed that as long as the ring is in the possession of the Laird, luck will stay on his side. If it passes out of the family it will be the end for him, his family, the castle...'

Ian could understand Xander's reluctance to give the story any credence. If he believed the legend, it would mean his own destruction. And to make it worse this laird appeared to have no heir. He could see where this was going and wondered if his resources were up to tracking stolen jewellery. It would have been sold on, possibly many times. It could be anywhere in the world. Needles in haystacks had nothing on this. 'I'm not sure I'm able to help,' he said. 'I know nothing about jewellery, forged or otherwise. And this was so long ago. I wouldn't know where to start.'

'You haven't heard the whole story yet,' said Bridget. 'We realise finding the ring is a long shot, although if you did it would be marvellous.'

'No,' added Xander. 'What we would like you to do is find the person who stole it.'

Didn't that amount to the same thing?

'Who we *think* stole it,' said Bridget.

'And you think you know who stole it?' That would make a difference, although possibly not a very *big* difference. Ian supposed it would depend how close they were to whoever they thought had stolen it. But if they knew them, couldn't they just ask? Well, perhaps not. Might spoil a friendship. 'Hey, nice to see you. Did you steal our ring?' No, that wouldn't do.

'We have our suspicions,' said Xander, opening one of the photograph albums. He flicked through the pages and settled on one, turning it to Ian. 'This is my sister, Ailish.'

Ian studied the photo. It was a young woman of eighteen or nineteen. She had waist-length hair and was wearing a very short skirt with knee high boots. She had false eyelashes and a sulky expression.

'Ailish was always difficult,' said Xander. 'She didn't get along with my father. My mother died soon after I was born, which must have been very hard for Ailish. She left home not long after this photo was taken.'

'When did your father die?' Ian asked.

'About twenty years ago.'

'And Ailish is older than you?'

'Considerably. She was twelve when I was born.'

'And when did you last see her?'

'1967. I was just a lad in short trousers. I barely remember her. No idea where she went or what she's done since.'

More than fifty years ago! And about the time the fake ring was made. Did they think Ailish had taken it when she left home? Was Xander asking him to find her?

'Has she been in contact since then?'

'Not a word.'

'And you think she had a copy made of the ring and then took the genuine one with her when she left?' He found that hard to believe. An angry teenager might steal the ring. But have a copy made? And exchange it for the real one without anyone knowing? It all seemed a bit far-fetched.

'The date seems right,' Xander continued. 'The experts think it was a 1960s fake. She could have taken it to Aberdeen or Inverness, even Edinburgh, and had it copied.'

'And have you any idea where she went after she left here?'

'My father thought she might have gone to London. Swinging sixties and all that. And she wanted to study art.'

'And he didn't try to find her?'

'To be honest I don't think my father really cared. They'd never got on. She looked a little like our mother and I think he probably found that hard. She was a constant reminder of what he had lost.'

Sad, Ian thought. A motherless girl whose father resented her for being alive was a miserable way to grow up. He didn't blame her for leaving, or for stealing the ring, if that was what she had done. He wondered if Ailish had believed the legend. Was she trying to destroy the family? Had she no feelings for the brother she'd left behind?

Ian sat back and stared out of the window. They hadn't asked him to find Ailish. Not in so many words, but he couldn't think what else they wanted after what Xander had just told him. He would be looking for a woman in her mid-seventies, who might or might not have stolen a ring. She wouldn't look anything like her photograph, but there was software that could age faces. He had one or two contacts who would know about that. She would most likely have changed her name at least once, but there would be records of marriages that he could check. She might have had children and again he could search birth records. She might not even be alive, but seventy wasn't so old. There was a good chance she would be. The hardest thing would be if she had moved abroad. He might need to look at foreign records and that would be time consuming and expensive. He wondered why Ailish had never returned home. She knew where they were and that they were not the kind of family to move around. Did she know that her father had died, or that her brother had married? Would it matter to her whether or not the estate had an heir? Would she prefer not to be found?

He took a deep breath. 'You want me to find her.'

Xander looked at him with a determined expression. 'I do, yes.'

'And if I find her, then what?' He could simply give them her current whereabouts and leave them to decide what to do. He could say that he had found her and that she was alive and well, or not, and leave it at that. Or was he expected to tackle her about the ring? And if he did that, what was the likelihood of her telling him the truth?

He explained all of that to Xander and Bridget.

'I think,' said Xander thoughtfully, 'that I would like you to talk to her. Just find out how things are with her.'

'And if she has a family?'

'There would of course be implications for the estate. I would need to reconsider my will.'

Ian wondered what was in his will, but felt it would be intrusive to ask and not relevant right now.

'So you'd be willing to take it on?' Bridget asked.

It wouldn't be easy, but yes, he would. It was something that would use his skills and his tenacity, and it would be a change from his usual work. A huge change. And he already felt involved with the family. A short meeting and he had become fond of them. Xander needed to know what had happened to his sister. Ian didn't think the ring had all that much to do with it. This was a man aware of his own mortality, who needed to reconnect with his past before it was too late.

But he mustn't get too emotionally involved. He should keep it businesslike. 'We'd need to draw up a contract,' he said. 'How many hours are you prepared to pay for? How much can I spend on expenses? That kind of thing.'

'What do most of your clients do?' Bridget asked.

She was the down-to-earth one here and Ian was glad of it. She would need to remind Xander of what was practical. Not let him raise his hopes too high and help him deal with disappointment if Ian failed. 'The most popular arrangement is a week-to-week rolling contract. I send you a report at the end of every week and you decide whether or not you want me to continue, leave it there or take a different direction.'

'That all sounds very satisfactory,' said Xander. 'What do you think, Bridget?'

'Yes,' she said. 'Let's go for it. When can you start?'

'Right away,' said Ian. 'If you have decided, it would be convenient if I could note a few things while I'm here.'

'How about some lunch first? Hope you don't mind eating in the kitchen. It's more comfortable than the hall.'

He'd hardly expected to be fed in the grand hall, which he imagined was only used for celebrations. A cosy meal somewhere warm was much more appealing.

The kitchen, he guessed, was a legacy of whoever had installed the plumbing in 1870. He doubted it had changed much since then. There were copper pans hanging from the ceiling, strings of onions and baskets of vegetables. The sink — a Belfast sink, he thought it was called — had two brass pillar taps of the sort much sought after by Edinburgh hipsters on the hunt for authentic fittings. In fact, the whole kitchen had an authentic feel to it, a mixture of generous Scottish hospitality and grim cold winters. He could see a scullery beyond the kitchen and imagined game hanging there before being carried into the hall to spit roast over the fire.

He was introduced to Maggie, who was standing by an Aga stirring something that smelt delicious.

'Maggie's lived in the village all her life,' Bridget told him. 'The Aga was her idea. Until ten years ago we were cooking on the original range. Maggie threatened to leave if she had to relight it one more time or break her back trying to keep it blackened.'

Maggie looked up and grinned. She didn't look in the least threatening, which he supposed was the effect an Aga could have after years of cooking on a Victorian range. She must be in her fifties, he thought, so wouldn't remember Ailish. 'Did your parents live in the village?' he asked.

'My mother still does,' she said. 'Ninety years old and still as bright as a button.'

Ian made a mental note to talk to Maggie's mum. With any luck she would remember Ailish. As a stroppy teenager she would have been noticed and hopefully gossiped about. He wondered if there were other locals who might remember her.

Lunch was a splendid lamb stew with mashed potato and spring greens, followed by fruit salad and cream. All organically produced on the estate, Bridget told him proudly. 'Xander and I went organic a few years ago.'

'Do you manage the estate yourselves?' Ian asked.

She shook her head. 'Xander and I are directors, but we employ a manager. We needed an expert in organic production. It's a minefield of red tape. He has an office here in the south tower, but he oversees all the farms on the estate and the fishing rights. We send the catch to Arbroath for smoking and doing that in a way that earns an organic label is full of pitfalls.

Ian had seen all of that on their website. The famous Arbroath smokie now raised to the status of organic produce, exported all over the world at several times the cost of its local counterpart.

Full of excellent food, Ian and Xander returned to the sitting room carrying cups of coffee. Lottie had been given a lamb knuckle to chew and Ian, worried about scratches on the polished wood floor, thought it best to leave her in the kitchen. By now he had a head full of questions, which he wrote down while he drank his coffee.

'Looks like homework,' said Xander.

'I'm hoping you can give me all the information I need to get started. Do you have a copy of Ailish's birth certificate, school reports, names of friends, places she liked to shop? Any knowledge about boyfriends?'

'We can get down to all of that this afternoon, but I usually take the dogs out after lunch. Do you and Lottie fancy joining us?'

'I haven't seen your dogs,' said Ian. 'Do you keep them outside?'

'Lazy buggers, the pair of them. They sleep in the boiler room at the back of the kitchen when they're not wandering around on the beach rolling in muck and picking up bits of nastiness to chew.' He whistled and two sleepy black Labradors appeared. Lottie had now strolled in from the kitchen. She pricked up her ears as the two dogs came into the room and wandered over for a sniff at the newcomers. They ignored her. 'See what I mean? We could be burgled, and they'd barely raise an eyelid.' He stroked them affectionately. 'We'll take a stroll to the beach and I can show you where the old castle used to be.'

The wind was fresher and stronger than when Ian had arrived. He wrapped his jacket around him and kept his hands in his pockets. The dogs livened up considerably in the fresh air, even acknowledging Lottie as a potential play fellow. A fifteen-minute walk and they were standing on a cliff that ended with a forty-foot drop into the sea. Xander pointed out towards the horizon. 'The old castle, really more of a fortress, was at the end of a promontory about fifty feet in that direction. Daft place to build anything, although it survived a few hundred years there. Built to spot Norse marauders, I suppose. It's said that on stormy nights you can hear the screams of those left inside. A lot of superstition if you ask me.'

Ian shivered. Apart from the castle there was nothing to see for miles. The village was behind him, hidden by trees and winding lanes. In front there was only the sea and the bare cliff. He looked to his right at the castle, which from this side seemed unfriendly, menacing even. From here all he could see were the fortress-like walls. They started walking back. Turning left from the promontory they could now see the friendlier east side with the picture window. Someone, Bridget he suspected, worked hard in the garden. It was a splash of colour in the middle of a grey, rocky landscape. He wondered what it had been like growing up here. Xander seemed happy. He'd been his father's favourite, the longed-for son, a consolation for the death of his wife. But a lively teenage girl? There couldn't have been much to interest her here. A few friends in the village perhaps, but it was a long way from any kind of teenage fun. And teenagers *had* fun in the sixties. Unless she was the quiet, nature-loving type, and her photo didn't suggest that, she'd have wanted parties and shopping trips. It didn't surprise him that she had escaped.

They returned to the living room to piles of photograph albums. Xander opened his bureau and indicated his filing system for family records. Ian looked at his watch. He'd promised to work until five and it was now two. He needed to get started. For now he'd concentrate on Ailish and try to build up a snapshot of her life in the year or two before she left. 'Do you have her birth certificate?' he asked Xander.

Xander opened a carboard folder. He found his own birth certificate, records of his parents' deaths and details of his father's will. But nothing about Ailish. Ian read through the will. She didn't even get a mention. Had her father been so angry with her that he'd torn up her birth certificate? Possible, he supposed, but was it more likely that Ailish herself had taken it? She'd need some kind of proof of her identity, for a passport for example, or if she wanted to get married. And if she'd planned her departure in the sort of detail that involved borrowing the ring and having it copied, slipping a birth certificate into her bag would have been easy. He wondered if money had gone missing at the time, and suggested this to Xander.

'I don't remember anything about money,' he said. 'There would have been cash in the estate office. They paid everyone in cash then. I don't remember any fuss about missing money but I was just a wee lad of seven and don't remember much about that time.'

'Do you have any memories about Ailish leaving? Anything your father said?'

Xander thought for a moment. 'Not really,' he said. 'My father rarely said anything about her. And of course, she'd been away at boarding school, so I was used to her not being here very much.'

A missing birth certificate wasn't a problem. A copy would be easy to get hold of if he needed it. They turned to a folder with her school records. Probably a more useful place to begin. There were reports from a prep school in Montrose where Ailish had been *lively but prone to stubbornness*, and also showed *a degree of artistic ability*. There were receipts for school fees – private education didn't come cheap even in the sixties – a newspaper article about a gymkhana in which she had won a red rosette and a few photos of her as a child with friends.

At eleven she had moved to Dorothea Prim's Academy for Girls, a boarding school in Edinburgh, where reports for the next six years described her as *intelligent but wilful*. No record of exams, but again, she could have taken those with her. While in the sixth year she had won a prize for art, awarded at the annual speech day by the wife of the MP for Edinburgh South. Ian jotted down details of the school, hoping that there might be some kind of alumni website with people who might remember Ailish.

He asked Xander if there was anyone in the village who might have known her.

'Apart from Maggie's mum, I can't think of anyone who lived in the village then. But we'll go up to the estate office. They'll have the ledgers for that period.'

They climbed up a flight of stone steps to a surprisingly modern office in one of the round towers.

'We moved the office up here about five years ago. Like I said, going organic meant a lot of paperwork and we had to modernise. I've never got to grips with all this technology, but the team here do a great job.' He grinned at four people sitting in front of computer screens and introduced Ian to the estate manager, Alan. 'We're looking for personnel records from the late sixties,' said Xander.

Alan pointed to the ceiling. 'They'll be upstairs,' he said. 'We don't keep digitised records from that far back, so they'll all be in hand-written ledgers. He pointed to a girl sitting at one of the computers. 'Sandy here is on work experience for one day a week. She'll show you where to go.'

Ian supposed Xander's role as a director didn't involve him much in estate admin. They followed Sandy up another flight of stone stairs to a room lined from floor to ceiling with shelves. Most contained box files, but Sandy led them to a shelf of ledgers all dated by year. Xander pulled out one dated 1966 and ran his finger down the pages of names. 'None that I recognise,' he said, 'but anyone who was working here then would be past retirement age by now.'

'You might do better looking at the rent records,' said Sandy. 'They record whole families, not just people working on the estate.' She found a rent book and Ian photographed the pages. He'd not spend time on it now. Better to let Xander read through the names. He could mark any he thought were still in the area and send them to Ian for a later visit.

'How do you like working here?' Xander asked Sandy. She blushed. Meeting the Laird, Ian supposed, wasn't a normal part of her working day.

'Very much, er, sir,' she said. 'Alan's really nice.'

'Good girl,' said Xander, nodding approvingly. 'Perhaps there'll be a permanent job for you one day.'

Sandy put everything back on the correct shelves and led them back down to the office.

'Did you find what you were looking for?' Alan asked.

'I've taken some copies,' said Ian. 'But I'm not sure how helpful they are going to be.'

Alan handed him a card with his email. 'Let me know if you need anything else,' he said. 'Sandy can email you copies of what you want.'

They returned to the living room where Bridget had tea ready for them. If nothing else this case was going to leave him well fed. 'I hope Lottie's not been a nuisance,' he said to Bridget.

'Not at all. She's been busy with her bone in the kitchen. No trouble, bless her.'

'Well,' said Ian. 'I've got enough to get started. I'll leave the two of you in peace and send my first report in a week.'

'Lovely,' said Bridget. 'We've really enjoyed having you here. Both of you.'

'Absolutely,' said Xander. 'You're welcome any time. Just give us a buzz and we'll try and have stuff ready for you.'

It had been quite a day. Ideas about how to start his search were spinning around in Ian's head. He had to find someone who had been missing for over fifty years and if he found her, which right now seemed unlikely, he had to find out if she had stolen a ring. And not just any old ring but a family heirloom with a legend attached to it. Ian already felt fond of Xander and Bridget. They were charming, but also a little sad. On one hand they had turned the estate into a thriving modern business, providing livelihoods for locals. Other landowners had turned similar estates into money-making machines with little thought to existing local economies; shooting weekends for bankers and murder mysteries in old castles for... who knew? But probably not for the locals. Drumlychtoun's green food venture was very much of its time, catching the *zeitgeist* for healthy eating and saving the planet and he admired them for that. On the other hand, while they were both fit and healthy now, they must worry about a time in the not-too-distant future when they might not be. An aging couple rattling around in an isolated castle with no immediate family to help them. He wasn't surprised that Xander wanted to find the sister who could possibly be his only remaining relative. *He'd do it,* Ian thought. Whatever it took, he would find Ailish.

It was a little before seven o'clock by the time he drove over the Tay Bridge and down into Greyport. He wasn't going to do anything useful this evening. He'd walk Lottie down to the waterfront and have a relaxed evening in the pub. He parked in the road at the end of his garden and let Lottie out, calling her as she started to climb the garden path. She looked at him as he waved her lead at her and she turned and wagged her tail. She was always up for another walk.

The *Thistle and Stone* was the smaller of the two pubs in the village. When hungry he'd go to the *Pigeon,* but he'd had a good lunch and what he felt like now was a pint and a friendly chat with the regulars.

It was a quiet evening in the bar. He hefted himself onto a bar stool and ordered a pint and a packet of bacon flavoured crisps. This evening both the landlord and his wife, Fred and Moira, were happy to stand and chat to him, breaking off to serve the occasional customer. They had worked here all their lives. The pub had been owned by Fred's father before being taken over by a local brewery. The walls were lined with photographs dating back quite a few years. Ian left his pint on the bar and strolled round for a closer look. Fred joined him and explained where they were taken and who was in them. One in particular drew Ian's attention. Fred lifted it down so he could take a closer look. It was of the pub which had, when the photo was taken, been called *The Fifie*. A crowd of people were standing outside the door.

'It was taken on the day the ferry crossed for the last time. No need for it once the bridge was open.'

'When was that?' Ian asked.

'Eighteenth of August 1966. The Fifies they were called. The last one back to Dundee left at closing time that evening. That's me,' he said, pointing to a small boy kneeling at the front of the group.

'That must have changed things for you,' said Ian, trying to imagine a time when the only way to Dundee would be a ferry crossing or a sixty-mile drive. His weekly trip to Tesco would feel very different.

'Oh, it did. My father thought it would be the end of the world. And it was tough for a few years, but by the time I took over in the early eighties things were looking up with the easy commute to Dundee.'

'Is Moira in the picture as well?'

'Aye, she's there.' He pointed to a young girl in a short dress with her hair in bunches. 'She's changed a bit since then. We both have.' He returned behind the bar to serve some customers who had just come in.

Ian took the picture back to the bar and studied it further. Yes, they'd changed, but they were recognisably the same people. It was one thing to have two people right next to him to compare with an old photo but possibly quite different if you didn't already know the person. Thinking about the photos he had of Ailish, he got out his phone and checked out face aging apps. They didn't get good reviews and looking at the pictures he could see why. All the app did was to add a layer of wrinkles over a picture of a face. They looked grotesque. Moira and Fred didn't look in the least grotesque. They just looked older.

Would Ailish be recognisable? Would it even matter? If he actually met Ailish he could just ask her to confirm who she was. Did he need to worry about trying to work out what she looked like now? The only reason he could think of would be if she had changed her name and didn't want to be recognised. And if that was the case, who was he to intrude on who she wanted to be? Unless she had committed a crime. He wondered what the police did if they needed to identify someone from an old photograph. He opened Google, tapped in 'forensic face aging' and discovered a whole new and vast area. The police occasionally issued pictures of children who had gone missing. Ben Needham and Madeleine McCann came to mind. He found two versions of a possible twenty-three-year-old Ben Needham which bore very little resemblance to either the missing toddler or to each other. He was in danger of disappearing down a very long and twisting blind alley. He drained the last of his pint, clipped on Lottie's lead and walked home. He would put everything Lyton-related out of his mind until tomorrow. He would find a thriller on Netflix and then get a good night's sleep.

4

The following morning Ian was awake early. He let Lottie out into the garden but that would have to do for now. She'd had plenty of exercise yesterday and he wanted to get down to work before breakfast while ideas were still fresh in his mind. It was going to be a day on the Internet. He made a promise to himself not to get side-tracked by interesting but irrelevant information. By the end of today he hoped to know enough about Ailish and her history to report to Xander and plan what to do next.

It was harder than he expected. His main hope had been that it was an unusual name that should be easy to find. But it wasn't easy. He began in the simplest way by typing her name into Google. Nothing. But in a way he found that encouraging. It meant he wouldn't spend hours researching the wrong person. She must be out there somewhere. She would be in some little corner of cyberspace. Not necessarily a nice corner, but she would be there. He was sure of that.

His next search was a trawl through social media. She wasn't a social media user herself, or if she was, she was very private about it. But again, he was sure he would find a tag or a mention somewhere. By mid-morning he was less sure. There wasn't a trace. But he must remember she was in her seventies and although there were thousands of silver surfers, there were probably just as many who never used the Internet. And thousands who did, but knew enough to stay under the radar.

He typed in 'Dorothea Prim Academy Edinburgh'. The school had closed down in 1975 but there was a Facebook page for past pupils. It wasn't an active page. The last entry had been made several months ago. But there was a contact button. He sent a message asking for anyone who remembered Ailish to get in touch. He wasn't hopeful that he'd get a reply, but it was the best he'd done so far. He couldn't remember many people he'd been at school with and that was less than thirty years ago. And if he *had* remembered them he couldn't imagine wanting to get in touch with them.

Then he turned to official record sites. He was able to log in and send for a copy of her birth certificate. It seemed she had never married, at least not in England or Scotland. If she'd married abroad, it would make his job even harder. But if she'd never married then it could be easier. Swings and roundabouts. On the plus side, she hadn't died either. He spent time trying to discover what happened with expat deaths. Normally, but not always, they were recorded by the British consul if it was believed there were relatives in the UK. A small chance, he supposed, that she might have died in some out of the way third-world country, but for now he would assume she hadn't and that she must be out there somewhere.

Then he struck gold.

He logged into the National Newspaper Archive. For a small subscription he had access to national and local newspapers going back over several hundred years. He typed in Ailish's name and there she was. She'd made it into the national press. Arrested for throwing flour bombs at Bob Hope in the Albert Hall during the 1970 Miss World contest. And that was only the first arrest. He tracked through several more accounts of Ailish at protests: Greenham Common, Twyford Down and a number of women's rights marches in London. He found a few photographs and checked them against the ones he had of Ailish. There was a definite likeness to her as a twenty-year-old flour flinger taken while being hauled out of the Albert Hall by a policeman. He had less luck with the Greenham Common women. Ailish would have been in her thirties and he couldn't find anyone who matched her photo even allowing for the fact that she would by then have been nearly twenty years older. Xander had shown him a portrait of their mother, which hung in one of the bedrooms. Ian had taken a photo of it on his phone and scrolled through to find it now. Either it was a very poor likeness or Ailish hadn't looked much like her mother. And there were hundreds of women at Greenham, many of them wearing hats and most of the pictures were grainy. It didn't mean that the Ailish who had been fined for lying down in front of an American transport convoy wasn't the one he was looking for.

He checked Twyford Down where an Ailish Lyton had been freed from the tree she had chained herself to by police officers with bolt cutters. There was a photo, again rather grainy, of a possibly forty-year-old Ailish. He lined up photos of Xander, Ailish at nineteen and the mother's portrait. Three people who looked nothing like each other and only a passing resemblance to a woman who had chained herself to a tree. In fact, tree woman looked more like Xander than either of the other two. As she had grown older had she become more like her brother? It was possible but was that enough? Yes. He was fairly certain that he had found the correct person. It did at least seem to be in character after what Xander had told him about Ailish being 'difficult'. Stroppy teenager to political activist didn't seem such a stretch.

He still had no idea where she was now.

He'd try local newspapers to see if they gave more details. The Albert Hall incident should have made the London locals. He clicked on late November and early December editions of the *Hammersmith and Kensington Gazette* for that year and was lucky first time. He found a short article. Ailish had appeared at Hammersmith Magistrates' Court where she had been fined ten pounds for causing a disturbance.

.   .   .

Miss Ailish Lyton of Hibernia Court, Kensington, appeared at Hammer-smith Magistrates' Court yesterday where she pleaded guilty to causing a disturbance at the Royal Albert Hall on Friday 20th November. Miss Lyton was fined the sum of ten pounds. This was paid for her by the Women's Liberation Movement.

So, in 1970 she was living in Kensington. He typed the address into Google and discovered that Hibernia Court was a mansion block five minutes' walk from High Street Kensington underground station. Ian opened Rightmove and saw that flats there sold for anything from two million up to around five million. But that was now. Fifty years ago – who knew? Unlikely that at twenty-one she would have owned a flat in Kensington, but he logged into the electoral register for that year and typed in the address. She'd lived in number sixty-seven Hibernia Court with a Joshua Remington. He trawled through registers for the following five years and they were still there. This was getting tedious. He would work in the other direction, going back in ten-year leaps. He brought up the register for last year, hardly expecting to find her. But there she still was. No Joshua Remington though.

He now had a lot of information; newspaper reports, photographs and electoral registers as well as photographs he'd taken at Drumly-chtoun. They were all in electronic form and littering up his computer desktop. It would be a lot easier to organise it in a more visual way. He'd not been a detective in the police but had watched enough crime drama to know what an incident room looked like. He needed a whiteboard where he could pin stuff up in some kind of timeline and study it all set out in front of him from the comfort of an armchair. He also needed a break and some lunch, so he loaded Lottie into the car to do some shopping. He drove to Dundee and an industrial estate where he'd noticed a supplier of office furniture and stationery. He bought the largest whiteboard he could fit into his car and stocked up on marker pens, Post-its, Blu-Tack and toner for his printer. After all that he deserved lunch. He had Lottie with him so he should do a quick stop off to buy some sandwiches, but then he remembered a café Caroline had told him about in the city centre which was casual and dog friendly. It would make a nice break and he still had plenty of the day left to set up his incident board and type up a report for Xander and Bridget.

When they arrived home the postman had been – no doubt glad of a Lottie free visit. There was an envelope addressed to him and Caroline, every word of which was written in a different colour. He opened it and found a picture of a couple holding a dog with a lot of glitter stuck to its nose and round its collar. There was also a letter:

Dear Ian and Caroline
Thank you for the box of crayons and paints and stuff.
I'm seven now.
Love from Jessie

A sweet wee girl, Jessie, and very observant. She'd drawn an excellent portrait of the lad who had stolen Lottie a few weeks back.

There was also a note from her mother, Sue, who said how thrilled Jessie had been to know that she had helped a real detective and was thinking of joining the police when she was old enough. Sue also thanked them for uncovering the mystery of Jessie's brief abduction and her relief at discovering that it hadn't been too serious.

Ian carried his purchases up from the car and set up his incident room. Considering that he'd not heard of Ailish Lyton until a few days ago, he had a lot of information and now it was time for a progress report to the Laird. He created a document with everything he had found including the various press cuttings and photographs. Too big for an email. He set up a shared document folder and emailed them a link, telling them they could add to it themselves if they found anything they thought might interest him. Then he made a copy for himself. Xander, according to Bridget, was IT-incompetent and Ian didn't want to risk anyone deleting the whole lot by mistake. He emailed Bridget and asked what they would like him to do next. This could be all they wanted, but he hoped that wouldn't be the end of it. He was intrigued by this family and his fingers itched to try and find out more about the ring and its whereabouts.

A good day's work, he thought. But he mustn't neglect his other clients.

He made a few calls to the employers named on the teacher's CV, all of which seemed genuine. He suggested that they confirm this by email to the headmaster concerned, logged the time and cost of phone calls and sent in his invoice. He advised the wife of the supposedly errant husband that she should send him any evidence she had before he started his own enquiries. With any luck it would be nothing more than a suspicion and he could let the whole thing drop. The false dog pedigree was more of a problem. The Kennel Club was now closed for the day. He assumed they would be able to validate – or otherwise – the dog's pedigree. The copy his client had given him didn't look like a forgery, but he was no expert. To get things moving he emailed the Kennel Club and attached a scan of the pedigree. They would be able to advise him, but he didn't expect to hear from them until after the weekend.

It was now early evening and time for food and an evening of crime drama.

5

T here was an email from Bridget the next morning.

Ian, you're a wonder. How did you find out so much in so little time?

Xander and I have been mulling it all over and we wonder if you would be prepared to go to London and meet Ailish. We think a face-to-face meeting with a disinterested person would be best. We've no desire to intrude on her life but don't want to let things go as they are.

When you have talked to Ailish and can tell us how things are with her, we will think about how to proceed.

We would still like to know what happened to the ring. Perhaps you could bring it up as part of the conversation – without actually accusing her, of course.

Brilliant. He could continue with the case and he got an expenses paid trip to London. He checked the train times. If he left Dundee early in the morning, he could be back home again the same evening.

His meeting with Ailish would be short and he didn't want to stay a night in a hotel in London. Yes, London was full of theatres, restaurants, cinemas and galleries, but on his own? Not a lot of fun. He would probably just end up in his room watching satellite TV. He would also need to kennel Lottie for a couple of days. It would feel like sending her to prison. Was owning a dog making him soft? Yes. Did he care? No. One day and he could ask Lainie, who was as soft as he was about Lottie. He went next door to ask her if she would look after her for a day and if so, which day would suit her.

'Oh, bless. I'll look after the wee dog any day you like.'

Then he went online to find a phone number for Ailish. He needed to know she was going to be there. London was a long way. He didn't want a wasted journey.

Apart from those with guilty consciences, most people were excited by the idea of talking to a detective. He hoped Ailish would be one of them. He called her straight away, hoping that she would be as intrigued as everyone else about why a detective was phoning her. She answered immediately with a curt, 'Yes?'

He introduced himself and referred her to his website where she could check his credentials. He told her he would be happy to call back a little later if she wanted to check him out first. Most people were too trusting. He had set up his website to be as reassuring as possible. To make sure everyone knew his background and how they could check up on him, he listed references, outlined earlier cases and had posted a picture of his certificate and medal. Worryingly, most people didn't bother checking and just took him at face value.

Ailish was one of them, which given her background surprised him. 'Just get on with it and tell me what you want,' she said, sounding irritable.

'I'm making a few enquires for a client. I wondered if I might call on you.'

'What client?' she snapped.

'I'm afraid I'm not at liberty to say over the phone. I'm happy to tell you everything when we meet.' Assuming that a meeting was a given was usually the best way to make sure that it was.

'Well,' she said. 'I will be here tomorrow at three o'clock. But I hope you won't keep me for long. I have an important meeting at four-thirty.'

Fair enough. He didn't need long and it worked well with the train times. 'That would suit me perfectly,' he told her.

'You have the address?'

'I do, yes. And I look forward to meeting you.'

She put the phone down abruptly.

He went next door to warn Lainie that it would be a very early start and probably a rather late finish. She told him not to worry. Lottie could stay the night with her – less to worry about in the morning. And if he was late back, then she could stay another night. Lainie would probably be happy to keep Lottie for a two-week holiday if he asked.

He returned home and thought about what he would need to take with him. Not much, but he didn't want to look too casual, so he found a moleskin notebook and some pens, charged his phone and made sure he had information about Drumlychtoun. Ailish might not know that her father had died, or that Xander had married. And she probably didn't know about the estate and its commitment to organic food production. A lot would have changed since 1967.

His alarm woke him at five and he crawled out of bed. Lottie's sleepover was definitely a good idea. No need for an early morning walk round the garden. Just grab a cup of coffee and go. He'd booked a taxi the evening before and by five-thirty he was at the end of the garden waiting for it.

How could taxi drivers be so chirpy so early in the morning? By the time Ian climbed out at Dundee station he knew the man's family history and his holiday plans for the next two years. At least they hadn't had time for a moan about local schools. He climbed out of the taxi and walked past potted plants, across the plaza and through a grand glass entrance into the station. He fed his credit card into a machine and collected the pre-booked tickets that would take him to

London and back as well as across the city by underground. Then he took the escalator down to the platform and waited for his train.

The London train was on time but not due for another fifteen minutes, so he walked down the platform to a snack bar where he bought another coffee and a bacon sandwich. Then he joined all the other sleepy looking commuters on the platform. His ticket told him the seat he had booked was in coach G. There was nothing to indicate where coach G would stop, so once he was on the train he could be in for a bit of a walk. That was fine. He was carrying very little. Everything he needed was in a small messenger bag slung from his shoulder. He placed himself midway along the platform and waited.

The train, when it arrived, was immensely long. It seemed to take several minutes to progress from the Aberdeen end to the Edinburgh end of the curved platform and when it finally came to a halt, he couldn't see either the front or the back of the train. He climbed through the nearest door into coach F and wandered back down the train, eventually finding his seat. There were not too many people travelling this morning and he had a window seat. He nodded at a woman in a business suit in the seat opposite his. 'Lovely morning,' he said, putting his bag down on the empty seat next to his own.

She agreed that it was a lovely morning and nodded at his bag. 'It'll fill up in Edinburgh,' she said. 'You'll need to move that.' Then she plugged in her earbuds and returned to her iPad where, from the little Ian could see, she was watching an action film with a great deal of violence. Not what he would choose for an early morning.

He had intended to sleep on the train, but it was such a beautiful morning he just sat back and enjoyed the view as it made its way down the Fife coast and over the Forth Bridge eventually arriving in Edinburgh – first Haymarket and then the sinister depths of Waverley. The woman had been right. Although she left the train at Waverley it soon filled up. He moved his bag and stowed it on the floor by his feet. A crowded train is a warm train and he soon nodded off, waking again as they arrived in Berwick-on-Tweed. He'd come for holidays here when he was a child. He'd not enjoyed it much at the time. He'd exchanged a cold, windy Scottish beach for a cold, windy beach in the North of England. As a teenager he'd longed for Spain or Greece. Hot, sun-soaked beaches and girls in bikinis. In Berwick girls wore sweaters and waterproof jackets. His one holiday in the sun had been two weeks with Stephanie in Narbonne where they ate the best pizzas he'd ever tasted, and he and Stephanie bickered constantly.

He woke again when the train stopped in Newcastle and after a nice view of the Tyne bridges a woman came round with a trolley. He'd had enough coffee. Any more and he'd be able to dance the rest of the way to London. Instead he bought a bottle of water and a Kit Kat. He sat back and mused about the weather. Scotland had a bad reputation – cold, mist and early snowfalls. But today he had left on a glorious, cloud-free May morning and as he got closer to London it got steadily gloomier. By the time they pulled into Kings Cross rain was streaking the windows.

Ian looked at his watch. He still had nearly two hours before his meeting with Ailish. He decided against the Tube and opted for the bus. He was only in London for a day; he might as well see as much as he could. He peered through the rain as the bus took him along Oxford Street, down Park Lane and then along to the Albert Hall. When it reached High Street Kensington the rain had thankfully slowed to a drizzle. He'd forgotten how slow buses were. By the time he got off it was nearly two o'clock. Not a problem. He still had plenty of time and the main lunch rush would be over. He found a fast curry place where he perched on a stool and ate Thai green curry, which he washed down with low alcohol lager. The curry came in a carboard box (fully biodegradable according to the label). He didn't particularly like eating out of a cardboard box, but this was delicious. Plenty of food like this in Edinburgh, he supposed, although as Grandad's carer they had usually eaten at home. He'd not really explored fast food in Dundee yet but assumed it didn't go much beyond McDonald's and Greggs. He was probably being very unfair to Dundee. He should explore further.

. . .

Hibernia Court was a big red-brick block of flats a few minutes' walk from the underground station. It was one side of a square of identical blocks with a garden in the middle surrounded by a fence and with locked gates on either side. Residents, he supposed, had their own keys. On the dot of three he pressed Ailish's bell and she buzzed him in. A lift took him to the sixth floor, and he rang the doorbell of number sixty-seven. The door was opened promptly, and he found himself face to face with Ailish Lyton. He wasn't sure what he had expected but it definitely wasn't the woman who stood in front of him now. She was tall and elegantly dressed in loose trousers and a silk Chinese shirt in bright red with gold dragons. She still had long hair but now it was piled up on the top of her head and secured with what looked like knitting needles. She wore a pair of spectacles on a chain round her neck. Her wrists jangled with heavy gold bracelets and on her feet she wore black slippers embroidered in gold. She had grown from the grumpy teenager of Xander's memory into a woman who exuded confidence and authority. He searched her face for a likeness to her brother but couldn't see any. Their only similarity seemed to be that they were both tall and athletically built.

'Mr Skair?' she asked, inviting him in. She led him into a living room which was sparsely but expensively furnished with a white-wood floor partly covered by a Persian rug, a silk covered chaise longue and a pale oak dining table with six chairs. He imagined dinner parties with similarly confident people having erudite conversations while they picked at delicately beautiful food from bone china plates and sipped wine that one or other of the guests had picked up while weekending with friends who just happened to own a vineyard in the Languedoc. Or would they drink cocktails? He'd only had cocktails once when Stephanie was trying to impress some new neighbours. He'd not enjoyed them. Give him a glass of fine whiskey any time.

There was a single print on the wall of a naked and extremely beautiful young man who gazed soulfully out of the picture with dark eyes. On the table was a square glass vase containing a single white lily.

'Please sit down,' she said, indicating a chair at the table. He sat and placed his bag on the floor next to him, stretching out his now aching leg under the table in front of him. Ailish sat opposite him and offered him lemon and ginger tea, which she poured from a china jug into tall glasses with metal handles. 'I don't drink anything with caffeine,' she explained.

Hence, he supposed, her clear, almost wrinkle-free complexion.

She took a sip of her drink. 'What have I done to merit a visit from a private investigator?' she asked. 'I've had a chequered past, but I don't think I've done anything recently to provoke enquiries. And,' she said with what he thought could be just a hint of regret, 'I'm too old to be anyone's mistress, if that's what you are after.'

He liked her intelligence and sharpness. She'd obviously looked at his website and discovered his usual line of business. He smiled at her and sipped his own drink. 'Nothing like that.' He paused, enjoying the fact that he had caught her interest. He'd keep her in suspense a little longer.

'No? What a pity. I quite like the idea that I might have stirred up a bit of jealousy somewhere. I've become far too respectable recently.'

He grinned. 'You weren't at the Extinction Rebellion demo?'

'Oh, I was there. I just didn't get arrested.' She laughed. 'I'm afraid the police can be quite ageist at times.'

'Perhaps you should have superglued yourself to an underground train.'

'I'm afraid someone else did that first. You've not come to find out if I'm some kind of eco fifth columnist, have you?'

'No,' he said. 'Your brother, Alexander, asked me to find you.'

'Good God, whatever for?'

Because he thinks you nicked his family ring. 'He wants to know how you are.'

'After fifty years? Well, you can tell him I'm fine. No thanks to our father.'

'You didn't get on with your father?' *Did she even know he had died?*

'To put it mildly. Wasn't too sorry when I heard the old boy had snuffed it.'

At least that was one bit of news he didn't need to deliver. 'So you quarrelled?'

'Nothing so engaging. Most of the time he ignored me. He just didn't have time for a daughter. My brother was born and my mother died shortly after that. And he couldn't care less about me, or my mother. The only thing he cared about was that he now had a son. Someone to pass everything on to. And I do mean everything. He made it quite clear that nothing would come to me, not a penny, not even a stick of furniture. He wanted to marry me off at the first opportunity and be shot of me.'

'And your brother?'

'He was quite fond of Alexander, who was no doubt quite an engaging little chap. But when I left, he was seven and of no interest to a teenage girl. As far as I was concerned, he was just a spoilt brat.'

'You've no wish to see how he turned out?' She'd like Xander's save the planet attitude to food production. She might even like Xander himself now he'd outgrown the spoiled brat stage.

'None at all. I'd have nothing in common with him. He's no doubt married and produced the next heir.'

'He's married, yes, but he has no children.'

'And I suppose when he goes the whole caboodle will be sold to some property developer who'll pull it down and replace it with tasteful holiday homes.'

'I can't see that happening soon. He seemed very sprightly.' And he cared deeply about his tenants. He might not have a son, but Ian was sure he would have ensured the future of the estate. He and Ailish probably had a lot more in common than either of them realised.

'So you're not here to arrange some kind of death bed reconciliation,' she said. 'Thank God for that.'

'No, just to see how you are. Although I'm sure if you have any wish to meet him, he would be very pleased.'

'Can't imagine why. We've not seen each other for fifty years and we had very little in common then. If that's what you were after, I'm afraid you're wasting your time. Have you come far?'

'From Dundee.'

'Today?'

He nodded.

'Well, that shows devotion to duty. You must have left at some ungodly time this morning.'

'Six o'clock train,' he said.

'And I know what train food is like. You must let me make you something to eat.' She disappeared into the kitchen before he had time to reply. Well, like Lottie he was always ready to eat.

While he waited, he wandered over to the window and a small balcony that looked out over the square of garden. 'It's a lovely flat,' he said as she reappeared with a plate of sandwiches.

'It is. I bought it with my lover way back in the late sixties. We picked it up for a snip with only a few years left on the lease. And when we started to do well, we renewed the lease and stayed on. Very convenient for central London.'

'He worked in London?'

'Yes, he was in imports and exports.'

'And you worked in London as well?'

'Of course. I have very strong feelings about not being a kept woman. I worked as an art journalist for a while, and I've been on various gallery committees.'

'You've never married, had children?'

'I'm wholly against marriage.' Yes, he'd worked that out. She turned away from him. 'I had a child once, but he died.'

'I'm so sorry,' he said, groping for comforting words.

'You don't need to be. I'm not mother material.'

'And your lover?'

'Died in 2000. Cancer.'

'Your brother was telling me about some family legend,' he said, trying to change the subject and work his way around to the missing ring.

'Oh, that bloody ring,' she said. 'Lost it, has he?'

'Not exactly. It turns out the one in his possession is a fake. He's wondering what happened to the original.'

She laughed. 'Well, I haven't got it.'

He hadn't accused her of having it. Was that too much of a denial? Hard to say. Anything he said about the family was going to be treated with hostility. He didn't feel there was any more he could ask. Had it been a wasted journey? 'Do you have any message for your brother?'

'Can't think of anything.'

'Then I'd better be on my way.' He took out his business card and left it on the table. 'Just in case you need to contact me,' he said. She already knew how to find him through his website, but a visual reminder would do no harm. Perhaps on a lonely evening she would spot it and ask him to reunite her and her brother. Probably not, but it was worth a try.

'Thank you,' he said as she showed him out. 'It's been an interesting visit.'

'I suppose you told Alexander that you had found me.'

'He knows you live in London, but I won't tell him more than that if you don't want me to.'

She shrugged. 'No, you can pass on my address. I don't mind him knowing that. I just don't feel like a touching family reunion.'

He hoped she would add 'yet' to that statement. But that was probably as much as he was going to get and she hadn't flatly refused to have any more to do with Xander. He couldn't have done a lot more. He hoped Xander wasn't going to be disappointed.

He took a crowded underground train back to Kings Cross. The bus was too slow and he had no wish to stay in London any longer. There was a lot to see but it was all too crowded and noisy and he longed for open spaces and the fresh air of Scotland. A bit pathetic when he'd only be here for a day but that's how he was.

He caught the five o'clock train, hitting commuter time. Thankfully he had a reserved seat. It made him feel tired watching exhausted workers crowd onto the train, many of them having to stand. Did people really commute from York? Hard to imagine spending hours of every day standing on a train. There must be better things to do, but if nothing else it made him appreciate his own free and easy life.

He stared out of the window at the gloomy North London houses. It would be dark before they got to Scotland and after eleven by the time he got home. It had been a long day. Had it been a wasted day? No, definitely not. He hadn't learnt much about the ring but then he hadn't really expected to. He couldn't imagine Ailish saying, 'Yes, I took it.' Why would she? She seemed to be far more occupied with making the world a better, less violent place. And good luck to her.

He reached down for his bag and took out his notebook and a pen. He needed to record everything he could remember of today while it was still fresh in his head. It was a pity he hadn't taken a photograph of Ailish. Xander would have liked that. But it had seemed intrusive to ask and he would be able to describe her in detail. He tapped open photos on his phone and studied the picture of their mother. A slight resemblance, he supposed, but really if Ailish looked like anyone it was Xander. Not so much in looks but there was a determined dignity about both of them.

He finished his notes and put the notebook away in his bag. They had just left York so there were several more hours to go. He leaned against the window and went to sleep.

6

T he next morning, still rocking from the motion of the train but after a reasonable night's sleep, Ian went next door to collect Lottie, who greeted him as if he had been away for two months rather than two nights. It was nice to be welcomed home with so much enthusiasm. Lainie bustled round insisting on giving him breakfast and asking about his trip. He hadn't really had time to see much of London. Had he somehow let her down? Perhaps he should make up stories about bumping into the Queen on the Tube or meeting the Prime Minister over a cup of coffee. All he had was a bus ride, a stint on the circle line and half an hour or so at Kings Cross. He hadn't been tempted by the Harry Potter shop which seemed to be the main tourist attraction at Kings Cross. Instead, he had bought a cup of tea and found a table where he could sit and watch the departure boards. As tourist visits go, it wasn't much. He told her he'd seen Oxford Street and the Albert Hall from the top deck of a bus and that he'd visited an upmarket flat in Kensington and she seemed happy to hear about those. She didn't get out much, Lainie. A trip over the bridge to Tesco once a week was about as adventurous as she got. One day he would take her to Edinburgh and buy her lunch in return for all the Lottie-sitting she did.

He returned home with Lottie, thinking about the report he would write for Xander and Bridget. He pinned a photo of Hibernia Mansions to his board and wrote a few notes next to it; lover (Remington?) now deceased, never touches caffeine (relevant?), Extinction Rebellion demo (not arrested). The file he typed was going to be a lot shorter than the last one he'd sent. And he couldn't tell them anything new about the ring. Not that they'd expected much. It was always unlikely that Ailish would admit to taking it and hand it over so that he could return it to its rightful owner. She hadn't seemed surprised that the ring now in Xander's possession was a fake. Did she know that already? And what did he think about her hasty denial? 'Well, I haven't got it,' was what she'd said. He'd not even suggested that she might have it. Was that too sudden and too quick? She knew at once that the legend and the ring were connected. None of which meant she was guilty. But it didn't mean she was innocent either.

What had he learnt from yesterday? He'd been fascinated to meet Ailish, a colourful character who'd led a full on life. Xander would now know where she was and how to get in touch if he wanted to. And he'd uncovered a couple of interesting facts. Ailish had lived with her lover, Joshua Remington from at least 1970 - when they bought the flat together – until his death. Even more interesting was that Ailish had had a child. He'd not found any record of a birth using her name, but he would now search again for a Remington birth. Even if they hadn't been married it wouldn't have been unusual to give the child his father's name. He wondered how long the child had lived. The way she told him suggested that he had been stillborn or died a short time after the birth. He also decided to research Joshua Remington. Did Ailish know him when she'd lived in Scotland or had they met in London?

He typed his notes and saved them to the shared folder. He sent Bridget an email telling her he'd added some more information, but that since they'd retained him for the rest of the week he would do some more online searches and let them know if he discovered anything of interest about Joshua Remington and Ailish's son.

. . .

By the end of the day he had discovered a lot about Joshua. As far as the Lyton ring was concerned, none of it very interesting. Ian started with Joshua's death and worked backwards. He had been chairman of an international exporter of luxury goods and had made a lot of money. He and Ailish were named on the deeds of the Hibernia Court flat from 1970. Ian guessed that he was older than Ailish and began a search of birth records from 1940. There was nothing among English births, so he turned, as he had for Ailish, to Scottish records. Joshua was, as he had expected, older than Ailish. He had been born in Edinburgh in 1945, so was older than Ailish by three years. Was it possible that they had known each other before Ailish had left for London? Further digging revealed that Joshua had been to school in Edinburgh, as had Ailish. Could they have met while Ailish was at school? Could Joshua have been a student there?

He'd drawn another blank with birth records for their child in both England and Scotland and decided to take a break. His eyes were sore from too much screen time and his back ached from sitting all day. It was time for a long waterside walk with Lottie. He decided to drive to Carnoustie where he knew the beach was dog friendly. He could throw a ball for Lottie on the long stretch of sand and when they'd had enough sea air, they could stroll into the town for something to eat.

Carnoustie is best known for golf and Ian discovered that, like St Andrews, the town catered for golfing visitors. He strolled past shops selling typical tourist stuff: expensive jumpers, leather goods, tartan rugs and traditional Scottish jewellery. He stopped suddenly outside the window of an antique shop. So suddenly that Lottie was jerked to a halt on her lead. She looked up at him indignantly. He took no notice and continued to stare into the window at a display of reproduction antique rings. It was the word *reproduction* that caught his eye. He had been so involved with piecing together Ailish's life that he had stopped thinking about the ring. The Lyton ring had been copied. If he could find where the copy was made, he would be on the way to finding *who* had had it made.

He tried to think himself into the head of a nineteen-year-old girl who was desperate to leave home. She'd need money. And she would need it without her father knowing about it. So what does she do? She takes the one thing she knows is valuable, has a copy made and keeps the original. But why keep it? Why not sell it? He needed a second opinion. Someone who might know how the mind of a teenage girl worked. Caroline. She knew all about teenagers and she had once been a teenage girl herself.

He looked at his watch. What would she be doing at six o'clock on a Saturday evening? She wasn't the type for a bit of Saturday night clubbing, but she might like the idea of a nice quiet meal somewhere. He pulled out his phone and called her. Yes, she'd love to go out for a meal, but he would have to pick her up. Her car was out of action.

'An accident?' he asked, concerned that she'd been hurt.

'No, just a repair. I've a friend who does them at weekends. It means I get it back for school on Monday.'

He knew just the place to take her. A small seafood restaurant in St Andrews. Probably fully booked on a Saturday evening but worth a try. He put Caroline on hold while he called them. They had just had a cancellation and would have a table at 8.30. Perfect. He had time to drive Lottie home, change into something more respectable and pick Caroline up. There might even be time for a quiet drink on the way.

She sounded delighted. 'Just time for a quick shower,' she said.

Now there was a thought. He found his mind wandering in a rather nice direction as he drove home. He must pull himself together. He didn't want to drive off the road, or worse, off the road bridge. Although he wasn't sure that was possible. People jumped off it from time to time. But that was probably not as a result of randy thoughts about women in showers. He slowed down and concentrated on the road ahead of him. He arrived home safely, fed Lottie and took a shower. He found a clean shirt. Not just clean but new. It was one his mother had bought him for his last birthday. For once she had been spot-on about both his size and the type of shirt that would actually suit him, a deep red brushed cotton. He looked at himself in the mirror. Not bad at all, he thought. He looked better since he had moved here. He was eating properly, not just mopping up what Grandad couldn't finish. And having Lottie meant that he got plenty of fresh air and exercise. He brushed his hair and put on his jacket. Lottie looked at him quizzically. 'Not tonight,' he said, stroking her ears. 'You stay here and behave yourself. I won't be long.' Thankfully she no longer wandered off on her own. He had now dog-proofed the house and garden. He knew she would be fine for a few hours.

'You look great,' he said as Caroline stepped out of her front door. Was that the right thing to say? He was rubbish at dating. But she did look great. She was wearing a dress. He didn't think he'd seen her in a dress before. She was usually in jeans. But then he didn't usually take her to posh restaurants. Green was a good colour for her, and he liked the way her hair was brushed down over her shoulders.

'You look pretty good yourself,' she said, smiling. 'So I assume we're not going to be grovelling round in dirty lock-ups this time?'

'I'll do my best.' He grinned at her. To be fair the dirty lock-up had only been once, and it had been her decision to join him there. He didn't bring that up now.

That reminded him. He'd brought Jessie's thank you letter, which he pulled out of his pocket and handed to her.

'That's sweet,' she said. 'She's quite talented for a seven-year-old, isn't she?'

'Yeah, she's captured us quite well. She's even drawn me with one leg longer than the other. I guess that's how someone with a limp looks to a wee girl.'

She brushed some glitter from her skirt. 'Sorry,' she said. 'I shouldn't mess up your nice new car.'

'It'll brush off,' he said. 'I'm not that car-proud.'

'You still like it then?'

'Can't imagine how I ever managed with the old one.' She'd never actually been in his old car and he didn't blame her. 'I've a new case as well. Thought you might like to hear about it.' She'd been very keen to help him with his rescue-Lottie-from-kidnap case. But that could have just been because she was a dog-lover, and it really should have been her dog that was kidnapped. Or should that be dog-napped?

Over their meal he told her about Drumlychtoun and that he'd been asked to trace a missing sister.

'Interesting,' she said. 'And rather more respectable than the dog-nappers of Dundee.'

'I wanted to ask your advice.' She looked pleased. She really had enjoyed helping on his last case. He hadn't just imagined it.

'Sure,' she said. 'How can I help?'

'Can you imagine for a moment that you are a nineteen-year-old girl who wants to leave home. Oh, and it's 1967.'

'Am I a Beatles fan?'

Wasn't everyone in the sixties? 'I've no idea. But you wear very short skirts and a lot of eye make-up. And you have hair down to your waist.' He showed her the photo on his phone.

'Very pretty and very swinging sixties. Definitely a Beatles lover. She looks like Jane Asher.'

'Who?'

She sighed. 'A well-known actress. She went out with one of the Beatles, Paul McCartney I think.'

He knew he needed to brush up on popular culture, but they were getting a bit off topic. 'She's still very striking. And she's feisty and determined.'

'You've already found her?' She sounded disappointed.

'Yes, but there's more to discover. Can you think yourself into her head?'

'I was always rather strong-willed, so I'll do my best.' She shut her eyes with the air of an actress trying to get into a role. 'Why do I want to leave home?' she asked, opening her eyes again.

'You don't get on with your father and you live miles from anywhere.'

'Yes, I can see why I might want to find somewhere with a bit more life.'

'How would you get the money to do it?'

'I'd go to university and get a grant. They had grants in the sixties, didn't they?'

'All college fees were paid, but I think living expenses were means tested.'

'And my father is too well off?'

'He lives in a castle, so very likely.'

She took a sip of wine and carefully de-boned her fish. 'I think I'd try and find a rich boyfriend or steal the family jewels.'

'Both of those could be in the picture. There's a valuable ring belonging the family that has recently been revealed as a fake, probably copied sometime in the 1960s. The father kept it in his bureau at the castle.'

'Did he keep the bureau locked?'

'I don't know.' That was something he could ask Xander. It was unlocked the day he'd been there, but that was because it was full of stuff Xander wanted him to see. He hadn't noticed a key, but he'd not been looking for one.

'Okay,' said Caroline, 'let's assume it wasn't or that she knew where the key was kept. Could she have had help from a friend?'

'I know she lived with a boyfriend in London a few years later. He was born in Edinburgh. And she was at school in Edinburgh so they might have met before she left home.'

'Assuming I'm her, I plan to escape with my boyfriend, and we need money. I could borrow the ring and get it copied. Pocket the original and slip the copy into the bureau before I leave.' She mopped up some garlicky sauce with a piece of bread. 'Is it a very unusual ring?'

That was a good question. He didn't know enough about

jewellery to say one way or the other. 'It's quite big,' he said. 'A bishop's ring so definitely for a man. But that's a good point and something to research.'

'If it's distinctive I don't think I'd try to sell it close to home. It could be recognised. I'd wait until I was in London.'

If it had been sold in London it could have had multiple owners and have ended up on the other side of the world. 'There wouldn't be much hope of finding it now, fifty years later. Unless...'

She looked up at him. 'What are you thinking?'

'This boyfriend became a rich businessman. I don't know when he made his money, but suppose he became successful quite quickly and there was no need to sell the ring at all. It would have been risky, even in London.'

'Then she'd still have it.'

'She's denying it, but she could be lying.'

'You're quite perceptive. Did you feel she was lying?'

He needed to think about that. Was he perceptive? It was the first time anyone had told him he was. 'I don't think she was telling me the *whole* truth.'

'You can't very well accuse her outright.'

No, he couldn't. That could lead to a lot of trouble. He definitely wasn't in the habit of making false accusations.

'Did she have a job in London?'

'She studied art and then worked as an art journalist.'

'They probably weren't short of money then. Which might mean they kept the ring.'

'The boyfriend died and I would guess he left her well provided for.' He wasn't sure how Ailish's feminist views would have coped with that, but she certainly looked as if she was very well off.

'Are you wondering where to go next with this?' Caroline asked.

He shook his head. 'My client wants me to keep going and find out as much as I can. I feel I've hit a bit of a brick wall, but I don't want to let him down and I did have a thought while I was walking Lottie today.'

'Okay, you've got my teenage girl perspective. What are you thinking now?'

'I don't think it's worth visiting her again, not yet. I need to concentrate on trying to find out who copied the ring.'

'Are there goldsmiths locally? You could start with them. See if their records go back that far.'

'I think there would be a problem with that. Her family were well-known around Montrose, which would be the obvious starting place. The ring appears in a family portrait and might have been recognised by local jewellers.'

'If they both had Edinburgh connections perhaps that would be the place to look.'

She was right. It had been good to have her to bounce ideas off. She was also very good company. He poured her some more wine and gazed into her eyes. 'Do you fancy a trip to Edinburgh to look at rings?'

'Oh my God,' she said. 'You're not proposing, are you?'

He nearly choked on his wine. He must have looked horrified because she started laughing.

'Oh, Ian,' she gasped. 'Don't look so terrified. I know perfectly well what you meant. I was teasing, okay?'

'Sorry,' he muttered, feeling stupid.

She reached for his hand. 'I'd love a day in Edinburgh.'

That made his next question awkward. But they had spent a lovely night together the time they found Lottie. He'd enjoy another night like that but could feel himself blushing as he made his suggestion. 'I thought perhaps we could go on Friday evening and find a hotel. Then we could spend all of Saturday looking for jewellers. Single rooms if you prefer,' he added lamely. He looked at her warily. She was still smiling, which was a good sign.

'No need for single rooms,' she said. 'But perhaps we should have a wee chat about *us*.'

'*Us*?' He didn't like the sound of that. 'Okay,' he said cautiously.

'We're both adults. We've unhappy marriages behind us. We are, I hope, good friends. Friends with benefits I think it's called. And that's absolutely fine with me.'

'Sounds perfect.' It really did. Why did he always feel he was walking into traps?

'So just clear your head of the idea that I'm out to snare you. I'm just an ordinary woman who enjoys your company. I'm not a different species. I don't have any hidden agenda.'

She was right. Of course she was. And as much as he was resistant to 'clearing the air' type conversations, it was a relief to have that out of the way. If he hadn't had to drive home, he would have ordered another bottle of wine. 'I'd better get back to Lottie tonight,' he said, trying not to sound as if he was making excuses and wishing he'd left Lottie with Lainie for the night.

'Of course,' she said, reaching for her coat. 'I've got work to do before Monday and need to keep a clear head.'

He paid the bill and they walked to his car hand in hand. He drove her back to her house in Cupar, saw her to her door and patted her dog, Angus, on the head. 'What time shall I pick you up on Friday?' he asked, kissing her chastely on the cheek.

She pulled him towards her and kissed him rather less chastely. 'Give me time to get home and change out of my schoolteacher gear. Would around six suit you?'

'Perfect,' he said, wondering what schoolteacher gear was. Something that wouldn't get the hearts of teenage boys racing, he supposed. He hoped it meant changing into something that might get the heart of a middle-aged private detective racing. Although on reflection, just the thought of a night in a hotel with Caroline was enough to do that.

7

Monday morning and Ian had two things he wanted to work on. First was to check names and addresses of all the second-hand jewellers, goldsmiths and jewellery designers in Edinburgh. There were going to be too many to visit in one day, so he narrowed them down to those that had been in business since before 1966. All he really expected was information. It was just possible they kept records going that far back but he wasn't hopeful. All he could expect was a feel for how usual it was for people to have jewellery copied. He needed to work out an itinerary for next Saturday or they would just spend the day wandering about. Pleasant enough but not helpful for his case.

He had just completed his list when a Facebook message popped onto his screen. He clicked it open.

Hello, it said.

Your message was passed to me by the administrator of the Dorothea Prim Facebook page. I was at the school for six years from 1965. Us old Primians are such a small group these days. The school closed in 1975 so we will dwindle even further until there are none of us left. It is good to know that there is still interest in it. I do remember Ailish Lyton although she was some years my senior. To us juniors she seemed such a glamorous figure, mostly I think because she had a boyfriend with a motorbike. I remember watching her speeding away from the school with her hair flying out behind her. I have scanned and attached the school photo from 1965. I'm not sure, but I think Ailish is the tall girl standing in the back row with her hair blowing across her face. I hope these memories are helpful. Regards, Aggie Trueman.

Ian zoomed in on the photo and studied the girl believed to be Ailish. He thought it probably was her. He couldn't be sure but compared it with Xander's photo of her and allowing for the lack of false eyelashes and the fact that in the school photo half her face was obscured by hair, he could see a similarity. She was taller than most of the others and the only one with her hair loose. The other girls all had plaits or ponytails. The photograph was one of those long pictures that used to line school walls. He remembered them from his own school days. Everyone out on the playing field. Little ones sitting on the ground at the front, the row behind on benches carried out from the gym, a line of prefects and teachers on proper chairs, another row standing behind them and then a backrow standing on more benches. He cropped Ailish out of the picture, enlarged it, printed it and pinned it to his board. He picked up one of his marker pens and wrote *'Ailish at school?' A boyfriend with a motorbike,* he thought. That was interesting, although trying to find young men who owned motorbikes in Edinburgh in 1965 wasn't going to be easy.

He wondered if Joshua Remington had ridden a motorbike, but had no idea how to find out. He had a lot of questions about Joshua and made a list.

Who might remember him from his school days? Find list of Edinburgh schools and try Facebook again.

Where did he go after he left school? University and college websites.

Did he have any family still in the city? Electoral registers.

Where might he have met Ailish? School dances, clubs, societies, sporting events?

· · ·

All a bit vague and time consuming. He'd start with the obvious.

He'd just typed Joshua Remington's name into the National Archive of Scotland website when there was a knock at the door. Lottie, as usual, barked and scampered towards it. Ian picked her up and stowed her under one arm, opening the door with the other. On the doorstep was a girl of about nineteen. She was dressed in a short flowery dress, bomber jacket, black tights and lace-up boots. He hair was a mass of frizzy blonde curls, which together with her brown eyes gave her an angelic look.

'Oh,' she said. 'What a cute dog. She's so adorable. Can I hold her?' She put her bag down on the step and held out her arms.

Lottie appreciated compliments. She wagged her tail and strained towards the girl. Ian passed her over. 'She's called Lottie,' he said.

'She's so sweet,' said the girl as Lottie licked her face.

'Can I help you?' Ian asked. 'Or have you just come to admire Lottie?'

She passed Lottie back and pointed to his door sign. 'Is this you?' she asked. 'Are you Ian Skair?'

'That's me. What can I do for you?'

'Can I come in or should I make an appointment and come back later?'

'I can see you now. Come into my office.' He put Lottie down on the floor and led the way. 'Have a seat,' he said, pointing to a chair on the far side of his desk. He couldn't imagine what she wanted to see him about. She was quite unlike any other client he'd ever had. Much younger for a start. Little more than a schoolgirl. He reached for a notepad and pen. 'Would you like to start by telling me your name?'

'Oh, yes, sorry. I'm Anna Lymington.' She brushed some hair out of her eyes and hung her bag on the back of the chair.

'And how can I help you, Anna?' Too young for marital problems, unless she was concerned about those of her parents. He didn't think she could be an employer worried about her workforce. Could she be adopted and looking for a birth parent? That seemed the most likely. Her answer surprised him.

'I just wanted to ask why you are working for my grandmother.'

Her grandmother? He mentally trawled through his client list. He couldn't think of any of them who were grandmothers. He supposed one of the women who had hired him to watch their husbands could be a grandmother, but she would have been a very youthful one. 'I'm afraid I can't reveal any details about my clients,' he told her. 'Everything they tell me is confidential. Even their names.'

She looked disappointed but then looked up and smiled at him. 'Perhaps if I tell you her name...'

He shook his head. 'No, sorry...'

Then something caught her attention. She stood up and walked over to his board, leaning in for a closer look at his photographs. She read what he had written underneath and tapped on it with her finger. 'That's her,' she said. '*Her* name's Ailish. Ailish Lyton. Is that what she looked like when she was young?'

Really? Ailish has a granddaughter? Why hadn't she told him? He couldn't have been more surprised. But it made a difference. Ailish wasn't his client and she had told him nothing in confidence. He smiled at Anna. 'You've got it wrong,' he told her. 'I was hired to *find* Ailish. What made you think she'd hired me?'

'I went to see her at the weekend and saw your card on her table. I took a photo of it on my phone. Look.' She held her phone up for him to see. 'That's your card, isn't it?'

He nodded. 'Yes, that's my card.'

'I live quite near here so I thought I'd get the bus and come and ask you about it.'

He was confused. 'You live near here but went to see Ailish at the weekend. In London?'

'A group of us from uni went to London for a party on Saturday. We stayed the night there, in Hampstead. We were getting the train back in the evening, so I got the Tube to Kensington and dropped in to see her before we left.'

'You're a student?' Yes, she looked like a student, bright and confident.

'At St Andrews. In my first year.'

'A long way to go for a party.' But he'd never been a student. Perhaps travelling five hundred miles for a party was quite normal.

Anna shrugged. 'Not really. We went on Saturday morning and came back last night.'

Fair enough. He'd been to London and back in a day.

'So, who hired you to find Ailish?' Anna asked.

No harm in telling her, he supposed. Xander would want to know about her anyway. And if she was up here at St Andrews, he'd even be able to meet her. He assumed Xander would be quite keen to do that. 'It was her brother. Alexander Lyton,' he told her.

'Her brother? And he didn't know where she was? That's a bit weird, isn't it?'

'Ailish fell out with their father and ran away from home when she was about your age and there's been no contact with her since. I went to London on Friday to talk to Ailish and tell her that her brother wanted to know how she was.'

'Is he very old?'

'No, he's quite a bit younger than Ailish. He was just a small boy when she left.'

'What did she say when you told her?'

'Not very much really. She didn't seem too keen to meet him again. And she didn't tell me anything about a granddaughter.'

'She didn't know anything about me until I dropped in yesterday.'

That must have surprised her. He wondered how she would have reacted. Joy at discovering a granddaughter or impatience at yet another family member looking for her? 'But you knew about her?'

'Mummy told me about her and where she lived. She said she was a cantankerous old trout.'

He could believe that. Ailish would probably have agreed with cantankerous. Possibly wouldn't be so pleased with the old trout bit. Although she'd probably prefer it to sweet old lady.

'She'd not spoken to Daddy since he joined the army,' Anna continued. 'She was a pacifist, Mummy said.'

That made sense, he supposed. Ailish had determined views and a history of pacifist demonstrating. But refusing to speak to her son seemed a bit much. It was sad, but then he remembered that his own mother didn't speak to him very much. That's how some families were, he supposed. 'She told me your father had died. But didn't give me any details. From the way she spoke about him I assumed he'd died as a baby.'

Anna looked sadly at him. 'He was killed by an IED in Basra when I was four. I barely remember him.'

'How dreadful for you. I'm so sorry.' He reached out and took her hand. 'Dreadful for your mother as well.'

'Probably much worse for Mummy. Like I said, I didn't really know what was going on.'

'So what made you suddenly want to see Ailish?'

'We moved to France quite soon after Daddy died. Mummy got married again about three years later and I grew up and went to school there. We both wanted me to go to uni in England but when Mummy said I had Scottish family I applied to St Andrews. Then I got interested in family history.' She opened her bag and pulled out a laptop. 'I joined this site where people make family trees. It's called *Forebears and More* and it has loads of information, records and stuff. Can I use your Wi-Fi?'

He handed her a card with the password. She turned the laptop on and logged into the site. She turned it towards him and showed him the family tree she had made.

'I've got loads about Mummy's family but practically nothing about Daddy's. Only what Mummy could remember.'

He looked at the tree. Her mother, Jeanette Le Brun, had been married twice and as Anna had said there were brothers and sisters and two generations of grandparents and great-grandparents. He looked at her father's side of the tree – father Pete Lymington, grandmother Ailish Lyton. Anna was right. She had very little about her father's family.

'I can fill in a little for you if you like.'

She looked excited. 'Oh, yes please. Have you got time? Will I have to pay you?'

'It's stuff I've already researched and I'm sure Xander will be thrilled to know he has a great-niece. I think I can waive my fee. You might be able to clear up one or two things *I've* been puzzled about.'

'I could be like your assistant.'

'Well, we'll see. Shouldn't you be going to lectures and writing essays and getting drunk in student bars?'

'I do all that as well. But I'm a good student. I can catch up later. And this is so exciting.'

'Okay, just for today.'

'So Ailish has a brother called Alexander.' She typed it in. 'Do you know when he was born?'

'He's twelve years younger than Ailish, so 1960. He's married to Bridget, but I don't have any dates for her. They don't have any children.'

She typed busily.

'Your great-grandfather was Robert Lyton. He died in 1990. I don't know the date.'

'You also have a great-great-grandfather called Alexander. And you can probably work back through several generations of Lytons who were alternately Alexander and Robert.'

'I absolutely must meet Alexander. Where does he live? Do you think he'll want to meet me?'

He was certain of it. How could he not? 'He lives in a place called Drumlychtoun. It's about forty miles north of here. Alexander is the Laird.'

'Wow.' She typed some more then looked up at him. 'What actually is a laird?'

'It's a title given to Scottish landowners.'

She looked puzzled. 'Can anyone be a laird if they own some land? Are you a laird?'

He laughed and shook his head. 'It's usually passed down through families. It's a title conferred by the Lord Lyon to people who are considered suitable. Although I believe there are some who buy their way in. There are websites I expect.'

'Lord Lion? Like Aslan?'

Ian laughed. 'He's not an actual lion. He's in charge of the Scottish

Court of Heraldry.' He hoped she wasn't going to ask too many more questions. That was pretty much the extent of his heraldry knowledge.

'What about my grandfather? Ailish wasn't married, was she?'

'I'll let you read the notes I made. You'll find Ailish very interesting. She's a lot more than a pacifist. She's a lifelong protester. Been arrested several times.'

'Was she a suffragette?'

He needed to remember that Anna had grown up in France. 'I really hope you are not reading history at uni. The suffragettes were years before Ailish. She was pretty much a founder member of the Women's Liberation Movement though.'

'That's so cool.' She paused and smiled at him. 'You were going to tell me about my grandfather.'

'I'm assuming he was the man Ailish lived with for most of her life. His name was Joshua Remington. He died about eighteen years ago.'

'I'll add it anyway. I can always change it if we find out anything different.' A few more moments of busy typing.

'Now,' Ian said, 'you can help me by telling me about your father. I've not been able to find any record of his birth, but I was looking for either a Lyton or a Remington. And you've recorded him as Pete Lymington.'

Anna rested her chin on her hands and stared at her family tree. 'It is a bit strange. I'd expected my grandfather to be called Lymington. Perhaps Daddy changed his name after the big falling out.'

'He could have done. Does your mother ever talk about your grandfather?'

She shook her head. 'I could ask her, but she didn't know them very well.'

She'd written the names one above the other on a piece of paper and sat staring at them. Suddenly she gasped and jumped out of her chair. She spread the paper out in front of him. 'Look,' she said.

He stared at the names. 'Sorry,' he said. 'You're going to have to explain.'

She sat down again and grinned at him. 'Some parents,' she said, using the tone of a primary school teacher talking to a particularly dim child. 'Some parents give their children double-barrelled names when they're not married.'

'But they didn't.'

'No,' she said. 'But look what they did instead.' She grabbed a pen and added Lyton to the top of the list.

Ian looked again and it began to fall into place.

'Can you see what they did?' she asked. 'That's so cool. Lyton – Remington. They squished them together and made Lymington.'

He watched her jumping up and down in excitement with Lottie joining in. She could be right. He hoped she was. She was so excited about her discovery it would be a shame to disappoint her. It was certainly worth running a birth search for Pete Lymington. Now he knew his date of birth it should be easy. He stood up and stretched. He was stiff and felt as if he had been sitting down for hours. He looked at his watch. He *had* been sitting down for hours. He'd not even taken his mid-morning break to walk Lottie round the garden. The morning had flown by and now he was hungry. 'Let's have something to eat,' he suggested. 'And then we'll try and find his birth certificate.'

'Can we do that?'

'We can. I'll need to pay for a copy, but Xander will want it so it can go on his expenses.'

'Shall I go and buy something to eat? I saw a shop where I got off the bus.'

'I've got bread, cheese and ham. I could make us some sandwiches.'

'I'll do that,' she said, jumping up. 'It's more of an assistant job, isn't it? You can start searching while I do it.'

He showed her where he kept everything in the kitchen and left her to get on with it, with Lottie gazing up at her with a look that suggested it was a long time since her last meal. He returned to his desk and glanced at her still-open laptop for Peter Lymington's date of birth. Some of the entries - including the one for Ailish - were grey with the names showing very faintly and he wondered why. As he was looking at the page a little red flag popped up at the top of the screen with a ping. He wondered what it meant, but that was none of his business. He didn't want Anna to think he had been snooping around her laptop. He jotted down Pete's date of birth and then turned back to his own computer. Logging into the births, marriages and deaths archive he typed in the name. He found it quickly, typed in his credit card details and ordered a copy.

Anna returned with a plate of ham and salad sandwiches and mugs of coffee. She put them down on the table in front of him. 'I made coffee. Is that okay?'

'Perfect.' He should think about getting an actual assistant. Visions of a desk clear of paperwork and a continuous supply of coffee and sandwiches appeared before him.

'Can Lottie have some cheese?'

'Just a small piece. We don't want her getting fat.'

'She's so gorgeous,' said Anna, scooping Lottie up and collapsing into the chair with her.

Ian took a bite of his sandwich. It was delicious. She'd found ingredients for a lovely mustard dressing. 'This is wonderful,' he said.

'I bet you usually just pick at stuff out of the fridge, don't you?'

He had to admit that this was exactly what he did.

'One thing about growing up in France, we take lunch very seriously. Normally we'd have a glass of wine with it, but I didn't know how long we'd stop for lunch. We want to get on with finding Daddy's birth certificate.'

Seemed like she might turn out to be a rather bossy assistant. But he was one step ahead of her. 'Already done,' he said. 'It'll be here in a couple of days. I'll scan it and email it to you. You should be able to keep it on that website you're using. I have Ailish and Xander's as well if you'd like copies of those.'

'Great.' She glanced at the still-open family tree. 'Oh,' she said, 'someone's sent me a message.'

'I noticed the red flag when I checked your father's date of birth.'

'It's because I've shared my family tree. Anyone on the site can see it, but it only shows people who have died.'

'Are living names the ones that are greyed out?'

'That's right. It's supposed to stop stalkers looking for victims.'

That seems sensible, he thought, although it didn't help people like him very much as he spent most of his time looking for the living. But it was nice to know that whoever set up the site was safety-aware.

Anna picked a tiny piece of cheese out of her sandwich and fed it to Lottie, who had been drooling next to her chair. 'Ailish and Alexander won't show up because they're still alive but I entered Robert Lyton this morning, so it could be from someone else researching the same family, or one with the same name.' She finished her sandwich and clicked open the message.

Interesting, Ian thought. He'd been so busy trying to find out about the family that it had never occurred to him that there might be others out there doing the same thing. 'What does it say?' he asked.

She looked at the screen and frowned. 'It's a bit weird. It's from someone called Orlando Bryson. He says he wants information about Lytons who are still alive. I think that's actually against the T&Cs for the site. I'd need to check.'

Ian felt uneasy. 'This guy has to be a signed up member of the site before he can send messages?'

'Yeah, he'll have a profile. And you can message people through the site. It's best not to give out any other contact details though. Even emails.'

Again, very sensible. 'He'll have seen your profile?'

'Yes, but there's not much on it. I didn't even upload a photo.'

That was good. He already felt protective about this girl who'd thrown herself trustingly into his life. There was too much dangerous stuff out there.

She had clicked on Orlando Bryson's profile. 'There's not much there. He's not even uploaded his own tree. I don't think I'll reply.'

He was relieved. 'I think you're right. You should be careful.'

She grinned up at him. 'I did some research on you before I just dropped in. I looked at your website and checked your licence. And it says you used to be police and you have a medal. I hope you don't mind.'

'I'm very pleased to hear it.'

She looked at her watch. 'I should be getting back. Do you know when the buses are?'

'Half-hourly from outside the post office. Or if you feel I'm sufficiently researched I could give you a lift back to St Andrews.'

'That's really sweet, but only if you are going out anyway.'

'Lottie needs a walk and dogs are allowed on the East Beach.' Lottie wasn't the only one needing a walk. He was stiff from sitting all morning. A nice windy walk along the beach would do both of them good.

'Can I come? I love the beach. And Lottie,' she added, ruffling the dog's fur.

'Sure,' he said. 'I'd be glad of the company. Lottie too. We'll take her ball, and you can throw it for her.'

'Does she go in the sea?'

'Yes, she likes to paddle.'

'Me too,' said Anna. 'Although it's a bit too cold here.'

Ian agreed with that. Nothing would persuade him to launch himself into the North Sea even though he'd been born and bred up here. He left that sort of thing to the tourists, as did most of his countrymen. He wasn't so sure about his countrywomen. They seemed altogether tougher. He'd had a great aunt who'd never had a day's illness in her life. She swam in the sea every day, even in winter, and she lived to the age of ninety-eight. Perhaps that was the secret to a long and healthy life. He didn't feel like putting it to the test though.

He grabbed his jacket, a towel and Lottie's lead while Anna packed up her laptop. Then they walked down the path to his car. 'Have you hurt your leg?' she asked, noticing his limp.

'I was shot.' She looked at him, alarmed. 'Long time ago,' he added.

'When you were in the police?'

'Yes. I was heading off an armed raid.'

'Did it hurt?'

'Like hell.' Not many people asked him that. He liked her directness. Came with her youth, he supposed. She wasn't much more than a child.

'I'm sorry,' she said, wiping away a tear. 'Bad things shouldn't happen to good people.'

She was thinking of her father, of course.

'Sometimes when I think about Daddy, I feel relieved that he was killed outright. I know there were people out there who survived terrible injuries... but... well, they never really recovered. Is that awful of me?'

'Of course it's not. No one wants to see someone they love in pain.'

'That's what Mummy says. They told her it would have been very quick. He probably didn't even know about it. He was alive one minute and then...'

'You're very close to your mother, aren't you?'

She nodded. 'I love uni, but sometimes I get homesick. And when I do I know she's always there for me.'

He began to feel quite fatherly. It was a good feeling. He liked the idea of having a daughter. He'd like to meet her mother. Tell her he'd keep a paternal eye on Anna for her. 'Come on,' he said. 'There's a beach waiting and then how about an ice-cream?'

'Yummy. And I've really enjoyed today. Was I a good assistant?'

'Never had a better one,' he answered truthfully. 'You've been a great help.'

'Have I?'

'Definitely. You've filled in some gaps in Ailish's story and you make great sandwiches.'

'I'd like to see Drumlychtoun.'

'I'm sure you will. I'm sending a report to Xander soon. I've a little to do in Edinburgh first. But can I give him your phone number and email? I'm sure he'd love to meet you.'

She nodded.

'And you know where I am. You be sure to keep in touch. Call me any time if you need anything.'

8

I t was quite strange being back in Edinburgh. He'd only left a few months ago so nothing much had changed. It felt different, though. Perhaps it was being here with Caroline. She'd grown up in Perth, but then moved to London where she went to university and began her teaching career. She'd had a miserable marriage from what he could work out, although she'd told him very little about it. She'd returned to Scotland five years ago after the divorce. They were alike, he thought. Caroline was more confident than he was; better at social things and also determined to throw herself at life. It was as if she'd been hurt and wanted to make up for lost time by enjoying life now. He'd been hurt, both emotionally and physically and still felt injured inside in a way that Caroline didn't. Or perhaps she did and was just better at covering it up. But they got on well and he was glad to have her with him now. She'd be quietly observant and note things that he might miss.

He had booked them into a hotel recommended by Jeanie. 'It's quite small and homely,' she told him. 'But you'll be able to come and go as you please. They'll not mind what you do. And,' she added, 'they do a grand breakfast and are only a few minutes from a tram stop.'

What on earth did she think they were going to get up to? A silly question really. She'd winked at him in a way that suggested she knew exactly what they would get up to. He rather hoped she was right. He'd rarely been a guest at a hotel. He spent more time sitting outside them spying on people. He was afraid it had given him a skewed idea of what went on inside. It was hard to rid himself of a vision of someone sitting outside in a scruffy car spying on *them*. Caroline had laughed when he told her that, promising that she had every intention of making him forget that he was a detective. And with a frisson of excitement, he realised that she was probably right. She'd make him forget what he was. She'd very likely make him forget *who* he was as well.

At breakfast the next morning he set out his plan for the day. Tram to Waverley and then a gentle stroll up to the Royal Mile, where he had made an appointment to talk to a jeweller who specialised in antique reproductions. They would drop in at a few more jewellers that he'd earmarked as having been there for many years. He didn't for a moment expect to find anyone who knew about this particular ring, but with any luck they might get a feel for the kind of people and places that Ailish, or whoever had taken the ring, might have dealt with.

By the end of the morning they had learnt a lot about jewellery reproduction and the kind of skills needed to copy rings. The dealers they spoke to had been interested and happy to talk to them. They had also learned a lot about ecclesiastical rings. Bishops are given a ring at their consecration and they are the property of the church. But they are also free to obtain and wear their own episcopal rings. This is presumably what Robert Lyton did or it would have been given back to the church on his death. The style of the episcopal ring had almost always been a very large, gold, stone-set ring. Roman Catholic bishops traditionally had their episcopal ring set with an amethyst. Was Robert a Catholic? Ian couldn't remember, and in any case there was so much religious turmoil at the time that the fact that this ring was indeed set with an amethyst probably didn't mean a lot and probably wasn't important.

Ian had photos of both rings, the copy owned by Xander and the one worn by the Archbishop. There were many similar rings, they were told. They could find him a fairly close match at a price, but not the actual ring. 'What would a genuine seventeenth-century ring be worth now?' he asked one dealer.

'Hard to say,' he was told. 'The value is mostly symbolic. But I believe one rather like the one in your picture was found by a detectorist in a field in Kent recently and fetched around £10,000 at auction. I would say that's an inflated price probably due to all the publicity around it at the time.'

By early afternoon they were flagging and had collapsed into comfortable chairs in a café in the old town. 'I'm not sure about the rate of inflation, or the comparative value of antiques in the sixties,' said Ian, biting into a bun, 'but I suppose the ring might have sold for enough to live on in London for a few weeks.'

'I don't think London was so different from the rest of the country back in the sixties, so you are probably right. But we still don't know if it *was* sold. And you'll never find it if it was.'

'No, I don't really expect to. I just want to piece together as much as I can for my client.'

'That laird?'

'Yes. I found his whole story quite compelling; the lost sister and the legend of the ring, all in a stunning setting.'

'It sounds like one of those epic quests. It would make a good film.'

'Yeah, with Ian McKellen as the Laird.'

Caroline laughed. 'And who would you cast as Ailish?'

'Joanna Lumley,' he said.

'And would they find the ring?'

'Of course. They'd have to lay the legend to rest.'

'You'd need a villain.'

'Ah, yes. I don't have an image of the villain yet. And the more I think about it the less I think it was Ailish.'

'She could have had an accomplice.'

'That's what I'm working on. I've not got much further with this Remington guy.' His research had been interrupted by the surprise discovery of Ailish's granddaughter and he'd been distracted from further Internet searches for him. He felt he was going off in several different directions at the moment, several strands of the same story. Was there going to be one thing that pulled them all together? And more importantly, was he going to find it? 'Well,' he said, draining his coffee cup. 'If you're ready, we'd better get going.'

As they left the café a young man thrust a leaflet for a flea market into Caroline's hand. She read it and then passed it to Ian. 'Do you think this might be interesting?' she said. 'It's not far from here and there'll probably be lots of old jewellery.'

'Good idea,' he said.

They followed the map on the leaflet down a narrow street and through an archway into a square that was packed with market stalls with awnings. They strolled past trestle tables groaning with second-hand books, rails of old clothes and boxes of worn shoes and boots. A little further on they came to piles of furniture and then went down some narrow stone steps into a small room with silver tableware, china and jewellery.

The jewellery dealer was having a quiet day and was happy to talk to them. Ian showed him the photo of the Bishop's ring and he upturned several boxes of rings, spreading them out on a table for them to sift through. There were several close matches, large chunky rings in gold coloured metal and set with a variety of different coloured stones. Most, Ian guessed, not particularly valuable and selling at bargain prices.

Caroline bought one of them. 'I couldn't look at so many rings and not be tempted,' she said. Ian liked it – a green agate set in pyrite. The dealer had given her a reduction on the price, which was already a tiny fraction of what the ring they were looking for would be worth. Even its copy was worth quite a lot more.

Ian texted the photo of the ring to the dealer who had told them he did a lot of house clearances and would call him if he ever came across one like it.

They bought cups of herb tea and sat at a wooden table watching the activity around them. A fun day out, but not getting him far with his case. Caroline looked at him and took a gulp of her tea. 'What next?' she asked.

'I've made an appointment to talk to Jane Crewe, the jewellery specialist at a museum on the other side of town. But after that I think we'll head home. We've probably done as much as we can.'

'It's not been a waste of time though, has it?'

'Not at all. I think I probably know enough now to steal a ring and have a copy made myself.' He laughed. 'And then of course it was worth coming for the...' He hesitated.

'Breakfast?'

'Breakfast was good, yes.'

They both liked the museum. They had arrived a little early so they wandered around looking at the jewellery collection on display until it was time for the appointment. There was little from the seventeenth century and even less that could be described as ecclesiastical. But museums only displayed a fraction of what they held in their vaults, so he hoped his interview might tell him more. They had done a lot of walking and his leg was tired and beginning to ache, so it was a relief when it was time to report back at reception. Mrs Crewe was ready for them, he was told. They were shown into an office with comfortable chairs and offered tea and biscuits. Mrs Crewe had a collection of ledgers with pictures of the museum's ring collection. Ian showed her the photo and asked if she'd seen anything similar. She found a few pictures which she passed to him. There was nothing that leapt out at him and he was beginning to feel he'd seen more than enough rings for one day. They were all beginning to merge together and imprint themselves onto his brain. It was warm in the room and as he looked at yet another set of ring pictures he clutched his cup of tea and hoped he could stay awake. He could easily nod off and it wouldn't leave a very good impression.

'It's interesting you're here today,' she said. 'I had someone last week asking very similar questions.'

'Really? About rings?'

'About the bishop's ring. The one in your photo.'

Suddenly he was wide awake again. He put his teacup down safely on a table and stared at her in surprise. 'What did he want to know about it?' he asked.

'Pretty much the same as you. Had I ever seen it? Did I know who owned it now?'

Someone else on the same search as himself. Must be a coincidence, mustn't it? Probably just someone who'd been at the Glasgow exhibition and found the ring interesting.

'Do you have their name?' he asked.

'Just a minute,' she said. 'I'll check the diary.' She turned to her computer monitor and scrolled through the pages of her diary for what he felt was an irritatingly long time. 'Sorry to keep you,' she said.

'No problem.' He hoped he didn't sound as impatient as he felt.

'Here we go,' she said. 'Last Tuesday. A Mr Orlando Bryson.'

He felt dizzy. Tuesday. A few days after his visit to Ailish. And more worryingly, the day after Anna had received a message from him asking for details of living Lytons. What the hell was going on? 'Do you have any contact details for him?' he asked.

She stared at her screen for another few moments, shifting her mouse and muttering under her breath. 'That's strange,' she said. 'I don't know who entered this appointment, but they should have asked for at least a phone number or email. But I'm sorry, we don't have anything.'

He felt Caroline's hand on his arm. 'You okay?' she asked.

He nodded, pulling himself together. 'Thank you so much for your time, Mrs Crewe.' He stood up and shook her hand.

'Not at all,' she said. 'Any time you need help just let me know.'

He couldn't get out fast enough. He dragged Caroline down the museum steps and towards the tram stop. A tram had just pulled in. They leapt aboard and found a couple of seats. He sat down breathlessly.

'You've got me worried,' said Caroline. 'You're not feeling ill, are you?'

'No, absolutely not. I'm fine. But I need to get home. I have to find out all I can about this Orlando Bryson.'

'Why? Who is he?'

'I've no idea who he is, but I need to know.' He got out his phone and sent a text to Anna. *On no account contact Orlando Bryson.* He'd no idea what he was going to discover, but it didn't feel good.

9

After the weekend Ian settled down to research Orlando Bryson. It was a fairly unusual name but with very little online presence. *A lurker,* Ian thought that was the word. He googled it to make sure. A lurker, he discovered, is a person who reads discussions on message boards, newsgroups, or chat rooms, but who rarely participates. They are considered malevolent, benign, or constructive, depending on their behaviour.

Bryson was clearly a lurker rather than a poster of information about himself. And something told Ian, although he had no idea why, that he belonged to the malevolent variety. He had found a couple Orlando Brysons on Facebook, but neither was based in the UK. He tried LinkedIn and had no more luck there. He did find an Orlando Bryson on a list of Glasgow businesses, where he appeared as CEO of a company called Bryson Office Solutions. That could be his man, but how could he tell? He could drop Office Solutions an email but what would it say? *Are you stalking my young friend on* Forebears and More? *What is your interest in ecclesiastical rings?* Probably not. It would look more as if *he* was the stalker. Should he call and claim he had an office with problems? Again, not a good idea. He was already getting sinister vibes about Bryson and didn't want him poking

around his home office. And he had no way of knowing whether this
Bryson was the one at the museum or if it was the one who had
messaged Anna. But it was an unusual name. He couldn't be dealing
with more than one person and office solutions man appeared to be
the only Orlando Bryson in either Edinburgh or Glasgow. It could all
be a harmless coincidence. Mr Bryson could be an entirely
innocuous person with interests in family history and antique rings.
But why *this* family and *this* ring? Anna had already told him that
Bryson hadn't shared a family tree on *Forebears and More.* Why join a
site like that unless you want to share your own family history? Had
he been there with the express intention of finding Lytons? That,
along with his connection to the ring, was making Ian feel uneasy.

He leaned back in his chair wondering what to do next. As far as
he knew, no crime had been committed, but this was where his police
connections might pay off. His best mate was a police inspector. It
would be a matter of minutes for Duncan to check this guy out. If
they had nothing on him, it would probably be safe enough for Ian to
call him as a person of interest in his Lyton enquires. And if they did,
it would give him a better idea of what he was dealing with. He called
Duncan and suggested meeting for a pint.

'I would,' said Duncan. 'But I've to clear the gutters this afternoon. It looks like rain and it's not been done since last autumn. Plus,
I promised Jeanie. How about this evening?'

Ian could hear some kind of discussion going on in the background. He waited for a few minutes wondering about his own
gutters. Was that a regular task on every house owner's maintenance
list? He'd not owned a house long enough to know. Grandad had a
man who appeared once a fortnight and pottered around the outside
of the house. Gutter clearing might well have been one of the things
he did. He would need to buy a ladder. Was it safe for him to climb
ladders? Perhaps there was someone in the village who would come
and do it. He'd ask Lainie.

It was a relief when his musing was interrupted. 'Jeanie says why
don't you come for your tea?' said Duncan.

As far as Jeanie was concerned tea meant a lot more than a cuppa and a biscuit. It would be a cooked meal. And Jeanie's cooking was too good to miss. 'Sounds lovely,' he said.

'She'll be wanting to quiz you about your weekend in Edinburgh,' Duncan warned.

Of course she would. She'd have been on the phone to Caroline as well. Ian laughed. 'I can live with that,' he said.

'It all went well then?'

'Yes, it went okay.' His private weekend arrangements were not something he wanted to share with the world. Share something with Jeanie and she would do her best to make sure the rest of the world knew about it. But yes, it had been a good weekend. Rather better than his 'okay' had suggested. 'It's actually something I found out in Edinburgh that I want to talk to you about.'

'Something about your Drumlychtoun case?'

'Possibly. I'm not sure yet. I was hoping you might be able to make some enquiries.'

'Sounds interesting,' said Duncan. 'We'll see you about six?'

'Great.' He could take Lottie for a nice long walk first, wear her out before leaving her on her own for the evening.

Pork chops with gravy and mash. One of his favourites. Ian cleaned his plate, sat back and smiled at Jeanie. 'That was the best meal I've had in a long time,' he said.

'Oh aye?' she winked at him. 'Better than a certain meal in a fish restaurant I heard about recently? Or a dinner last Friday in Edinburgh?'

Was there nothing she didn't know about his personal life? 'Different,' he said.

'I'll bet.' She nudged him playfully and started to clear away the meal. 'Well, I'll leave the two of you to your wee gossip.'

Wee gossip? When she'd clearly extracted every detail of the last two weekends from Caroline.

'Don't mind her,' said Duncan. 'She means well. And she's that fond of you.'

'I know,' said Ian. 'But she seems to have taken over where Grandad left off.' It had been Grandad's dearest wish to see Ian happily paired off and he had taken every opportunity to try and make it happen. No female acquaintance between the ages of twenty and fifty was safe from his scheming. Ian had firmly resisted every one of Grandad's matchmaking attempts. Well, most of them.

'We'd both like to see you happy,' Duncan was saying as Jeanie reappeared from the kitchen with a pot of tea and some mugs.

'That's right,' she said. 'You'd be quite a catch now you've your own house.'

A good catch? No, he'd never be that. It made him feel like a giant salmon. Why couldn't he be happy without being paired off? Did he have *helpless man in need of female intervention* stamped across his brow?

'You needed some information?' asked Duncan, pouring tea and pulling him out of his reflection.

Ian passed him a page he had printed with the little information he had collected about Orlando Bryson. 'I wondered if you knew anything about this guy?'

Duncan studied it. 'That name seems a little familiar. I don't think we have anything on him locally, but I can find out if Edinburgh or Glasgow do. Is there a Drumlychtoun connection?'

'I'm not sure. His name has come up a couple of times. It could just be coincidence, but I'd like to know more about him.'

'Okay,' said Duncan, folding the paper and tucking it into his pocket. 'Leave it with me and I'll get back to you in a day or two. But right now, I think we could sneak out for that pint. I've done my bit with the gutters. I've earned a bit of freedom.'

Two days later Ian received the copy of Pete Lymington's birth certificate. It confirmed what he and Anna had worked out. Pete was born on September 29th 1974 in the Kensington and Chelsea Hospital. His mother was Ailish Lyton, a journalist and activist. Interesting that Ailish had considered activism an occupation. But she had been prepared to be arrested for it, so it was obviously a big part of her life. Pete's father was Joshua Remington, a designer and company chairman. That was even more interesting. Designer? What did he design? Clothes, furniture, cars, interior decoration? Or was it just possible that he designed jewellery? In particular, copies of antique rings.

Ian scanned the certificate and emailed a copy to Anna repeating his advice not to have any contact with Orlando Bryson. She replied quickly:

Thank you so much. What's with Orlando Bryson? I don't understand. How's Lottie?

Anna xxx

He replied:

Not sure yet. I'm making enquiries – just don't trust him. All fine with Lottie. I'm just about to send a report to Xander. I'll get in touch when I hear from him.

Work hard.

Ian

He didn't add kisses. He'd never sent email kisses. It wasn't his style and sending kisses to a teenage girl felt a bit creepy. He pressed send and then thought of something and started another email:

Were you going to upload the birth certificate to the forebears website? Can you hold off for now. Safer to keep your father's connections to the Lytons private.

She replied:

Will do. Or rather won't do!

There was a lot to add to the Drumlychtoun file. Most exciting was his meeting with Anna, which he outlined in detail. He added a copy of Pete's birth certificate and a brief paragraph he had found in a newspaper about his death. *Poor old Xander*, he thought. It was going to be a shock for him. Two new relatives he'd known nothing about – one he would be thrilled about and another he was never going to meet. He'd have very mixed emotions about it. He must ask Anna if she had photos of her father that he could scan and send to Xander.

She's keen to meet you, he wrote, feeling sure that Xander would feel the same.

He outlined his trip to Edinburgh, adding that it was rather inconclusive and that Xander shouldn't build up his hopes of finding the ring. He decided not to mention Bryson yet. He'd no evidence that there was any connection beyond a vague enquiry about the family. His interest in rings was probably irrelevant.

He was just finishing his report when Duncan called. 'I've found out a lot about your guy.'

'Interesting?'

'Oh, yes. There's a big file on him,' Duncan paused. 'Probably best if I don't email the information. Can we meet?'

Why? What on earth could he have discovered? Or was he just being cautious? Police emails, he supposed, could be intercepted. A lot had changed since his days in the police. Everyone was so much more security conscious than they used to be. Ian had been quite low down in the police hierarchy and he supposed that reaching inspector level meant being more careful about the information one handled. 'Shall I come to your office?'

'Best if we stay under the radar for now. I'll come to you. This evening okay? Will you be on your own?'

That sounded even more intriguing. Was this something Duncan couldn't risk his immediate colleagues knowing about. 'Sounds very cloak and dagger,' he said. What the hell had he got himself involved with? 'Yes, I'll be on my own. Apart from Lottie.'

Duncan laughed. 'I daresay we can trust the wee dog.'

'She does have a history of mixing with the criminal classes.' He stroked Lottie's head. 'But I think she's reformed now.'

'Pleased to hear it.'

Duncan arrived to a great deal of tail wagging from Lottie. 'She remembers the sausage your PC fed her,' said Ian.

'Aye, they miss her at Bell Street. You'd best drop in for a visit some time.'

They'd both been well looked after at Bell Street police station after Ian's brush with a local drug dealer and his daring escape from a fire. He'd had a hot shower, a change of clothes and a check up from a doctor. Lottie had been walked to the local chippy for a sausage and received a great deal of attention from one of the WPCs. 'Hear that, Lottie? Want to visit your fan club?' Lottie wagged her tail.

Ian made tea and they sat at his desk. Duncan opened a file and spread out some papers in front of Ian. 'Your Mr Bryson is definitely a person of interest in Glasgow, and probably further afield. He's not actually been arrested for anything, but that could just be a matter of time. He operates, as you discovered, from a company called Bryson Office Solutions. But that's probably just a cover. He's being investigated for tenant harassment and possible money laundering.'

'He's a property owner?'

'No, at least not any more. He inherited a family business but pretty much ran it into the ground with gambling debts. Now he provides thugs to make people's lives miserable. Mostly to clear properties and open the way for developers to move in and make obscene profits.'

An unpleasant sounding type, but Ian couldn't for the moment work out why he was interested in the Lyton ring.

'What's your interest in him?' Duncan asked.

'His name has popped up a couple of times. I have a young friend who is into family history and he sent her a message through the website she uses. She'd never heard of him and I advised her not to reply.' At the time it had just been a general piece of advice about not replying to unsolicited messages but it turned out to have been just as well.

'Good advice under the circumstances. You said a couple of times?'

'Yes. That's why Caroline and I were in Edinburgh. I told you about the Laird? Well, he asked me to find his sister who he hadn't had any contact with for a very long time. He suspected her of taking a valuable ring that belonged to his father. We trekked around jewellers asking for information and ended up at the museum. Quite by chance the woman we spoke to mentioned that Bryson had been at the museum a few days before we visited, making very similar enquiries about the ring. I was thinking of going to visit him, but something didn't feel right so I thought I'd consult you first.'

'Ah, your well-known feeling for things that don't seem right. Well, your instinct is usually correct, and you were right to contact me before you did anything.' Duncan tapped the folder he had left on Ian's desk. 'I'll leave this with you. There's quite a lot of background on him in here. But be careful. He's not someone to mess with. Don't even think of making any kind of contact with him without some back up from us. And make sure your friend knows to stay clear of him.'

10

Ian, I can't tell you how thrilled we are with your latest report. We're very sad to learn about the loss of Ailish's son under such dreadful circumstances. How awful that must have been for her and, of course, for his wife. But how wonderful to learn that he had a daughter and to know that she's in Scotland. Xander can hardly believe it – news after so long. And yes, of course we want to meet Anna. Can I suggest that you both come for a weekend soon? We want to make Anna feel as welcome as we possibly can, and I think she might feel more comfortable if she has someone here that she already knows. And of course you can drive her here. I don't like to think of the poor girl having to come by train and be met by total strangers. Have a chat to her about dates and let me know.

He liked that idea because it meant another visit to Drumlychtoun and the place had intrigued him; the family, the history and the castle itself. This case had landed him in a different world, a fascinating and rather beautiful one. Not that it was without a darker side of family quarrels, missing relations and early deaths – he hoped it would be only the one early death, but after reading the file on Bryson that Duncan had shared with him, he couldn't be sure. He was certain there were secrets waiting to be discovered and also felt a shiver of fear after Duncan's emphatic warning. *Do not tackle Bryson without back up from us.* He needed to find out if Xander knew anything about Bryson that might shed light on why he was interested in the ring and the Lyton family. Should he also warn Xander and Bridget? He didn't want to scare them. On the other hand, he didn't want to leave them exposed to any kind of danger. Could Bryson perhaps be working for someone who had an interest in the estate? Ailish's remark about some property developer getting their hands on it and Bryson's connection to tenant harassment made him wonder. But he couldn't work out how that could happen. The Drumlychtoun estate seemed to be a well-run and highly respectable organisation. It presumably had teams of legal people to ward off dodgy developers and protect tenants from threats. A day visit would have been good, but a weekend would be much better. He already knew how hospitable Xander and Bridget were and he expected them to, as it were, kill the fatted calf, or more likely roast a well hung slab of venison, for a great-niece they'd known nothing about. At the very least he expected more of Maggie's excellent lamb and a new batch of shortbread.

Anna was going to be very excited. Not that she ever seemed completely calm. At nineteen the world was still an exciting place and here was a girl who was exploring a new country, making new friends and hurling herself at university life. And on top that she had discovered a connection to an ancient Scottish family who lived in a castle. It was a young girl's dream. He clicked on her name in his contacts and called her wondering if she was working; a lecture or a tutorial perhaps. His experience of students told him she was just as likely to be still in bed nursing a hangover.

She answered at once.

'I hope I haven't interrupted anything,' he said. 'I wasn't sure of your timetable.'

'Not at all. I've just finished some notes for an essay and now I'm headed out to the library.'

A model student, he thought. 'Have you had a chance to read all the notes I sent about Xander and Drumlychtoun?'

'Yeah, I read them last night,' she said breathlessly. 'You didn't tell me they lived in an actual castle. I googled it and it looks so cool. How's Lottie? Have you got any more news? Do I get to meet them?'

'Yes,' he laughed. 'If you'll let me get a word in. They've invited us for a weekend. They didn't like the idea of you struggling up there on the train, so I've been employed as your chauffeur.'

'Oh wow!' she shrieked. 'When?'

She was also, he imagined, jumping up and down in excitement. 'My weekends are loose – just let me know when you want to go.'

'I can't wait. Can we go next weekend?'

He guessed waiting was not an idea she'd take to. 'As soon as that? Well, I don't see why not. Shall I check with them and let you know?'

'Oh, yes please, and text me as soon as you know. I'm so excited.'

He laughed. 'I guessed you might be.'

'Will we take Lottie?'

'Of course. She came with me last time I was up there. They're very dog friendly.'

'Have they got any dogs?'

'Two black labs.'

'Oh, so sweet. I do love dogs.'

'I had noticed. But I must let you get on. I'll call you back soon.'

He ended the call and phoned Bridget. 'She's very keen to come,' he said. 'Would next weekend suit you?'

'Lovely,' said Bridget. 'Xander's going to be thrilled. I'm not sure he really believes it yet. Shall we say Friday evening?'

'Perfect.' He wondered what the weather was going to be like. The castle must look stunning in the setting sun. 'We'd better leave on Sunday afternoon. Make sure she's back for college on Monday.' He didn't want to be in trouble from university authorities accusing him of keeping students from their work.

'You must tell me all you know about her. She's not a vegetarian, is she?'

What did he know? She'd shared ham sandwiches with him so

probably not a vegetarian. 'No, I don't think so but I'll make sure. I'd say she was a pretty normal teenager. Very chatty and excitable and she loves dogs.'

'Then she's going to fit right in. Tell her to bring warm clothes. I know what teenage girls are like with their skimpy little skirts.'

He remembered the skimpy skirt she was wearing when she turned up on his doorstep. He didn't know which part of France she was from, but it had to be warmer than Scotland. But she'd enjoyed the beach at St Andrews so she must know how cold and windy it could be. 'I'll pass that on,' he said.

'Lovely. I'll get Maggie cooking and see you both on Friday.'

He ended the call and sent Anna a text.

We're on for Friday evening. I'll pick you up near Hamish at 6.30 - do you know where I mean?

Hamish was the statue of a well-loved local cat. He was sure Anna would know it and he'd be able to wait in the car in the road nearby.

Of course I know Hamish. I'll be there. She'd added a cat emoji.

Should he get to grips with emojis himself or would it seem like a dad trying to be down with the kids? In other words, embarrassing. He typed, *Bridget says to bring warm clothes and to let me know if you have any food likes or dislikes.*

She replied, *Fantastic. I'll wear my thickest jumper and a hat. I eat EVERYTHING. See you Friday.* This was followed by a mass of smiley faces, ice creams and dogs.

On Friday evening she was waiting for him with a group of friends, most of them looking as excited as she did. They saw her off with hugs and kisses and made her promise that she would send them photos of the castle. Lottie greeted her with a wagging tail and Anna picked her up so that her friends could take photos of them both. Ian thought this might be how teachers feel trying to herd over-excited students on a school trip. He put Anna's bag in the back of the car and hinted that they should get going.

'How far is it?' she asked, jumping in beside him and buckling her seatbelt.

'About fifty miles. If the traffic in Dundee isn't too bad, we'll be there in a little over an hour.'

She looked out of the window and waved to her friends as they drove away from the town. 'I've not been to Dundee. Some of my friends go clubbing there but it sounds a bit scary.'

'It's very different from St Andrews, and you're probably quite right to keep out of the clubs.' Too many drugs, and drunken fights were commonplace. Although he supposed with all the students, St Andrews wasn't immune from those kinds of problems. 'You should think of going during the day.' He was beginning to feel like he had as a copper in Leith, rounding up truanting kids and marching them back to school. 'You should visit the V&A,' he said, trying to sound a bit more upbeat. He'd been meaning to visit it himself since he'd moved here and hadn't got around to it yet. He'd go when this case finished, although right now it seemed to be taking more and more of his time.

As usual he enjoyed the drive up the coast pointing out places he'd known all his life.

'Have you always lived round here?' she asked.

'I was born in Aberdeen. Lived in Edinburgh for a long time and then moved back here a couple of months ago.' That must seem very dull to someone whose parents had travelled the world and who'd moved hundreds of miles to go to university.

'Mummy and Daddy moved all over the place with the army. But I can only remember living in France. I was born in England, but we left when I was too small to remember.'

'Why did your mother choose France?'

'Mummy *is* French. After Daddy died, she wanted to move near to her family. She got a job with Mathias and then married him. It was really romantic. I was seven and I had a pink dress and flowers in my hair.'

'What does Mathias do?'

'He has a vineyard near Roussillon, Clos le Brun.'

That sounded like heaven. 'And you actually chose to come to Scotland?'

She nodded. 'It's not that weird. St Andrews is not so different. Small town with very old buildings.'

'And generally about twenty degrees colder.'

'I don't really mind that. My room in halls is lovely and warm. And it snowed in the winter. We sometimes go skiing in France but we have to drive a long way up into the mountains. It never snows at our house. But here I woke up one morning and there it was. About six inches right outside my window. We had snowball fights and built a snowman. I've got pictures on my phone. I'll show you when you're not driving. My sisters were *so* jealous.'

'Sisters?' That was a surprise. Was Xander's family even bigger than he thought? Apparently not.

'They're half-sisters,' she explained. 'But they feel like real ones. Papa treats us just the same. They're twelve and they've just started collége – that's like middle school, I think.'

So her mother had had twins soon after she'd remarried. Pete was Daddy and Mathias was Papa. Anna seemed unfazed by it all.

'Have you got brothers and sisters?' she asked.

'Just an older brother. He works on the oil rigs. Makes a fortune. But we don't get on all that well.' *Just like the rest of my family*, he thought, turning off the main road into the lanes and the Drumlych-toun Estate. 'Nearly there,' he said. 'Keep an eye out. You'll get a glimpse of the castle any minute.'

'Oh, wow,' she said as it came into sight. 'That looks amazing.'

He stopped so that she could take a photo. Then he drove on, over the bridge and into the courtyard where Xander and Bridget stood waiting for them. Anna climbed out of the car as Xander stepped forward and wrapped her in his arms.

'Anna, my dearest girl. It's so good to meet you.'

'Don't keep her out here in the cold,' said Bridget, leading them inside. 'I've lit a fire,' she said. 'Even in May it can be quite cold in the evenings. I'll show you to your rooms then I thought we'd have soup and sandwiches by the fire.' Ian picked up their bags and Bridget led them up the grand staircase. 'This is your room, Anna,' she said, opening the door into a pretty room with flowered wallpaper and a view of the garden through leaded window panes. 'I believe this was Ailish's room,' she said. 'But there's not much trace of her now.'

'It's such a long time ago,' said Anna. 'I don't suppose she took much with her. I wonder what happened to all her things.'

Ian had wondered that as well. Did Ailish have toys? A rocking horse or a dolls' house? More likely that at nineteen she would have had a Dansette and a collection of singles. But she wouldn't have taken them with her. Particularly if she'd left on the back of a motorbike.

'I'll let you settle in,' said Bridget. 'Come and join us downstairs when you're ready and we'll have a good chat.'

'She led Ian and Lottie to a room further along the landing and opened a door. 'This was the old Laird's room for the last few years of his life. We turned it into a guest room after he died. Xander and I have the room at the end of the landing. All the other bedrooms are in the old part of the castle and rather draughty. We sometimes open them up later in the summer for fishing parties.'

Ian unpacked his bag and then joined the others in the sitting room he remembered from his first visit. Bridget was right. It was a chilly evening and the fire that crackled in the grate was very welcome. Lottie sidled up to it and growled softly. 'Sorry,' he said. 'She's never seen an open fire before.'

Anna laughed and scooped her up in her arms. 'It's all right, Lottie,' she said. 'It won't hurt you and you'll be lovely and warm soon.'

'Ian told us you were a dog lover,' said Xander. 'When we've eaten you can meet our dogs, take them for a wee walk.'

'Oh, yes,' said Anna, grinning. 'Can I explore the castle as well?'

'I'll give you the full tour,' said Xander.

'Is it haunted?' she asked.

'Well...' Xander started.

'No,' said Bridget firmly.

'There's some silly story about the old castle,' said Xander.

'There's an older castle?'

Xander laughed. 'Oh, this one is really quite modern. Built in the seventeenth century. The old one was washed into the sea during a storm. It's said you can hear the screams of the residents drowning on windy nights.'

'Have you heard them?' she asked.

'Never,' said Bridget. 'It's just a silly story.'

'She's right,' said Xander. 'You'll be quite safe with us. And I promise we'll explore thoroughly tomorrow.'

Sometimes, thought Ian, as he sat drowsily by the fire listening to Anna chatting and laughing, *I actually do a worthwhile job.*

By the time they had eaten and walked the dogs it was getting late. Anna stopped chatting and yawned. 'I'm quite sleepy,' she said. 'I think I might go to bed.'

'I'll come up with you,' said Bridget. 'Make sure you remember the way and that you've got all you need.'

They said goodnight to Xander and Ian.

'How about a nip?' asked Xander, reaching for a bottle of Glenlivet.

Ian nodded. His leg was aching and it would help him sleep.

'You've done a grand job, laddie,' said Xander, filling his glass. 'You've found Ailish and brought me a wee angel.'

Yes, he'd found Ailish. Anna had actually found him, but he supposed if he hadn't done a thorough job of finding Ailish that would never have happened. 'I'm happy to have helped, but I don't think it's over yet. I've not found the ring.'

Xander took a sip of his drink and sighed. 'It was never likely, was it? And what you've done is splendid. But you look a little worried. I'm happy to pay for your time if you think there's more to know.'

How was he going to explain to Xander? That a known violent criminal was showing an unexpected interest in them. But he had to know. Ian couldn't risk Bryson finding them out of the blue. Even if his intentions were entirely benign, and having read the file on him Ian doubted that they were, he was reluctant to spoil the weekend and Xander's obvious pleasure at having found Anna. 'I don't want to take too much of your time when you've Anna here,' he said cautiously. 'But if you can spare a few moments before we leave, something's come up that's worrying me a bit.'

Xander drained his glass and slapped him on the back. 'Of course. We'll have a chat before you leave on Sunday.' He offered Ian the whiskey bottle. 'One more?'

Ian shook his head. 'I won't, thank you. It's been a long day and I need my sleep.'

'Quite right. And that wee lass is a bundle of energy. I've a feeling that tomorrow she's going to keep us all busy.'

There was something about the air here. Ian had had one of the best night's sleep he could remember. He woke refreshed and remembered this was a day off for him. He would be happy to laze around the castle, looking at Xander's books and taking strolls with Lottie around the grounds. He'd stay in the background and let them all get to know each other. It was good to hear the three of them chatting and laughing together. Anna was an excellent guest, clearly enjoying the whole experience, marvelling at everything the castle had to offer and eating everything that was put in front of her with gusto.

Xander kept his word and Ian joined them as he took Anna on a tour of the castle, starting with the great hall. Anna looked up at the gallery.

'For musicians,' Xander explained. 'The Lytons are known for their hospitality way back through the generations. Even now we still have a big party for Hogmanay. New Year's Eve to you,' he added, noticing that she looked puzzled. 'And another in the summer for everyone who works on the estate and their families.'

'How do the musicians get up there?' she asked.

Xander pointed to two doors at the back of the gallery. He pulled back a heavy curtain that hung below the gallery revealing two more doors. 'This one,' he said, opening the one on the right, 'leads to a short passage and a stone staircase that takes you straight up there. The one on the left goes to the kitchen and at the back of the kitchen there is another staircase which leads up to the other door in the gallery.'

'Why are there two ways in?'

'I suppose musicians were treated as servants. They wouldn't have been welcome with the main body of guests and they needed to be able to come and go discreetly. But there were also times when perhaps someone made a speech and needed a direct route.'

'Can we go and look?' Anna asked. 'You can show me the way through the kitchen and Ian can go up the other stairs. We'll see who gets there first.'

It wasn't much of a race. Ian was never speedy on stairs. Anna and Xander had further to go, but they all arrived at the same time. They stood at the edge of the gallery and looked down at the hall.

'It's so brilliant,' said Anna. 'I can see it with all the candles lit and something roasting over the fire and people dancing. What kind of music would it have been?'

Xander laughed. 'We're not talking about the Dark Ages,' he said. 'As I said, we still have parties here. Have you heard of ceilidhs?'

Anna shook her head.

Xander put an arm round her shoulder. 'Look down there and imagine the men in their kilts dancing to music played by a couple of fiddle players, maybe a flute and an accordion.'

'Not bagpipes?'

'Not for the dancing. We've had a piper here for Burns Night to pipe in the haggis. An ear-splitting sound though. The pipes are not really for indoors. We open those double doors at the back and let him do a circuit of the room. That's usually enough.' He laughed.

'So does everyone wear a kilt, men and women?'

'People these days wear pretty much what they like. The tradition is kilts for the men and long tartan skirts or plain dresses for the women with a sash worn over the left shoulder. I'll get Bridget to show you.'

After lunch and with great ceremony Xander told them he intended to update the family bible. They trooped into his study and sat watching as he went to his bureau and pulled out an enormous book. 'Many families, not just Scottish ones, traditionally used bibles to keep records of births and deaths,' he told them. 'This one's been in the family since Robert's day.'

'I thought there were lots of Robert Lytons,' said Anna.

'Aye, but this was the one who reclaimed the estate back in the eighteenth century. See his name at the top here?'

Anna was fascinated. Not something her French family did apparently.

Robert had been a bit of a family historian himself, Xander told them. He had painstakingly copied out parish records from around 1600. 'We can't be sure how accurate they were,' said Xander. 'I suspect Robert made some guesses from papers he found and of course the portraits.'

'He didn't spell his name the same though,' she said.

'It's a common name around here with all sorts of different spellings. It took a few years after people began keeping records for the spelling to settle down. Before that I suppose a lot of people couldn't read or write very well and it was mis-recorded in the parish records.'

'It's really interesting. I never thought I had so many ancestors.'

'The Scots are very good at keeping track,' said Ian. 'Although that's not always such a good thing. They became very tribal and a lot of clans were quite violent.'

'We'll take a look at the portraits later,' Xander said. 'It'll help to put names to faces. But first we need to add you.' He picked up a pen and below Ailish he wrote *Pete Lymington* and below that *Anna Lymington.*

'Can I take a photo?' she asked breathlessly, pulling out her phone.

'Aye,' he said in amusement. Anna had already photographed every inch of the castle. 'You'll be sending that off to all your friends, I don't doubt.'

She nodded excitedly. 'And to Mummy. Oh,' she said. 'I forgot.' She scrolled through her photos then passed her phone to Xander. 'This is Daddy.'

Xander sat down suddenly and took the phone from her. He looked at the picture of the man in his uniform and wiped away a tear. 'Oh, my dear,' he said. 'My nephew, and I never knew him. I wish I'd had a chance to meet him.'

'Shall I send it to you?' she asked, squeezing his hand.

He nodded. 'I'd like that.'

Xander turned back to the bureau and from another drawer he extracted a book of newspaper cuttings and photographs. There were some of him and Ailish as children – rarely together, his own parents and grandparents. He showed her newspaper accounts of family weddings and clippings about wills. There was information about the estate: maps, details of houses along with household ledgers and rent books. It was a family historian's paradise and Anna photographed enthusiastically.

With Xander and Anna engrossed, Ian scanned through the family details in the bible looking for any record of a Bryson. There was nothing and he felt reassured. But why *was* Bryson interested in living Lytons? He must warn Anna again about posting on *Forebears and More*. He could see how excited she was about all these documents and hated to dampen her enthusiasm. But until they knew more about Bryson, she shouldn't take the risk.

Bridget joined them, rubbing her hands enthusiastically. 'We're pushing the boat out this evening,' she told them. 'Maggie's been cooking all day. We're going to light a fire in the hall and eat in there.'

'We should dress up,' said Anna. 'But I've not brought anything dressy.'

'I'll find you something,' said Bridget. 'And we'll get Xander to wear his kilt.'

'What about you, Ian?' Anna asked.

'Me?' he said, shaking his head. 'I'm afraid I haven't brought anything either.'

Bridget looked at him with her head on one side. 'Well,' she said. 'You're a bit broader than Xander, but I think I have just the thing for you if you're not too picky about the tartan.'

'Are you thinking of the Ogilvie?' Xander asked. 'He was a cousin of some sort. I forget why we have his kilt here, but it should fit you.'

'You wouldn't object to wearing an Ogilvie tartan, would you?' Bridget asked.

He wouldn't object at all. He'd be honoured. The Ogilvies were a highly respected family. His only regret was that he hadn't thought to bring his own kilt.

'Ian's actually related to us,' said Xander. He reached for the bible again. 'Here,' he said, pointing at one of the entries. '1747, David Lyton married Anne Skair. They had six children.'

Ian looked at the names. David's entry was off to the side of the page. A rather distant cousin. He'd no idea if there was an Anne Skair in his own ancestry. But it was a nice idea. Maybe he was somehow connected to the Lytons of Drumlychtoun.

'So,' Xander continued. 'If he's related to us, he's also related to the Ogilvies.'

'That's so exciting,' said Anna, giving Ian a hug. 'We're cousins.'

Later, dressed in Cousin Ogilvie's kilt, Ian watched as Bridget set the table for the evening meal. Maggie had been busy all day in the kitchen and the smell of cooking was wonderful. A fire was lit in the hall and as it grew dark Bridget also lit candles. 'In the old days,' she said, 'they would have roasted a deer on a spit over the fire, but it's out of season and anyway with only four of us it would be way too much. We'd be eating venison sandwiches for months.' She smiled at him. 'You look very fine,' Bridget told him.

She looked good herself, he told her. She was wearing a long tartan skirt with a white shirt. 'Wait until you see Anna,' she said. 'Ah, here she is now.'

They had really gone to town with her outfit. She was wearing a long, navy blue, velvet dress, her hair brushed up on top of her head and a tartan shawl draped over her shoulders. Angora, he suspected, or alpaca. He didn't know a lot about yarns. Most of his wool experience was with tweed or Fair Isle. His grandmother was forever knitting him Fair Isle jumpers which were scratchy and which he hid away in drawers knowing the jeers he'd get from his school mates.

Anna did a twirl for them. 'I'm going to buy a dress just like this,' she said. 'It makes me feel really Scottish.'

'My dear,' said Bridget. 'Keep it. I'll never get into it again.'

'Oh,' said Anna, flustered. 'I couldn't. I didn't mean... I wasn't asking you to give it to me.'

'I didn't think that for a moment. And I'd love you to have it. Something to remind you of the weekend.'

'I won't ever forget it,' said Anna. 'I can't wait to tell Mummy all about it.'

Xander had gone quiet. Looking rather sombre, Ian thought.

'Anna,' Xander said. 'It's right that you should feel Scottish because you are, or at least partly. Was your grandfather Scottish? The man Ailish lived with?'

'I don't know,' said Anna. 'I don't know anything about him at all. Would it make a difference?' She looked worried.

Xander patted her hand. 'Not to me. Not in the least. I just wondered.'

It did matter, Ian thought. He didn't know why, but it seemed to matter a lot. 'I've more research to do,' he said. 'But it looks as if he was born in Edinburgh.'

'Ah,' said Xander. 'That's good. Find out all you can. I'd like to know about him.'

'Let's eat,' said Bridget.

Ian thought she was trying to distract Xander. Something had brought on a fit of gloom and Ian couldn't work out why.

'Local lamb,' Bridget continued, 'and carrots and potatoes grown on the estate. Did Ian tell you anything about what we do here?' she asked Anna. 'Our tenants run a co-operative growing organic vegetables. They sell in local markets and are doing very well.'

'Yes,' Xander agreed, appearing to throw his gloom aside. 'We went through a bad patch a few years ago trying to deal with supermarket supply chains who always seemed to get the upper hand. They paid miserably and usually very late. I was sceptical at first, but we had this young lad – grew up on the estate then went to agricultural college. He got interested in organics and it all snowballed from there. He manages the estate now. Our stuff is pricey but there's a demand for locally grown food these days. It's what's kept us going.'

'Do you ever open the castle to the public?' Anna asked.

'We've thought about, but there are so many regulations it would probably cost more than we ever made. And I don't like the idea of people trooping round my home and snooping into every corner.'

It must be a worry for him, Ian thought. He couldn't imagine how much it cost to keep a place like this. He'd no idea of the economics behind it all and was quite glad that he only had his small house and business to run.

'Dessert?' asked Bridget when they'd finished their lamb. 'We've done something rather special to celebrate.'

Maggie appeared from the kitchen carrying a baked Alaska lit with sparklers. She set it down on the table and they waited as the sparklers died down. She served it into glass bowls and handed round silver spoons.

'That's amazing,' said Anna, reaching for her phone to take a photograph.

'You'll be wearing that phone out,' Xander laughed, as he dug his spoon into the white meringue.

'I don't want to forget a single thing about this weekend,' said Anna.

With the fire and candles the room felt warm. Ian removed his jumper and noticed that Anna was unwrapping her shawl. She turned to drape it over the back of her chair and something caught the light.

As she turned back, Xander gasped and dropped his spoon with a clatter. He stared at Anna. 'It's... it's...' he stammered. 'She's got...'

'What is it, darling?' Bridget asked, then gaped at Anna, speechless.

What was the matter with them? Ian wondered, looking across the table at Anna. When it had first caught the light he'd assumed it was a pendant, but now realised with a shock that it wasn't. *Oh my God,* he thought. It couldn't be.

'What?' asked Anna, looking from one to the other in confusion. 'What have I done?'

Xander, his hand shaking, pointed to the chain she was wearing round her neck. 'That... that round your neck,' he stammered. 'Why are you wearing it? Where did you get it?'

'This?' she asked, holding it up.

'But it's the ring...' Xander spluttered.

'I have to wear it on a chain like this because it's too big for me. It would slip off my finger.'

'You took it out of my bureau?' he growled.

'No, of course I didn't,' she said, looking horrified at the idea.

Xander stood up and walked around the table towards her, his expression furious.

Bridget reached for his arm and held him back. 'Xander, get a grip,' said Bridget. 'You're upsetting her. For God's sake sit down.'

He didn't answer her. He turned and disappeared into his study. Bridget put her arm round Anna. 'It's okay, sweetie,' she said. 'He's just a bit tired. Finding out about Ailish and your father. It's all been too much for him.'

Xander returned a few minutes later with a wooden box which he slapped down on the table in front of Anna. 'Open it,' he said angrily.

Anna looked up at him warily. Then she opened the box and gasped. 'It's the same as mine,' she said, staring down at the contents.

Xander looked down at the box and turned pale. 'It's still there,' he muttered.

'Of course it's still there,' said Bridget. 'You didn't really think Anna had taken it, did you?'

Xander seemed a bit shaky on his feet, so Ian helped him back to his chair. He sank into it and put his head in his hands. 'I thought... I don't understand...' he whispered. 'I don't know what's going on.'

Bridget put a hand on his shoulder. 'I'm sure there's a perfectly good explanation,' she said kindly.

'Perhaps we should let Anna explain,' said Ian.

Anna was sobbing quietly, and Bridget passed her a tissue. She wiped her eyes and looked up at them. 'I don't understand either,' she said. 'I didn't mean to upset you. I'm sorry...'

'Anna, it's okay,' said Ian, giving her arm an encouraging squeeze. 'Bridget's right. Just tell us about your ring.'

'Daddy left it to me,' she said, starting to cry again.

'Take your time,' said Ian, passing her another tissue.

'When troops are deployed in conflict zones they write letters and leave things for their families in case... well, you know. Daddy left this for me with a letter to open on my eighteenth birthday.'

'Had you ever seen it before?' Ian asked kindly.

She shook her head. 'Mummy hadn't seen it either but...'

She'd started to shiver and Bridget reached for her shawl and wrapped it gently round Anna's shoulders. 'Pour her a drink,' she said to Ian. 'A brandy from Xander's study.'

Anna wiped her eyes. 'I'm okay.'

'You were going to tell us about your mother. Did she say anything to you about the ring?'

'She told me Daddy hadn't spoken to either of his parents since he'd joined the army except just one time. His father was in hospital, and he sent a message to Daddy's CO asking him if Daddy could visit him urgently. He and Mummy were in Aldershot then and they gave Daddy a day of compassionate leave.'

'Did your mother say why?'

'Not really, but my grandfather died not long after that and Mummy thought that he might have given Daddy the ring then.'

'You say your father wrote you a letter,' said Ian. 'Did he explain anything about the ring?'

'He just said that he hoped one day I would find out more about who I was. Mummy thought he might have meant something to do with finding my Scottish family. That's why I came to St Andrews and not an English university. And it's why I joined *Forebears and More*.'

'And it's why you went to see Ailish?' Ian asked.

'Yes, although Ailish said she had nothing to tell me. She wasn't exactly unfriendly but I could tell she didn't really want me there. Then I saw Ian's card on her table. It was an address in Scotland.'

'And you went to see him?' asked Bridget.

'I hoped he'd be able to tell me more about her.'

'Which brought you to us. And I'm very glad it did. Xander, you must apologise to Anna. Look how much you have upset her.'

Xander pulled up a chair next to Anna's and put his arm round her shoulder. 'My dear, I don't know how to apologise. I don't know what came over me. It's just... well, it was such a shock seeing it like that.'

'I don't understand,' said Anna tearfully.

'Of course you don't, my dear. Let me try to explain. Come with me.' He reached for her hand and led her to the stairs, to the portrait of Robert. In the dim light he held up a candle. 'Bishop Lyton,' he said. 'Look at his hand.'

'Oh,' said Anna. 'It's the same as mine... yours... I'm sorry, I'm really confused. Why are there two rings the same?'

Xander led her back to the table. 'They're not the same,' he said. 'One was made in the sixteenth century, the other is a copy made about fifty years ago. The two were switched. I have the copy. Yours must be the genuine one.'

'Who switched them?' Anna asked quietly.

'I didn't find out about the fake until quite recently. We had it very carefully examined by experts and once they told me the likely date I began to wonder if Ailish had taken it.'

'Is that why you hired Ian? Not because you wanted to find Ailish, but because you thought she had stolen the ring?'

'I'm afraid that was part of the reason, yes. I'm very ashamed of that, but finding Ailish, and then you, was far more important.'

Anna turned to Ian. 'So you knew about the ring and you didn't tell me.'

'Ailish told me she didn't have it,' said Ian, 'and I wanted to believe her. I didn't want you to know that she might be a suspected thief.'

'I'm afraid it's all to do with that silly legend,' said Bridget. 'Xander always says it's nonsense. He's right, of course, but it does make you wonder.'

'Legend?'

'The story is,' said Ian, 'that as long as the ring is in the possession of the Laird then both he and Drumlychtoun are safe.'

'Then you must have it back,' said Anna, unclasping the chain and handing the ring to Xander.

'No, my dear. It's rightfully yours. I've been without it for fifty years. If something bad was going to happen to either me or the estate, it would have happened by now. And what this has done is make me see sense and not put any faith in silly stories.'

'But if Ailish took it that makes it stolen property.'

'Ailish was desperate to get away. If she took it then she needed it more than I did. In any case, if I die before Ailish, she inherits Drum-lychtoun. It would become hers anyway.'

'But that's not very likely. Ailish is a lot older than you.'

'If she dies before I do, it will pass to her heirs. Your father would have inherited it if he had lived, but as he didn't it means that *you* are the heir so you would be the owner of the ring. But more importantly, your father wanted you to have it. And I absolutely respect his wish. You are its rightful owner. And all I can say is that I hope you can forgive my stupidity just now.'

'Of course I do,' she said, throwing her arms around him.

'Hey,' said Bridget, putting an arm round both of them. 'This has all been a bit emotional. What we need is a nice cup of tea and a chance to calm down.' She chivvied them all into the more comfort-able sitting room and disappeared into the kitchen to put the kettle on. Anna was twirling the ring in her fingers. 'I think it should stay here,' she said. 'I don't think it's safe with me.'

'But your father...' Xander started.

Ian was more concerned that *she* might not be safe. 'Can I make a suggestion?' he interrupted. 'Why doesn't Anna take the fake ring for now and leave the genuine one here for safekeeping. I'm sure you could put something in writing in case there's any misunderstanding in the future.'

'That's a great idea,' said Anna. 'I'd feel much better if it was here.'

'Better still, let's get the damn thing locked up at the bank,' said Bridget, as she returned with cups of strong tea and a plate of shortbread.

'Do you think Daddy knew what it was?' Anna asked.

'It's hard to say. All I know is that he and Ailish didn't get on, so I'm not sure how much she would have told him,' said Xander.

'Isn't it strange that my grandfather had it, not Ailish?'

Ian was thinking the same thing. Could Ailish have been telling the truth all along? Should they actually be investigating Joshua Remington?

'Can you remember exactly what your father wrote to you?' Ian asked.

'It's at home. I don't really remember. He wished me a happy eighteenth birthday and like I said, there was something about finding out who I was or where I came from. I don't remember exactly. I could get Mummy to scan it and send me a copy.'

'Do we need to look into it any further?' asked Xander. 'We know where the ring is now. Isn't that enough?'

'Let's sleep on it,' said Ian. He didn't think they had the full story yet, but it was probably best not to ruffle them any further. He'd have a quiet word with Xander before they left tomorrow.

Ian woke early on Sunday morning. He shifted Lottie off his feet, climbed out of bed and opened his window. It was another glorious sunny day. He took a long breath of sea air. It was quite different from his Tayside window. Here it was merged with the scent of peat and bracken.

Last night had been surreal. For a moment he wondered if he'd dreamt it. It had been a shock to all of them, seeing the ring like that, glinting in the firelight as if it was welcoming itself home. And then there was Xander's reaction. His sudden flash of anger when he'd always seemed so even tempered. What memories had it brought back? And was his case now over? Both the ring and Ailish had been found but he had an uneasy feeling that it wasn't over yet. Perhaps worse was to come. Had things been stirred up that might have been better left alone?

He could smell bacon cooking, so he dragged on his clothes and descended to the kitchen, where Bridget was cooking breakfast. She was singing quietly to herself and smiled at him as if nothing had happened last night.

'Xander about yet?' Ian asked, tucking into bacon and eggs as Bridget poured him coffee.

'He and Anna have taken the dogs for a quick run.' She tossed Lottie a piece of bacon. 'Missed out on the walk, didn't you, my sweet?'

'Xander's okay, is he?'

'He's fine. Why wouldn't he be?'

'He seemed a bit on edge last night.'

Bridget shrugged. 'Oh, that,' she said. 'Just some memories stirring. He feels dreadful about shouting at Anna like that. He said you wanted to talk to him about something this morning so I thought Anna and I might go for a stroll round the village. Maggie can't wait to introduce her to her mother, and I expect there are one or two others who are curious.'

'Curious about what?' asked Anna, bouncing in rosy-cheeked and windswept from her walk. She greeted Lottie as if they hadn't seen each other for years. All the trauma of last night apparently forgotten.

'About you,' said Bridget. 'Our surprise great-niece. Word gets around quickly so expect a lot of questions and be ready to eat cake and drink countless cups of tea. I'll just make a light lunch before you and Ian are on your way,' she added.

'Okay,' said Anna, tucking in as Bridget put a plate of bacon and eggs down in front of her.

'Don't give Lottie any more bacon,' said Ian, 'or she'll get fat.'

Anna made a sad face. 'Hear that, Lottie?' she said. 'No bacon for you.'

Ian finished his breakfast and rinsed his plate in the sink.

'You wouldn't like some more?' Bridget asked.

'He'd better not,' said Anna. 'Or he'll be the one getting fat.'

She was very chirpy this morning. Ian was relieved that she hadn't been upset after last night. It was such a lot for her to take on board. Memories of her father, suddenly finding she was the heir to a castle, realising she was the owner of a priceless piece of jewellery. Although he wasn't sure how much the ring was worth. But that wasn't the point. It was priceless to the family and probably couldn't be seen in terms of money. He wondered vaguely about insurance, but that was none of his business.

'Ian, would you be a dear and take Xander a coffee? He had breakfast earlier. He's in his study.'

'Of course,' said Ian, pouring him a cup.

He found Xander sitting in a chair by the window. The same chair, Ian thought, that he'd been sitting in the first time he'd visited the castle.

'Thank you,' Xander said as Ian handed him the coffee.

'Bridget and Anna are walking to the village so would this be a good time for a chat?'

'Of course,' said Xander. 'Have a seat.'

Ian sat down in the chair opposite. Xander looked tired. 'Everything okay?' Ian asked.

'Didn't sleep too well.'

'I'm not surprised. It was quite an evening.'

'I feel so bad about snapping at Anna. She's such a sweet girl. How could I even begin to think she'd have done something like that?'

'She is a sweet girl, but she knows what it's like to lose someone, the way grief can make you a bit irrational. She'll have understood.'

'You're right, of course. I've such a lot spinning round my head – knowing where Ailish is, discovering Anna, knowing that I've lost a nephew without ever having known he existed.'

'And finding the ring?'

'Yes, of course. Although I wish that could have happened without it confirming that Ailish was guilty of stealing it.'

'You hoped I'd find out that Ailish didn't take it?' Ian suggested.

'I suppose I did, yes.'

'I'm still not convinced that she did. I know the evidence is against her at the moment, but I still don't think we know the whole story. Think about it, Xander. Isn't it more likely that it was Pete's father who gave him the ring, not his mother? There's no evidence that Ailish had ever had it. Couldn't it be possible that Joshua took it?'

'Without Ailish knowing? Do we know if he ever came here? And if he did, how would he know about the ring?' Xander asked. 'I suppose Ailish could have told him the legend in all innocence.'

'It's possible,' said Ian. 'Would you like me to find out more about him? And I'm not just angling for more work. If you say you'd rather leave it, that's fine with me.'

'Is that why you wanted to talk to me this morning. You think there's more to discover?'

'I do, yes. But I wanted to talk to you about something quite different.' Although he didn't know how different it was. The ring was a connection but it might not be the most worrying one. 'There's been someone poking around. Trying to find information about the family. First it was a message on this website Anna uses. If it had just been that I probably wouldn't have worried. But the same name cropped up when I was asking about the ring at the museum. Does the name Bryson mean anything to you?'

Xander leant back in his chair and looked puzzled. Ian could have sworn he was blushing. Not the reaction he expected at all.

'Yes,' said Xander. 'That's a name that brings back memories. Can't imagine what it's got to do with Ailish or the ring, though.'

'So who was he?'

'She,' Xander corrected. 'Someone I knew way back.'

From the look on his face it wasn't an unpleasant memory. 'Can you tell me about her?'

'If you really want to know, but I'm sure it's not relevant. Sheila Bryson was my first love. I must have been eighteen or nineteen. Sheila was maybe a year or two older. She was a botany student at Glasgow University. Up here one summer on a field trip.'

'Staying at the castle?'

'No, she was camping with a load of other students up the coast from here. They were looking for some wild orchids that they thought were only found in very specific parts of Scotland. I'd just left school and was taking a break before learning about running the estate. But this isn't the most interesting place for a bored teenage boy, so I joined them most days while they were here. About six weeks. Joyful evenings singing round a campfire and then escaping together into the woods, or barns, once even the sand dunes. I'm sure you get the picture.'

Ian did, and was doing some calculations in his head. 'So this would have been late seventies?'

'Sounds about right, yes.'

About right for Xander maybe, but all wrong for the ring, which the experts were sure had been copied at least ten years earlier. Could they be wrong about that? But even if they were, it didn't explain how Anna's father had got hold of the original. Someone could have stolen it later, but he still couldn't escape the fact that at some point it had made its way into Anna's family. And the only explanation had to be that Ailish or Joshua had taken it. And neither of them had been back here since the late sixties.

'You've come across the name Bryson recently?' Xander asked.

'I have, but I think it must be just coincidence.' Ian explained what he knew about the message to Anna and the enquiry at the museum. 'This was a man called Orlando Bryson. Probably no connection at all. But if he does find his way to you, be very careful. I checked him out with the police, and he doesn't sound like a nice character at all. I've already warned Anna not to respond to his messages.'

'That's good. I'd never forgive myself if anything happened to her. We agreed on our walk this morning that I'm going to let her have the copy. I'll take the original to be authenticated and keep it in a safe at the bank along with a certificate of ownership for Anna.'

Ian and Anna left for St Andrews after lunch; Anna promising to return very soon and Ian having been contracted to make further enquiries, focussing on who'd had the ring copied.

Xander and Bridget waved them off from the front door.

Ian was exhausted and he'd just been an observer. Not much more than a fly on the wall. Thank goodness for Bridget and her down to earth good sense. It had all been way too intense. He'd be glad to get home, just him and Lottie, and no emotional revelations.

He glanced at Anna, who seemed as cheerful as ever, and marvelled at the resilience of the young. He hoped Xander would be that tough because he had a feeling that there were going to be more revelations before they finally got to the bottom of things.

11

Sheila Bryson. Orlando Bryson. Coincidence? Bryson wasn't such an unusual name. But with a connection to Drumlych-toun? Although in Orlando's case a rather tenuous one.

Ian needed some thinking time. He'd take Lottie for an early morning walk down to the shops for croissants and a local newspaper. Then what? Xander was happy for him to keep delving into the recent history of the ring – two rings. The original was now safely returned. But how had Pete got hold of it? The obvious answer was that, as they had originally assumed, Ailish had taken it and given it to her son. But from what Anna had been told by her mother, Ailish and Pete hadn't spoken for a long time – not since he had joined the army. When would that have been? Pete was born in 1974. If he had joined the army when he left school or university that would have been in the early nineties, and he was killed ten years later. So there would have been ten years of Ailish not talking to Pete. Could she have given him the ring before that? Perhaps for his eighteenth birthday. He had left it for Anna on her eighteenth so that might make sense. It would also mean that Ailish hadn't been lying when she said she hadn't got the ring. She'd just been a bit economical with the truth.

Ian decided that wasn't a line he was going to follow today. He might learn a bit more when Anna was able to show him her father's letter. For now, his thoughts turned to the Brysons. He wrote down what he knew.

Sheila Bryson – a couple of years older than Xander so currently in her mid-sixties.

Had been in the Drumlychtoun area for six weeks during the summer after Xander had left school.

Had an affair with Xander which sounded like it was a lot more than a bit of innocent hand holding.

Orlando Bryson – age not known but old enough to have ruined the family business so probably somewhere between thirty and fifty.

Known to local police as a hit man running a team of thugs.

Ian stopped writing and thought about that for a while. Bryson must be well known among the criminal classes, and those edging towards the criminal. But how had he become well known? He could hardly have advertised himself online as *Rent-a-Thug*. That would be a catchy name, Ian thought. Perhaps one could advertise on some dark corner of the Internet with one of those search engines that required a subscription and several complicated passwords. Not something he fancied doing himself, even if he had thought up a catchy name that Bryson could use. He'd leave that to the serious crime squad and hope information would filter through to him via Duncan. He continued his list.

Interested in the Lyton family.

Interested in the ring.

According to Duncan's file Bryson had single-handedly run a family business into the ground – when, and what kind of business?

Both Brysons – live or lived in Glasgow.
    Both have or had tenuous connections to the Lytons.

Question
    Could they be related?
    Where is Sheila now?

Ian began to plan his day. He logged in to the Glasgow archive but wasn't sure what he was searching for. It would be better to go there. People who worked in archives were always happy to help. It would be long day with an hour and a half drive in each direction. He'd need to leave Lottie with Lainie for the day.

Monday proved to be a good day for a visit. The archive was quiet, and he found a young man called Greg who was sitting behind a desk looking bored and who was only too pleased to help him. Greg suggested they start with birth records, which led to eye opening discovery number one.

Sheila Bryson was the younger of two siblings. Her father was Harold Bryson, and she had a brother called George. Nothing spectacular so far, but then Ian discovered that Sheila had given birth to a son, Orlando, in March 1979. No father was named on the birth certificate. It hit Ian between the eyes. Nine months earlier Sheila had been cavorting in the heather with Alexander Lyton, heir to the Drumlychtoun Estate. He was sure Xander had known nothing about it. For him it had been no more than a rather pleasant teenage memory.

Ian was just wondering how he was going to break the news to

Xander when he was hit by eye opening discovery number two. He'd told Greg that he thought the family had been in business in Glasgow, but that it had likely gone bankrupt some time in the last ten or fifteen years. Greg suggested local newspaper reports currently stored on microfilm. Ian typed in *Bryson* and searched year by year starting when Orlando would have been about twenty. If a son was going to ruin a business, he guessed, the most likely time to do it would be in his twenties or thirties. He trawled through several years' worth of articles. After an hour his back was aching, and his eyes were itching. Time for lunch. He'd take a break and come back after a bit of fresh air and a sandwich. And then there it was. *Death of Local Businessman George Bryson.* Ian enlarged the article and read:

We are sad to report the death of Glasgow businessman George Bryson following a short illness. Mr Bryson was respected locally as the chairman of Bryson Holdings, a company formerly known as Bryson Remington, which traded in precious metals. Mr Bryson lived at White Lodge in Bearsden with his sister Sheila and her son Orlando.

The name jumped out at him *Remington.* Could this be the same Remington, Ailish's lover? He needed to know more about the company formerly known as *Bryson Remington.* It couldn't be Joshua Remington. He'd left for London when he was in his early twenties. Could it be his father? Back to the desk to ask Greg's advice. He was directed to a different room where he could find company records.

Bryson Remington was founded by Harold Bryson and Gideon Remington in 1945 at the end of the war. Harold became sole chairman on Gideon's death in 1980 when the company name changed to *Bryson Holdings.*

Ian made some notes.

1. *Find Joshua's birth certificate.*
2. *What did Joshua do after he left school and did he spend time at*

Drumlychtoun? Perhaps he'd camped in a tent in a field the
way Sheila had done ten years later.
3. *Find Sheila Bryson.*

Sheila seemed to be the best starting place. He found a free computer
and typed *White Lodge, Bearsden* into Google Maps. He printed the
page, thanked Greg for his help and left, pausing for a cheese roll and
a cup of tea in the cafeteria.

Bearsden, he discovered, was an upmarket suburb about six miles
from the centre of Glasgow. Ian noticed new developments of flats
and maisonettes and larger houses converted into apartments. White
Lodge, as its name suggested, was white. Built in the 1920s, he
guessed. It was now a B&B. He'd hardly expected to find Sheila still
living there. He was actually quite relieved that she wasn't there with
Orlando, who didn't sound like someone to sit down and chat to over
a cup of tea. And at least at the B&B he was likely to find someone at
home.

He parked in the road, walked up the drive and rang the doorbell.
It was opened by a woman in a flowered crossover pinafore and with
a scarf round her head tied and knotted at the front. She was carrying
a yellow duster and a tin of lavender polish. She looked like a char-
lady from a 1950s film, and he expected a cockney accent. Ian handed
her his card and introduced himself.

'I'm Elsa Curran,' she said, not sounding in the least cockney. She
didn't sound particularly Scottish either, at least not the thick
Glasgow accent that even he had trouble understanding. And she was
younger than he'd first thought. He mentally ticked himself off for
making sudden assumptions about people's appearances.

Elsa glanced down at her overall. 'You wouldn't think it to look at
me now, but I own this place.'

'I'm sorry to disturb you,' said Ian. 'But I'm making some
enquiries about the Bryson family.'

'No worries,' she said. 'Glad to take a break. Will you come through to the kitchen? I'll put the kettle on.' She pulled the scarf from her head and let a cascade of red hair fall over her shoulders. She led him to the kitchen and offered him a chair. 'Tea or coffee?' she asked, removing her apron and hanging it on the back of the door, revealing jeans and a bright pink cardigan which contrasted strikingly against her red hair. Right in front of his eyes, she'd morphed from Mrs Mopp into Christina Hendricks.

Ian looked around the kitchen and noticed an expensive machine on one of the worktops. He opted for coffee, hoping for a rich brew of freshly ground beans.

'So how can I help you?' Elsa asked, pouring beans into a grinder, and pressing a switch.

Ian waited for a moment so that he didn't have to shout over the sound of grinding coffee. 'Did you buy the house from the Brysons?' he asked, once the noise had stopped.

She tipped the coffee into the machine and added some water. 'Aye, we did. About five years ago.'

'We?'

'Me and my sister, Kate. She's away down the shops right now. She's the oldest so she gets all the best jobs. I'm stuck here with the cleaning. Mind, it's easier now. Right mucker of a place it was when we moved in.'

'Did you meet the Brysons?'

'Just Sheila Bryson. She had a studio at the top of the house. That was a grand mess. She wasn't a tidy painter; paint on the walls and the floor, reeked of alcohol and cigarettes.'

'She was an artist?'

'Some kind of illustrator. Flower paintings and the like. Quite successful once, I think. That would be before she took to the drink.'

'And the son?'

'Never met him, but he wasn't liked by the neighbours. Got himself into trouble more than once, fighting and the like. Mind you, it helped us. Not everyone likes a B&B in their road. They think it will be noisy with people coming and going at all hours, and parking problems. People are very possessive about the bit of road outside their houses. That's why we had the front garden paved. We've space for eight cars so no one needs to park in the road.'

'So you were a welcome change for the neighbours?'

'We tried to make sure we were very quiet and respectable in comparison. And we tidied everything up: painted the outside, saw to the garden, worked hard and kept quiet. Just what they all wanted.'

'Do you know where the Brysons moved to?'

'The son moved into the city centre somewhere. I don't have an address. Everything was forwarded to Sheila. She moved into some kind of artists' community up in the Trossacks.'

'I don't suppose you have an address for her?'

'Aye, somewhere. It'll be in the office. If you can just hang on for a minute, I'll find it for you.'

While she was gone Ian looked round at the kitchen. It was well organised and spotless. He wouldn't mind staying here himself. He imagined they provided excellent breakfasts and probably very comfortable beds. He was just daydreaming about freshly laundered Egyptian cotton sheets when Elsa returned and handed him a card, which he photographed on his phone. Elsbeth Mackay Art Village, Balloch. He wondered if he should have heard of it, but Scotland was littered with little communities of artists and craftsmen. Few of them ever became famous. He put his phone away and stood up.

'Do you live in Glasgow?' she asked, as she showed him out.

'Tayside,' he said. 'A little village called Greyport.'

'Pity,' she said. 'I'd a mind to ask you out for a drink.'

He'd have accepted it too. Possibly just as well he lived fifty miles away. He didn't need any complications. All the same... 'Another time perhaps,' he said.

She looked at the card he had given her. 'Whenever you're over here again. I'll text you my number.'

He returned a little reluctantly to his car and fed Sheila's address into his satnav. Just over half an hour's drive from here. Two hours from Greyport. It made sense to go there now. He looked at his watch. He could be there by four o'clock and home at around seven. He sent Lainie a text and asked if she could keep Lottie a bit longer than planned. She replied immediately. *Always happy to have Lottie. I've a tin of dog food left from last time, so I'll feed her for you and take her for a wee walk.* Lottie, he knew, would be happy to stay for a couple of hours extra spoiling.

Driving through picture postcard Scottish scenery, Ian's thoughts were first, he wished he had brought Lottie, and second, there must be B&Bs up here with fabulous breakfasts and beds with freshly laundered Egyptian cotton sheets. He should have waited until Caroline could come with him. But, of course, he could easily come again with both Lottie and Caroline. A little break together. Perfect.

Ian found the Elsbeth Mackay Art Village a few miles outside Balloch. It was a collection of wooden chalets dotted around a field on the side of a hill, behind a pair of iron gates. He parked outside the gates and went in through a smaller gate at the side. Once inside he found a larger building with a door labelled *Reception*. It was deserted, but a laminated plan pinned to the door told him that the chalet he wanted was on the far side of the field at the top of the hill. Just his luck. There was no one to unlock the gates, and in any case a quick look at the field told him that there was no way he could drive his car across it without getting stuck in the mud. There were a couple of Land Rovers parked next to the reception building, but no ordinary cars. He could see why. How did people get food up here? The nearest shops were miles away. He didn't imagine delivery drivers taking kindly to driving their vans up the field. He supposed everything would have to be left at the gates. It brought a whole new shade of meaning to his idea of starving artists. Thinking of which, there seemed to be very few artists about – starving or otherwise. Probably all escaped to a pub in Balloch.

Just then a chalet door opened and a bearded man in a paint-stained smock appeared. Give him a palette and a velvet beret and you'd have a caricature artist. Were they all like this? Perhaps they only admitted people who fitted the stereotype. Perhaps stereotypes were the only people who wanted to come here. Too affectedly eccentric to fit in anywhere else.

'Can I help you, guv?' the man shouted, sounding as if he had come straight from Billingsgate on a busy Friday.

'I'm looking for Sheila Bryson,' Ian said, showing the man his card.

'Up there,' he said, jerking his head towards the furthest chalet at the top of the hill.

'Do you know if she's there now?' Ian asked, rather hoping she wasn't and that he could sit in his warm car at the bottom of the hill and wait for her to come home.

'She's always there. Best of British if you're 'oping to get any sense out of her though.'

'Sense?'

'She's a bit of a one for the...' He tipped an imaginary bottle towards his mouth and winked.

Great. A steep climb up a muddy hill and no guarantee that he'd get anything useful from her. What was he hoping for anyway? It crossed his mind that he could just get in his car and drive away. He knew she was alive and that she was Orlando's mother. Was there anything more she could tell him that would be any use? But no. He'd come this far. He might as well go and see what she was like. And she might elaborate on the details of her affair with Xander.

She'd probably changed quite a bit from the rosy-cheeked young student of Xander's memory, who flitted around in the heather looking for orchids and who sang songs around a campfire. Perhaps when the artists were all in residence, they had campfires and singing, but he doubted it.

He knocked on the chalet door and it was opened by a woman who looked considerably older than the couple of years Xander had suggested. She had thin, grey hair that was scraped into a knot at the back of her head and secured with bailer twine. She was wearing a baggy pair of tartan cotton trousers with more bailer twine knotted around her waist and a jumper that might once have been red, but which now had so many stains and patches that it was hard to tell. Never mind two years, Xander was a stripling in comparison. She looked as if she hadn't had a square meal for several months. Should he offer to drive her down to Balloch and buy her some food?

'Yes?' she said, holding the door open and frowning at him.

'Sheila Bryson?' She nodded. 'My name's Ian Skair. He handed her his card. 'Could I come in and ask you a few questions?'

She stood back and let him inside. Walking to a table, she snapped shut the lid of a laptop. An expensive Apple one, Ian noticed.

'Drinkie?' she asked, picking up a plastic tumbler that could possibly have been washed half a dozen drinks ago.

'No thanks.' He looked around at the room they were in. It was actually quite cosy if you ignored the untidiness and lack of washing up. He pushed some newspapers off one of the chairs and sat down. Once this had been a nice room, with a pine table and chairs, polished floorboards and a wood burning stove. It still wasn't too bad. A bit of a clean, a clear out of bottles and some dishwashing and he could see why someone might want to live here.

Sheila poured herself a drink. 'What questions?'

'Do you remember spending a summer at Drumlychtoun when you were a student?'

She smiled, and for an instant he saw the pretty young student of Xander's memory.

'I remember, yes.'

'And you remember Alexander Lyton?'

'Xander, yes of course.'

'Have you seen him since then?'

'No,' she said. 'Why? Has he gone missing like his sister?'

Ah, she knew about Ailish. 'Did you ever meet Ailish?'

'No, darling, long gone by the time I was there. Bit of a black sheep by all accounts. But then so was I. We could have been soul-mates if we'd ever met.'

'Did you ever go to the castle?'

'God, no. Not for the likes of me. The old Laird would have gone for me with a shot gun if I'd gone near the place. Can't say I blame the sister for legging it. Xander was a sweet boy though.'

'So if you never went to the castle how did you and Xander meet?'

She scratched her head. 'Not sure. He spent a lot of time in the camp with us. I guess he'd been friends with one of the other students.'

That was possible. Not a lot of social life in Drumlychtoun, so a visit from a fellow student would have been welcome.

'Ciggie?' she asked, passing him a battered tobacco tin with a few skinny rollups, her fingers stained with nicotine.

'I don't smoke, thanks.' Apart from the occasional illicit cigarette behind the bike sheds at school, he really was a walking cliché; he'd never smoked. And he wasn't sure that the ones he was being offered contained only tobacco. He didn't like to imagine Lainie's face if he turned up to collect Lottie high on whatever it was artists smoked. Anyway, he'd seen too much of the damage drugs could do during his police days. He'd never been tempted.

He was running out of things to ask her. She'd never been inside the castle. The ring was probably long gone by the time she was there. Any kind of fling she'd had with Xander was probably irrelevant. But then there was the son and there was no escaping the coincidence of his date of birth and the dates Sheila had been at Drumlychtoun. 'Tell me about your son.'

'Orlando?' She seemed surprised to be asked. 'Bloody nuisance he turned out to be. Trouble from the day he was born.'

'He was born a few months after you were at Drumlychtoun?'

'Yes, I suppose he was,' she said vaguely, exhaling and waving smoke away from her face.

'It's an unusual name, Orlando. Was he named after his father?'

She shook her head. 'I was into Shakespeare at the time so probably not.'

Probably? 'You don't remember his father's name?'

'Darling, I don't know *who* his father was. Could have been one of several,' she giggled. 'Made my father spitting mad.'

It would have done. Ian thought of himself as reasonably broad-minded, but if he had a pregnant daughter unable to name the father of her child, he imagined he might have been spitting mad as well. Either with the daughter or with the likely candidates, depending on the circumstances.

'So is it possible that Xander is his father?'

She considered this for a while. 'I'd say it's unlikely. If he is then Orlando is nothing like him either in looks or temperament. And there were plenty of other contenders. You'd be surprised what can go on in a sleeping bag. There were at least ten men in the camp. Not that I slept with all of them, of course.'

Good grief. How had she found the time? Or the energy? But it was a relief. It seemed less likely that Xander was the father of what was by all accounts a member of Glasgow's equivalent of the Mafia. How on earth was he going to break it to Xander? Should he even mention it? Yes, he had to. Orlando's interest in the family had taken a dangerous turn. At least he now had some idea why Orlando was interested in them. He wished he could talk to him, although if his mother didn't know who his father was, then it wasn't likely that Orlando would be any the wiser. And anyway, he respected Duncan's warning. Duncan didn't issue warnings unless there was a very good reason to. Ian had no intention of tackling a thug who by all accounts was surrounded by henchmen of even greater thuggery, and asking him questions about his paternity.

Sheila's whole situation was sad. She may have had a riotously happy summer in 1979 but it didn't seem to have done her much good. She had a son of the type that every mother must dread, a career wrecked by drink and housing that might be fine in the summer but must be miserable in a long damp Scottish winter. He wanted to do something to make her life a bit more comfortable. He didn't like to offer money. It would be patronising and probably not get her further than the nearest off-licence. He rummaged through his pockets and found a bar of chocolate, which he gave her. It wasn't much but the sugar would give her a bit of energy and might just tide her over until her next meal. He only hoped there was someone to see that she ate now and then. If there'd been anyone at reception, he would have asked them to make sure of it. He reluctantly told himself he'd done what he could and thanked her for her time. As he was leaving, he noticed the card he had given her still on the table. He picked it up guiltily, hoping he wasn't her only lifeline. Orlando probably didn't visit his mother, but he wasn't taking any chances.

12

It was a relief to leave Balloch behind him and head for home. Not that it wasn't a beautiful part of Scotland. He might well come back for a bit of a holiday one day. That is if he could get the Brysons out of his mind. He had yet to come face to face with Orlando and wasn't relishing the prospect. But Sheila had made him feel sad. How had she gone from a lively, if flirtatious student, into this alcohol-ridden wreck? What a waste. And how had it happened? He supposed it had all gone downhill since the death of her brother. She'd have watched the smart house in Bearsden deteriorate as her son systematically ruined the family business. Then she had to move into a cabin in a field. That must have been a shock to the system. By all accounts, they had left the house in a mess. Was that because of the alcohol or was it somehow connected to Orlando? Did he make her life a misery? And when had he started on the road to ruin?

He could speculate all he liked but it was unlikely to bring him any closer to the truth. He must try and concentrate on the case and separate fact from supposition. As he drove home, he began a mental list.

.   .   .

Find out more about Joshua Remington. He'd rather let that drop until the name popped up in connection with the Brysons.

Work out how to tell Xander about Orlando.

Talk to anyone in Drumlychtoun who might have been there in the late sixties.

Stay in touch with Anna in case of any more contact from Orlando.

It occurred to Ian that he hadn't talked to Anna about messages from Orlando since he had spoken to Duncan. He would do that first. Anna should know how dangerous Orlando might be. He didn't want to frighten her, but she did need to be warned now that he knew more about the Bryson connection to the family. He arrived home and collected Lottie, who, even though she was devoted to Lainie, was ecstatic to see him. That was the nice thing about owning a dog. Someone was always pleased to see you. How many times in the past, he wondered, had he arrived home to a scowling Stephanie? But wasn't it time he put all that behind him? Stephanie was in the past. There had been many angry words and recriminations. Both his marriage and his career had ended with a single gunshot, or that's how it had seemed at the time. But that was water under the bridge. Life right now was good. Better than before really. He had a house he loved, a career that was thriving, new women in his life and a dog who never scowled, well hardly ever. She wasn't nice to the postman although he didn't think that was personal.

He texted Anna, *Fancy a walk on the beach tomorrow? I'll bring Lottie and some sandwiches.*

Okay, she replied. *Five o'clock? See you near the café we went to before. Can we get chips instead of sandwiches?* She added her usual row of smileys and dogs.

He was able to park near the beach. The café was open, but he sat in his car waiting for Anna. A cup of tea and a snack and he'd probably not feel like a windy beach. First things first. No chips without a brisk walk to earn them.

Anna bounded up a few moments later looking excited and pleased with herself. Ian let Lottie out of the car and they set off along the beach.

'Have you discovered some more about how the ring disappeared?' she asked, hurling Lottie's ball along the sand. 'That's very quick. I only saw you a few days ago. Not that it isn't nice to see you.'

'A little,' he said, as Lottie returned and dropped the ball at his feet. He picked it up and threw it down the beach into the shallow waves. She emerged from the sea and rolled in some foul-smelling seaweed. She'd make the car reek of damp dog and seaweed, but she loved the beach and she'd sleep soundly tonight so it would be worth it. 'I just wanted to update you,' he told Anna. 'I didn't bring it up at the weekend because I didn't want to worry you. But a bit of research I did yesterday reminded me that I should warn you.'

'Warn me? That sounds scary.'

'Probably not,' he said, hoping he hadn't sounded too alarmist. 'Just be careful. Remember what I said about not answering messages on the *Forebears* site?'

She nodded. 'I didn't reply to the message.'

'That's good. I've discovered a bit more about Orlando Bryson and it's not very nice.'

'Who is he?'

'I can't really tell you that yet, but I talked to a police friend of mine and he warned me off him. Also there does seem to be a connection between the Bryson family and your grandfather and I'm trying to find out more. If you do hear from Bryson again, can you let me know right away?'

'Okay. That's interesting, about my grandfather. Do you think that's why Orlando Bryson wants to know more about the Lytons?'

'It's possible. It's looking more and more likely that Joshua and Ailish knew each other in Edinburgh, but there's more work to do on that so keep it to yourself for now.'

'Don't tell Xander, you mean?'

Don't tell anyone, was what he had meant. 'Just keep it to yourself for now, okay?'

Was that too much to ask of an excitable teenager? He hoped she had other things to distract her. 'You're looking rather pleased with yourself today,' he said, hoping that now he'd warned her, he could change tactics and get her to talk about something else. 'How's uni going? Nearly the end of your first year, isn't it?'

'Yes, it's great. And actually... well, there's this boy I met.'

'Oh yes, tell me more. What's his name?' That could be just the distraction he was hoping for. Something to take her mind off family history.

'Robin Walter. He's a philosophy student. He's been helping me with an article I've started for a blog I subscribe to.'

'That sounds interesting. How far have you got with it?'

'I've only just started. Talking about Daddy at the weekend made me think there may be more people like me who've had a letter from someone who hasn't been in their life for a long time. It sounds a bit spooky, doesn't it? A letter out of the blue. But it wasn't at all. It was like getting to know someone you've not seen for a long time. It made him feel more real.'

'And your friend Robin was able to help?'

'More encouraged really. I know what I want to write but it's nice to have someone to try it out on.'

'Where's he from?'

'He grew up here. His father's a maths lecturer. I'm going to their house for dinner tomorrow.'

This was definitely good news that should help to keep her right away from Bryson's prying messages. The last thing he wanted was for her to start digging into Brysons and Remingtons on her own and possibly putting herself in danger. This sounded ideal - a boyfriend with a local family made him feel a lot better. Did he really need to think like this? There had been no sign of Bryson after that first message and no one had contacted him to say he'd been back to the museum. With any luck Bryson would have lost interest in her. There had never been anything to suggest that he'd had any more than a fleeting interest in the family. But after what Duncan had told him and his warning to keep away, it was as well to be careful.

The son of a maths tutor sounded highly respectable, even if he was a philosophy student. In Ian's mind philosophy students sat around all day having long and pointless discussions about the futility or otherwise of human existence. He had an idea it was all about squirrels running round trees and cats in boxes who might be both dead and alive at the same time. But he probably shouldn't write off an entire discipline on the grounds that he found it incomprehensible. Perhaps he should sign up for a philosophy course. It could while away the winter evenings and it might change his life. Unlike maths. With all due respect to Caroline, he couldn't see how that could change his life. He wondered how close-knit the maths community was around here. Would Caroline have heard of Robin Walter's father?

By now they had turned and were heading back to the café. Anna nudged him. 'You were miles away,' she said.

'Sorry, just thinking about someone.'

'Lady friend?'

'Well...'

'It was, wasn't it?' she teased.

Was he that transparent? He'd been well and truly rumbled. 'Yes, as it happens,' he said cautiously.

'So, who is she? Go on, do tell me.'

'Her name is Caroline. She's a maths teacher at a school in Dundee. I was just wondering if she and your boyfriend's father knew each other.'

'I'm not sure he's actually my boyfriend, well not yet anyway.'

'And I'm not sure she's actually my lady friend, so I guess we're quits. And how come you get to call him a boyfriend, but I'm stuck with lady friend not girlfriend? It makes me feel quite Victorian.'

She thought for a moment. 'It's probably it's because you are very, very old.'

'Cheeky young monkey,' he said. 'I suppose I asked for that, didn't I?'

'Fell right into it. I'm glad you've got someone. I thought you seemed a bit lonely.'

You and every other woman I know.

'He's called Adrian,' she said.

'Who is?'

'Robin's dad. You can ask Caroline if she knows him. Hey, we could all go to the pub together and they can chat maths to each other. Is that what maths people do? I can't see them being quite like philosophy or poetry students somehow.'

'I've no idea. She rarely talks about maths when she's with me. Probably afraid I won't understand.' To be fair that was quite likely.

'What about our chips? I'm starving. Lottie is too. Can we get them now?'

They were almost back at the car. 'Race you,' she shouted, scampering off with Lottie.

Not a chance, he thought, opening the back of the car and reaching for a towel. She'd forgotten about his limp. And he liked that. He was someone who limped. Not a limp with a person attached.

She was holding Lottie by the collar. 'Come on,' she shouted. 'We're hungry, me and Lottie.'

Oh, to be nineteen again. Writing serious articles one minute, demanding chips the next. 'Won't be a minute,' he said, walking towards a tap at the edge of the car park and calling Lottie. 'I'll just give her a rinse and rub her down so she doesn't stink the place out.'

'But she can have some chips when she's stopped being stinky, can't she?'

'Just a small one,' he said, laughing.

A couple of days later Anna sent him a link to her blog and it terrified him.

She had called it *A father's gift*. It started with the letter her father left for her before he was killed. Her mother must have scanned it and sent it to her. It was a good letter. Pete must have thought long and hard about what he was going to write. He began by saying that, if she was reading the letter, it would mean the worst had happened and he would never see her grow up. He promised that she would have been in his thoughts right up to the final moment of his life. He told her he had left her something that he hoped would help her to know who she was. Then Anna described the ring and how it had connected her to her previously unknown family. She hadn't actually named any people or places, but if Bryson recognised her name, he would be able to work it all out.

What on earth was he going to do? He couldn't demand that Anna take it down. She'd been so excited about it. He must try to calm down and think it through. How likely was Bryson to stumble across it? He typed Anna's name into Google and came up with a list of Anna Lymingtons that were either obviously not her or that were blocked from any further searches. Bryson must have been on the lookout for Lytons and would have found the family tree when she entered Robert Lyton that day while she was in his office. Ian wondered vaguely if Bryson had signed up for a lot more family history sites and how long it had taken him to find the right one. *Forebears and More* wasn't one of the better-known sites so he could have been searching for quite a while before he struck gold. Anna's username on the Forebears site was Annilym. She had used her real name on the blog. It wouldn't take a genius to notice the similarity. What could he do? He tried very hard to tell himself not to be too concerned. It wasn't going to go mainstream. It would be hidden away somewhere in cyberspace and forgotten about. All the same, he was going to keep an eye on it

13

A few days later, and as he had done every morning since she had told him about her blog, Ian clicked on the link to Anna's story. It was becoming part of his morning routine to check through the comments section. It was the first item on his daily list of tasks. He wanted to check every time he sat down at his computer but persuaded himself not to. That would be overdoing it. More paranoia than protection.

So far there had been nothing to worry about. There were a lot of encouraging comments, many from fellow students, and one that he suspected was from her mother. Then there were some sad accounts from others who had lost a father when they were young. Many telling their own stories and all agreeing that letters and small gifts had helped them come to terms with their grief.

He was on the lookout for anyone who wanted more direct contact with Anna – people who asked for private messages from her or suggestions about friending her on Facebook or WhatsApp. But so far all seemed well. He also kept an eye on Facebook, looking for mentions on other people's pages or photographs of her that had been tagged, but again there was nothing. He regularly typed Anna's name into Google but up to now he had drawn a blank – nothing except a link back to the blog. Hopefully today's students were well trained in Internet security. She hadn't, for instance, posted either photos of Drumlychtoun or details of the ring, other than the fact that it had been in her family for many generations. It was clear from the comments of other students that she was at St Andrews, but she was one of several thousand and he assumed student contact details weren't handed out to anyone who asked for them. Could someone print her photo from the blog and wander round St Andrews hoping to bump into her or ask about her in shops and cafés? Possible, he supposed. Should he warn her about that? He was walking a thin line between cautioning Anna about who might be out there and not wanting to scare her. For now he'd just keep an eye on things and hope he was worrying unnecessarily.

He needed a distraction and moved to the next item on his list, which was to talk to any residents of Drumlychtoun who had been there fifty years ago. He also needed to break the news to Xander that there was a fleeting chance he might be a father. And that would also mean telling him that his first love might not have been all that he remembered. He wasn't sure how Xander would take the news that she was now a borderline alcoholic living in what was little more than a hut in a field. But it had to be done. Apart from anything else he had a horrible suspicion that Orlando Bryson's interest in the family would eventually lead him to Drumlychtoun, and Xander should be prepared for that. He wasn't at all sure how Xander would take someone turning up on his doorstep claiming that he was an unknown son. It didn't help that he had no idea how much Orlando knew. Whether as the result of a poor memory or the alcoholic haze that she lived in, or both, Sheila had been vague about the whole episode. Had she told Orlando anything about her summer of camping and fornication? She must have mentioned the Lyton name. Why else was her son showing an interest in it? But other than contacting Orlando himself, something Duncan had forbidden him to do, he had no way of finding out.

After the wonderful hospitality of the previous weekend, Ian felt he shouldn't go to Drumlychtoun empty handed. He loaded Lottie into the car and drove to one of his favourite places, a farm shop on the way to St Andrews. It was a bit of a detour, but he was in no hurry, and it had the best delicatessen counter he knew. Drumlychtoun produced food, but apart from exorbitantly expensive smoked herrings, most of which went abroad, it was not exotic fare. He loaded up with olives, local cheese, some grapes – probably not local – and a box of handmade chocolates. He was never able to resist the bakery and in any case, they would need bread with their cheese, wouldn't they? The loaf he bought was fresh from the oven and warm. It would probably not be when he arrived at Drumlychtoun, but it would still be very fresh. Then he thought he should add butter and a jar of chutney. By the time he'd finished he needed to keep the trolley to get it all to his car.

He'd left Lottie tied to a fence near the entrance. She wagged her tail and sniffed curiously at his shopping. Ian broke off a corner of cheese which she swallowed in a single gulp and looked at him expectantly for more. 'Maybe later,' he said, untying her and returning to the car. He left the trolley in a fenced off area of the car park which suggested he wasn't the only one loading up a car with impulse purchases.

As ever, he enjoyed the drive to Drumlychtoun. He suspected Lottie did as well. She must recognise the road by now and he knew she enjoyed poking her nose out of the window for a sniff of sea air. She leapt out of the car the moment he pulled up outside the castle and rushed around chasing her tail and kicking up gravel on the drive.

'This is an unexpected pleasure,' said Bridget, appearing from the back of the castle with a pair of shears and two black Labradors who greeted Lottie by sniffing her lazily. 'I've just been doing a bit of pruning, but I could do with a break. I'll go and put the kettle on.'

'I hope you don't mind me just turning up like this so soon after the weekend.'

'Not at all. It's lovely to see you.'

'There's something I need to talk to Xander about and I didn't think I could do it by phone or email. It's a bit sensitive.'

'Sounds intriguing.'

You could say that. Intriguing was an understatement. He was about to deliver a blow of possibly epic proportions. He opened the back of his car and lifted out his bags of food. 'I've brought lunch,' he said, suspecting that it might not do much to make his news more palatable. Or perhaps Xander would be thrilled. Thrilled to know he was the possible father of a thug that he'd been warned off by the police? Probably not.

'Let me help you carry it,' said Bridget. 'We'll have lunch in the kitchen, then you can cosy up with Xander in his study and have a nice chat while I get on with the pruning.'

Nice chat? She'd no idea, had she? How was *she* going to take the news? Presumably they'd tried to have children. But that was all far too personal to ask about.

He tried not to look embarrassed and changed the subject. 'I was hoping for a word with Maggie's mum as well. She might remember any friends Ailish had around here.'

'I think she'd love that. There's nothing old Morag enjoys more than having someone to listen to all her memories. She's a spry old biddy. Could keep you occupied well into the evening with her yarns.'

At least lunch was a success. They were full of good food, which might help to soften the blow of what Ian was about to reveal. Or perhaps he was putting too much faith in the power of a good meal.

But Xander had enthused about Ian's gift. 'You might need to bring us regular hampers,' he said, spearing the last olive with a knife and breaking off some cheese for the dogs.

'Ian's here to talk,' said Bridget. 'Go through to your study. Ian can carry the coffee tray. Maggie's going to take you to see her mother when she's finished here. About four o'clock, is that okay?'

Ian nodded and followed Xander into the study. He sat down and poured them both coffee.

Xander took the cup from him. 'So,' he said, 'I can see you've something to tell me. You've been fidgeting like a dog with fleas since you got here. So come on, laddie, spit it out.'

Ian sat down, swallowed a mouthful of coffee and took a deep breath. 'I went to see Sheila Bryson.'

'Blimey, I wasn't expecting that. How did you find her?'

'I spent a day in Glasgow going through local records. That led me to an address where she'd lived until a few years ago and the current owner was able to tell me where she'd moved to.'

'But she was here long after Ailish left. She can't have had anything to do with the ring.'

'No, I don't think she did. I was trying to find out more about Joshua Remington.'

Xander looked confused. 'Ailish's Joshua Remington?'

'That's right. What I found out was that there used to be a company in Glasgow called Bryson Remington. It went out of business about ten years ago.'

'So there's a connection between Sheila and Ailish's boyfriend? I don't understand.'

'Neither do I right now. And I've not confirmed the connection yet. It could be just a coincidence of names. But it does seem quite likely. There's a lot more to find out about Remington. I need to see Joshua Remington's birth certificate.'

'Tell me more about Sheila. How is she?'

Ian didn't really want to say too much about the condition he'd found her in. 'She's an artist and living near Loch Lomond. I actually went to see her because I've made some discoveries about her family.' He drank another mouthful of coffee. Now for the hard bit. 'As far as I can see the fact that Sheila was here was coincidental and nothing to do with Joshua Remington. But she did tell me something you need to know.' He paused, feeling awkward.

'Go on.'

'Sheila has a son. Name of Orlando.'

Xander laughed. 'Nothing odd about that. A lot of women have sons. Probably not so many called Orlando though.'

'Orlando was born in March 1979.'

Xander looked puzzled. Ian could almost see the calculation going on in his head. Then he looked up at Ian and roared with laughter. Not what Ian was expecting at all.

'You think I'm Orlando's father?'

Ian shrugged. 'Sheila said she didn't know and that Orlando is nothing like you. She also said that there had been others around that time. I'm afraid you weren't the only one.' He looked at Xander, hoping that he hadn't just shattered all his illusions about his first love.

Xander was still chuckling. 'I knew that. I may have been young and innocent, but anyone could tell a mile away that Sheila was not a one-man type of girl.'

'But she didn't rule out the possibility.'

'So you're still thinking the child could be mine?'

That was exactly what he had been thinking. 'Well, yes.'

Xander pulled out a handkerchief and wiped away tears of laughter. 'Highly improbable. I took precautions.'

They didn't always work though. 'You seem very sure?'

'Ian, Bridget and I have been married for thirty-five years. It's been a normal, loving marriage, if you get what I mean. We always hoped for children, but it didn't happen.'

Had they taken any steps to find out why? He really couldn't ask that and Xander didn't look as if he was about to tell him. And it didn't really matter what Xander and Sheila thought. What might matter a lot was what Orlando thought. He could still turn up and claim to be Xander's son. 'This Orlando, he doesn't seem to be a very nice person.' To put it mildly. 'I've been warned to keep away from him by the police. He's a bit of a thug apparently.'

'And you think he might come here and try to claim his birthright?'

'It crossed my mind. I don't know whether Sheila would have told him who his possible fathers were, but she might have done.'

'What makes you think that?'

'A couple of things. He messaged Anna on the *Forebears* website asking for details about Lytons, and he was at the museum in Edinburgh asking about antique rings.'

'Did Anna reply?' asked Xander, looking alarmed.

'No, I told her not to.'

'That's good. If he's a dodgy type, we don't want him anywhere near Anna.'

'And if he contacts you?'

'I'll tell him to bugger off. And if he persists there's some test he can get, isn't there?'

'A DNA test. You'd need to do one as well.'

'That's okay, if it gets him off my back. But if it's any comfort, we'll double lock our doors at night and I'll warn the estate office to be on the lookout.'

Ian hoped it was that simple. Hard to imagine a hardened criminal agreeing to a DNA test and quietly going away. And what if the test proved Xander *was* his father? The extent of Bryson's involvement in organised crime networks made him shudder. But there wasn't very much he could do about it other than warn Xander. Better, he thought, to change the subject. He took out his phone and clicked into Anna's blog. 'Anna wrote this. I thought you might like to see it.'

Xander took the phone, put on some reading glasses and read it. He smiled. 'That's lovely. She's a clever girl.'

'I was a bit concerned about it actually. She's posted it online for anyone to read.'

'You're not worried this Orlando could trace her through it, are you?'

'I hope not. I'm keeping an eye on the comments just in case.'

'She's not mentioned any names or places, has she?'

'No, and she knows to be careful about who she allows to contact her.'

Xander nodded. 'Sounds like you've got it all under control.'

Ian wished he felt the same.

Bridget peered round the door and tapped her watch.

'And now you're off to see Morag?' said Xander. 'What are you hoping to learn from her?'

'I'm just wondering if she can fill me in on Ailish as a teenager. How much she was out and about when she was here, boyfriends, that sort of thing.'

'Well, she's got a remarkable memory. If anyone can tell you, Morag can.'

He joined Maggie in the kitchen, where she was packing some plastic boxes with food and stowing them into a shopping bag. 'For mother,' she explained. 'She enjoys her food and it's easier for me to do all the cooking while I'm here. Bridget's fine with it,' she added.

He was sure she was. Bridget obviously cared about both Maggie and her mother. Probably everyone who worked on the estate. 'Shall we take my car?' he asked.

Maggie shook her head. 'I'd rather walk,' she said. 'It's only a few minutes and I like to feel the wind in my hair.'

He could do with a bit of fresh air himself and Lottie would enjoy a walk. He fetched her lead from his car, although there was no real need for it here where there was so little traffic. He'd only ever driven to the castle and it was nice to walk over the bridge and have time to look around at the lake with the sea and the hill in the distance. 'Are there fish in the lake?' he asked.

'A few,' said Maggie. 'Not enough for anything commercial but the village children enjoy fishing. It's a pity there are no children at the castle. Haven't been any since Xander was small, I suppose. But now there's a great-niece to take over that could all change.'

That was a bit of a leap into the future. But who knew? He could see Anna here with a brood of children and dogs. Stranger things had happened.

When they arrived, Maggie introduced Ian to her mother. Xander hadn't been wrong. Morag was thrilled about Ian's visit. She was ready for him with her best tea service and an embroidered tablecloth.

'Sit yourself down,' said Maggie, disappearing into the kitchen with her shopping bag and reappearing a few moments later with a teapot and a plate of food which she set down on a table in front of her mother.

'Maggie's cooked drop scones,' said Morag, handing him a plate with a small pancake dripping with butter. Lottie sat drooling at his side.

'Och,' said Morag. 'Give the wee doggie a piece.'

He broke off a piece and gave it to Lottie, making a mental note to cut down on her dog biscuits that evening. He smiled at Morag. 'I was hoping you could tell me a bit about Ailish. Do you remember her?'

'That I do,' she said, looking slightly offended at the suggestion that she might not. 'What do you want to know?'

'What was she like as a teenager?'

'I felt that sorry for her after losing her mum. But she was a wild one. Worried the life out of her poor father, some of the capers she got up to.'

'Was she here much? I thought she was at boarding school in Edinburgh.'

'She was here a fair bit. Holidays of course, but quite often weekends as well. More so when she met that lad with the motorbike.'

That was interesting and it confirmed what Aggie Trueman from the Facebook page had told him. He'd wondered how Ailish had got around. She might have used a bike locally, but Edinburgh was a long way, and he didn't suppose the old Laird had been generous with pocket money. A boyfriend with a motorbike meant that Ailish had plenty of chances to visit jewellers with the ring. But was the boyfriend Joshua Remington?

'Mind,' Morag continued. 'Her father didn't like that. Not one bit. Tried to forbid it. But she took no notice. No one could stop Miss Ailish from doing what she wanted.'

'This lad with the motorbike,' Ian asked. 'Do you remember his name?'

She took another bite of scone and thought for a moment. 'Can't remember. I think it was something out of the Bible, but I'm not sure.'

Joshua was a biblical name, but then so were many more. 'Do you know what he did?'

'A student, I think. Oh, and he worked for his father in the holidays. I remember that because one time he arrived with dirt on his fingers. Said Ailish had dragged him away from work before he'd time to wash them.'

'Do you know what work he did?'

She shook her head. 'Ailish always said he was artistic though.'

'Did he ever stay at the castle?'

'No. The old Laird would never have allowed it. He didn't approve of Ailish having a boyfriend. Mind you, he shouldn't have been surprised. She was a bonnie wee thing with her long hair and that look in her eyes.'

'So, this lad wouldn't have visited the castle?'

'Not as a visitor, but Ailish used to smuggle him in. They'd go up from the beach and through the cellar door.'

Joshua Remington had just risen to the top of the prime suspect list. Assuming Joshua and motorbike lad were one and the same person. Morag seemed to have nodded off, so Ian got out his notebook and made a list of the evidence against him:

1. *He had access to the castle*
2. *He had a motorbike so traveling back and forth from Edinburgh was easy*
3. *His father ran a precious metal company*
4. *He got his hands dirty at work – making jewellery?*
5. *He was artistic*
6. *His son Pete had the ring*

Morag was now snoring gently. It was time to go. 'Thank your mother for me, won't you?' he said to Maggie. 'She's been so interesting and helpful.'

'She'll have enjoyed it,' said Maggie, wrapping up the remaining scones and handing them to him. 'She loves a visitor. We don't get so many, not living out here. You'll come again, I hope.'

'I'll drop in next time I'm up here.' He'd bring her something. She obviously enjoyed her food, so another visit to the farm shop deli was on the cards.

Maggie waved them off at the door and Lottie trotted at his side as they walked back to the castle, where he'd left his car. Bridget was still in the garden, so he popped in to say goodbye to Xander.

'Was she able to help?' he asked.

'I think I've made a friend for life. Lottie certainly has. And yes, she's given me plenty to think about.'

'That's grand,' said Xander, patting his shoulder. 'Come again soon. And look after little Anna.'

'I'll do both of those,' said Ian, loading Lottie into his car and climbing in after her.

14

It was part of his daily routine now, an early morning walk down to the village shop with Lottie. Possibly not so good in winter when the pavements would be icy and with a raw wind from the estuary. But for now he wouldn't miss it. And Lottie expected it. If he slept late, she would jump onto his bed and lick his face. Once he was up, she would run round in circles, jumping up and down until he put on his boots and clipped on her lead.

This particular morning he looked out of his window and was greeted by a sullen grey sky and drizzle. He had little to do today and was tempted to go back to bed with a cup of coffee and a good book. He headed in that direction, but Lottie was having none of it. She skittered to the door and stood there whining. Then she picked up one of his boots in her mouth, trotted into his bedroom and dropped it at his feet. She stood looking up at him and wagged her tail hopefully.

'Oh, all right then,' he growled grudgingly, struggling into some clothes. Single booted, he padded into the hall to find its pair. He pulled on a waterproof jacket that he hadn't worn since... he couldn't remember. It had been a lovely spring, but he should know by now that it didn't necessarily mean a lovely summer. A quick check of the kitchen told him he was nearly out of coffee and getting low on fruit. He found a hessian shopping bag with *Save the Planet* and a picture of a daisy stamped on it and set off.

By the time they reached the shop his hair was soaked, and Lottie's fur was glistening with drops of rain. Should he buy her a raincoat? He'd seen dogs in coats, but it never felt quite right. He bent down to scratch her back and found that underneath a topcoat of rain she was quite dry. All she'd need when they got home was a good towelling. As would his own hair.

The shop was used to dog owners. Ian tied Lottie to a low railing next to a bowl of drinking water and went inside. He bought a loaf of bread, coffee, some apples and a North Fife newspaper. He was tempted by jars of local honey displayed near the checkout. His mouth watered at the thought of fresh bread and honey. He picked one up and put in his basket. But then he remembered he had to climb back up the hill carrying his shopping and replaced the jar. He'd get one next time he was down here with the car. Two perhaps. He thought Xander would enjoy one next time he went to Drumlych-toun. Maybe three because Morag would like one as well. He could imagine both as a honey lovers. He wondered why they didn't have their own hives. There was plenty of heather around the castle. Perhaps one of them was allergic. Bee stings could be very nasty.

Enough daydreaming. He was ready for breakfast. He paid for his purchases and went outside to untie Lottie. She seemed in no hurry to go home, in spite of the drizzle. She was getting a lot of attention from a group of children waiting for the school bus. They had been in the shop buying sweets and he hoped they weren't now feeding them to Lottie. They would be her friends for life, but at the expense of her waistline. Lottie had no appetite control whatsoever. She'd eat anything and everything. He'd already had lectures from Caroline, whose own dog Angus was similarly greedy. He shouldn't let Lottie become overweight. And not just for Lottie's health, although that was important. If he let her put on weight Caroline would probably never speak to him again. And that would be a shame.

The school bus arrived, and the children climbed aboard. Lottie watched longingly as it left. She probably needed to offload a few calories and the rain had eased so he chose the long way home – a twisting lane that was less steep than the direct route and took in a small park on the way. Once in the park he took off Lottie's lead and let her scamper around for a while, chasing imaginary squirrels. Occasionally they saw actual squirrels here, but Ian knew they were safe. Any squirrel could outrun Lottie. Usually up trees where they would perch on a branch and tease her.

When they arrived home, it was well after their usual breakfast time and Ian was hungry. He made coffee and tucked into the bread, which he spread generously with butter and jam. How would he spend the rest of the day? He hadn't had a free day for a while and liked the thought of a few hours of not very much. He reached into the shopping bag for the newspaper he'd bought, made a second cup of coffee and padded into the living room where he settled into a comfortable chair, planning to catch up on local events.

It was a short-lived plan.

He unfolded the paper and was grabbed by the headline:

St Andrews police issue warning to students

Following a recent attempted mugging outside a St Andrews pub, local police have warned people to be vigilant. A nineteen-year-old student was leaving the King's Arms recently when she was set upon by two men who attempted to steal a piece of jewellery, believed to be a family heirloom. Luckily, she was followed out of the pub by a group of friends who were able to ward off the attack, although the two men escaped down a side road.

In a press briefing Inspector Duncan Clyde praised the quick actions of the students. He promised a greater police presence in the area but warned everyone to be alert and to keep valuables out of sight. He stated that attacks like this were extremely rare and recommended not going out in the town alone at night.

· · ·

Ian grabbed his phone and called Anna. No reply. He sent a text. *Call me ASAP* followed by several exclamation marks. He hadn't been able to find an emoticon that suggested urgency. Why hadn't she answered? There was no suggestion that she had been hurt in the attack, but perhaps that was something the police didn't release. All kinds of frightening images flooded his brain. Anna lying in a hospital bed somewhere. Or shut in her room, too scared to go out. Or held at gunpoint by the two men who hadn't after all escaped but had returned to finish what they had started. *Get a grip*, he told himself. There was nothing to suggest any of that had happened. She was in a lecture with her phone turned off, or somewhere with no signal. All the same, he needed to do something.

He called Duncan. 'I need to see you,' he said. 'Urgently.'

'Okay,' said Duncan. 'Calm yourself down and tell me what's so urgent.'

'It's about that attack in St Andrews.'

'The one with the students?'

Ian took a deep breath and tried to sound cool and professional. 'Yeah, I may have some information.'

'I'm in Dundee this morning. Can you meet me there?'

'Sure. I can be there in about twenty minutes.' Not the most convenient of Duncan's workplaces to get to but at least there was parking nearby. And Lottie would get a fuss made of her. The last time they were there Ian had been patched up by a doctor, having been hit over the head and then escaping from a burning building. Lottie was fed sausages by an adoring young constable. She didn't forget acts of kindness like that, particularly if they involved food.

Duncan welcomed them into his office and offered Ian a cup of tea. 'What can I do for you?' he asked. 'You sounded quite scared. I hope you've not got yourself mixed up with the local criminal fraternity again.'

Ian pulled the newspaper out of his pocket and unfolded it, pointing to the news of the attack in St Andrews. 'Can you confirm that the girl who was attacked was a student called Anna Lymington? If so, I believe I know who was responsible.'

'You know the girl?'

Ian took that as confirmation that it had indeed been Anna who was attacked. 'She's a great-niece of the laird I'm working for. It turns out she's the owner of the ring that was lost.'

'She stole it?'

'No, no, she's the legitimate owner.'

'You're losing me here,' said Duncan. 'You mean the ring wasn't stolen after all?'

'It was stolen, but then it found its way back into the family again.'

Duncan shook his head. 'Can't help thinking police work is more straightforward than being a PI.'

'Yeah, well, I didn't have a lot of choice about that, did I?'

'Fair enough. Let's start again. You found the ring and its owner. Family harmony duly restored. End of case, surely?'

'There's more to it than that.'

'I was afraid there might be.'

Ian reached for his phone and tapped the link to Anna's blog, passing it across the desk for Duncan to read.

'A very heart-warming story,' said Duncan. 'But I can't for the life of me see how it's connected to Miss Lymington being attacked. This,' he said, tapping the screen, 'is about a ring. The muggers were after a pendant.'

Ian shook his head. 'Anna wears the ring on a chain around her neck. See her photo?' He pinched the photo Anna had uploaded to the blog and spread his fingers to enlarge it.

Duncan squinted at it. 'I suppose if you knew it was a ring... but it's still unlikely, isn't it? Who is going to read a blog and decide to hunt down the person who wrote it on the off-chance she'd be wearing it at the time?'

'That's not all,' said Ian. 'Anna's into family history. She uses a site called *Forebears and More*. She had just added some of the Lytons to her family tree when she was sent a message by Orlando Bryson asking for information about living Lytons.'

'Yes, I remember you telling me that. Something about the museum as well.'

'He's definitely interested in the family.' Should he tell Duncan why Bryson was really interested in the family? He'd prefer not to go into details of Xander's personal life unless he had to.

'You think it was Bryson who attacked Anna?' Duncan asked.

'Maybe not him personally. You mentioned henchmen.'

Duncan looked doubtful. 'It doesn't sound like Bryson's usual MO, and we have little in the way of a description. Just two men in black hoodies. And I don't see how a vague interest in the family could lead to him attacking the girl. Is the ring very valuable?'

'It might raise a few thousand at auction but...' He stopped.

'You need to tell me everything if you want me to take this seriously.'

'Okay,' Ian said reluctantly. 'But I'm telling you in confidence, right?'

'At this stage we'd have no reason not to keep private information to ourselves.'

'There's a chance, a small chance I think, that Orlando Bryson is Alexander Lyton's son.'

Duncan looked at him wide-eyed. 'The Laird of Drumlychtoun is the father of a violent criminal?'

'Possibly, but even Bryson's mother thinks it's unlikely. What worries me is that Bryson himself might think he is.'

Duncan sighed and put his head in his hands. 'What the hell have you got yourself involved in now?' he asked. 'I'm not sure it's grounds for putting out an arrest warrant. Bryson's probably done much worse than that. I'm guessing the Glasgow police would rather get him for something a lot more serious.'

'But you can't rule him out, can you? Not after what I've just told you.'

'I suppose not. And I'll get someone to look into it. But I repeat my warning. In no way are you to get involved with Bryson yourself.

You could seriously mess up an ongoing investigation. He's volatile and dangerous. If you get the slightest hint of where he is, you let me know right away.'

Ian nodded. He had no intention of getting caught up in anything Bryson related. At least not head on. Unless he absolutely had to.

'I mean it,' said Duncan. 'I'd hate to see you get hurt again. And believe me, Bryson has no scruples about hurting people if they get in his way. If it was him, or one of his team your young friend was extremely lucky. She has some very brave, quick-witted friends.'

'So what are you going to do to protect her now?'

'We've extra patrols in the town in the evenings. We're upping security at the halls of residence. And we're checking ANPR for that evening.'

'But will that keep Anna safe?'

'We're doing our best, but other than giving her twenty-four hour protection there's not much else we can do.'

Not enough, Ian thought. What chance did a nineteen-year-old girl have against professional hitmen? Even if she had protective friends. They could be following her, waiting for when she was on her own. Next time she might not be so lucky. 'You managed to keep Prince William safe,' he said, frowning. 'Can't you do the same for Anna?'

'Protection of royals is quite different. You know that. They have their own units. Costs a fortune.'

'But...'

'Look, Ian, I promise we'll do all we can. She has some good friends. She'll be as safe at the university as anywhere. And term ends soon. She'll be away home in another two or three weeks.'

He'd have to be satisfied with that. He would do all *he* could. Stand outside her door all night if necessary.

As he and Lottie walked back to his car, his phone rang. Anna.

'Hi,' she said. 'You asked me to call you. Is it urgent?' She sounded her usual cheerful self.

'Are you okay?' Ian asked, trying not to sound too much like a mother hen.

'Yes, thanks. Why?'

'I heard you were mugged.'

'Oh, that. Yes, it was a bit scary. But I was with friends. They chased them off.'

How could she sound so cool about it? Hadn't she made the connection? That if they had been after her ring, then they might try again. 'Can we meet? I think we need to have a chat.'

'I'm staying with Robin and his family.'

Robin? Oh yes, the boyfriend. 'Was Robin with you when it happened?'

'Yes, and another student. They were great. But Robin's dad said I would be safer staying with them for a bit. They live well out of town. He's driving me to classes.'

Thank you, Robin's dad. At least someone was taking this seriously. 'Are you at his house now? Do you think he would mind if I dropped in?'

'I'm sure he wouldn't mind. He said I needed protecting. You can tell him you're a detective.'

'Is he there now?'

'Yes. We're all here. Robin and I are revising. Adrian's writing something in his study and Maura, that's Robin's mum, is in the garden. They've got this really fantastic dog.'

Hopefully a large dog with a fierce bark and sharp teeth. 'I'm in Dundee right now. I'll be there in about half an hour. Can you text me the address? Oh, and just check that they don't mind.'

The address arrived as he was unlocking the car along with a message that said, *Adrian and Maura said great and would you like some lunch? Is Lottie with you?* Then her usual row of smiley faces. He sent a small picture of a dog and a thumbs up sign. He was either getting used to teenage communication or he was becoming like an embarrassing uncle. Could he be an embarrassing uncle *and* a mother hen? It conjured up an interesting image. Perhaps Jessie could make him a drawing of it.

He tapped the address into his satnav. It was a village a few miles inland from St Andrews. That was good. It was better for her to be out of the town. Apart from anything else she'd be less likely to go wandering around at night. And she would be harder to find.

The house was larger than he'd expected – double fronted with gable windows in the roof and surrounded by a big garden. There was a front door with a storm porch and double-glazed windows, hopefully with security locks. Best of all, as he approached the front door, he heard barking. Definitely a fierce bark. It wasn't a high pitched yap like Lottie's. This was a scary bark belonging to a large dog. He picked Lottie up and held her under one arm as he rang the bell. The door was opened by a tall, friendly looking man in a checked shirt and corduroy trousers, with a pair of spectacles pushed on top of his head. He was holding the collar of an enormous dog – it was even larger than he'd hoped – with thick brown fur. Ian recognised it as a Bernese mountain dog. Sweet natured but with a bark that would scare any intruder. It probably gave the postman nightmares. He should probably stop obsessing about postmen and dogs.

The man held out his hand, which was large and had a firm grasp. 'Hi, I'm Adrian,' he said. 'Anna's been telling us about you. I must say I'm very pleased and relieved to meet you. I think the police should be taking attacks like this far more seriously.'

Yes, he agreed with that. 'It's very good of you to let Anna stay here. I was worried about the lack of protection in the halls.'

Anna bounded up to him and scooped Lottie into her arms. 'My favourite dog,' she said. 'Apart from Hector of course.' She grinned down at the large dog and put Lottie down on the floor next to him. Hector showed very little interest in her. Lottie was doing her best, running in circles round Hector and trying to nip his tail. Hector had just yawned, and Ian suspected he was about to stroll off for a snooze. Somewhere well away from this annoying little bouncing bundle. He smiled at Anna. 'So Lottie's now second best, is she?'

'No,' said Anna, laughing. 'I love both of them.'

'Seems to me,' said Adrian, smiling at her, 'that you fall for anything with four legs, fur and a bark. But let's not stand around on the doorstep. Come in.'

He led them into a living room with hundreds of books, a piano and an enormous dog basket. They sat down in comfortable chairs. Hector loped over to the basket and lay down in it. Lottie watched him with her head on one side and then jumped into Anna's lap.

Ian took out his notebook and turned to Anna. 'Tell me exactly what happened the other night.'

'We were in the King's Arms.'

'In the town centre?'

She nodded. 'It's just off Market Street.'

'And what time did you get there?'

'About half past eight. We'd been to a lecture that finished at seven, got burgers in the student union and then walked through the town.'

'You were with friends?'

'Yes, Robin and Stefan. Stefan's Polish. He's doing the same course as me and we buddied up because we're both doing an extra course for students from abroad who aren't used to academic writing in English. It's a bit boring because Stefan and I are both bi-lingual, but we still have to go. We usually sit at the back and pass notes to each other.'

'And it was busy in the pub?'

'Very, loads of other students and it was someone's birthday.'

'And what time did you leave?'

'About nine-thirty. I had some work to finish so I didn't want to be out late.'

'Did you all leave together?'

'Robin, Stefan and I left at the same time, but there was a crowd near the door, and we had to push through it, so we got separated. I got outside first and waited on the pavement. There were two men leaning against the wall. When they saw me one of them grabbed my arms from behind and the other made a grab for the chain round my neck.'

'The one with the ring?'

'Yes. I was shouting when the others came out of the pub. Robin and Stefan grabbed them and I kicked the one that was holding me in the shins. By then a whole lot more people had come out. There was a bit of a scuffle, and the men ran off. We went back into the pub and called the police.'

'You must have been very frightened.' Although she seemed unfazed by the whole thing. *Not unlike her grandmother*, he thought. Ailish would be proud of her.

Anna shrugged. 'Not really. It can get quite rowdy in the evenings. I thought they were just messing around until one of them made a grab for my chain. That was a bit scary but by then Robin and Stefan were there. It only lasted a few seconds, and then they were gone. The woman behind the bar at the pub made us some tea while we waited for the police. She put way too much sugar in because she said it was good for shock, but it tasted horrible, so we didn't drink very much. And anyway, the police were there quite quickly. They took the names and numbers of everyone in the bar. Then they drove Robin, Stefan and me to the police station. We made statements and Robin called Adrian who drove us back here.'

'And Stefan?'

'He shares a flat with some of the other Polish students and one of them came to pick him up.'

'I thought it would be safer for Anna to stay here for a while,' said Adrian. 'Hopefully they'll catch these louts soon. But until then it doesn't seem like any of them are safe in the town.'

'I'm afraid that's why I needed to talk to you urgently. I don't want to scare you, any of you, but I don't think this was a random mugging. I think they were targeting Anna.'

'What makes you think that?' Adrian asked, suddenly looking a lot less laid back.

'Anna,' said Ian. 'You remember that message you had on *Forebears and More*?'

'From Orlando Bryson.' Ian nodded. 'You told me not to reply to it. I promise I didn't.'

'Just as well, as it turns out. I made some enquiries about Bryson.

There's a possible connection to Drumlychtoun which I won't go into now. But I checked him out with a police friend of mine and he's a nasty piece of work. I've been absolutely forbidden to have any contact with him without police protection.'

'So why don't they just arrest him?' asked Adrian.

Ian had wondered the same thing. 'I'm told he's part of an ongoing investigation. But I suspect that they don't actually know where to find him. He gets his henchmen to do his dirty work for him. He's best known for an unpleasant business getting tenants out of flats, but I think he's probably the go to person for anyone who needs a spot of violent enforcement. He operates around Glasgow, so this was a bit out of his way.'

'I still don't understand why he's targeting Anna,' said Adrian.

Anna turned pale. 'It's the ring, isn't it?'

'I think it could be, yes.'

'Do you think he read my blog and made the connection that way?'

'There's no sign that he did. I've been checking the comments every day. But of course, he wouldn't need to add anything. Just discovering your name was probably enough. He knows your father's name from *Forebears*, knows your Lyton connection and was probably on the lookout for anything to do with the ring.'

'So it's my fault,' Anna said, becoming tearful.

Robin put his arm around her. 'It's absolutely not your fault,' he said.

'Robin's right,' said Adrian. 'But it's worrying. Do the police know all of this, Ian?'

'Yes, I spoke to Inspector Clyde this morning. He's already putting extra patrols around the pubs, and I'll let him know that Anna is here. He can probably arrange regular checks around the village.' He remembered Duncan's other suggestion. 'How would you feel about a panic alarm?'

'I should go back to hall,' said Anna, wiping away tears. 'It's too much trouble for you to let me stay here.'

'Don't even think about it,' said Adrian. 'This is the safest place for you.'

'But...'

'Not another word, young lady. You agree, don't you, Ian?'

'I do, yes. This house looks far more secure than the halls of residence. Very few people know you are here and,' he grinned at her, 'you've got Hector for company.' He turned to Adrian. 'Do we need to alert the university authorities?'

'Already done. And they'll keep it confidential.'

'What about Anna's family?' Ian asked. 'We don't want them worrying that they can't get in touch with her.'

'I'll let Mummy know I'm staying here for a bit. I don't want her to know about the attack though. She'd fuss.'

'Won't she want to know why you are staying here?'

'I'll tell her I'm staying with my boyfriend.' Robin squeezed her hand. 'Actually,' she added, blushing slightly, 'I was going to ask if he could come and stay with us in the vac.'

Robin smiled at her. 'I'd love that, but Dad says I need to work.'

'I said you should keep busy and out of mischief,' said Adrian. 'I think, if Anna's family will have you, a stay in France would be an excellent idea. You could improve your French while you are there.'

'Papa can give you a job in the winery,' said Anna, making a sudden recovery and grinning at all of them. 'He pays me to show English speaking tourists around. You could do that too.'

'I should probably talk to your parents,' said Adrian. 'But if they agree, I'll book flights for you to leave immediately term ends.'

'Brilliant,' said Anna. 'You can meet Fifi.'

'Fifi?' asked Robin.

'My dog. She's like Lottie only white and fluffy.'

Ian reached down and patted Lottie on the head. 'Poor Lottie,' he said. 'You're no more than a Fifi substitute.'

'Oh, you're not,' said Anna, scooping Lottie into her arms. 'I adore you.'

'But she's only in third place behind Fifi and Hector,' said Ian, relieved that he could tease her again.

'Do we know what this Bryson fellow looks like?' Adrian asked. 'If we catch sight of him lurking around, we could call the police.'

'Good idea,' said Ian. 'There's probably a mugshot of him on the police database. I'll get Duncan to send me a copy.' He tapped a message into his phone.

'And you mentioned panic alarms? Would the police see to that as well?'

'They probably contract it out. I'll make enquiries.'

15

Confident that he'd done as much as he could for the moment, Ian drove home. So much for his day off. He'd stop off on the way and give Lottie a run in the woods. It would help to clear his head as well. Perhaps he'd go and see Caroline this evening. It was a busy time of year for her with school exams, but she probably needed to take time out as much as he did. He looked at his watch. School would have finished for the day. He'd call her now. He reached into his pocket for his phone and as he got it out, it pinged with a message and then started to ring. It was a number he didn't know. He could ignore it, but with so much going on he'd better not. If it was a new case, it would be unlikely to be urgent. He could stall and say he'd call back later. He pressed answer.

'Hi, Ian. It's Elsa Curran.'

A picture of a waterfall of red hair came into his head. The way she had untied her scarf and let it fall to her shoulders. 'Good to hear from you,' he said. He wanted to add 'so soon', but that sounded as if he thought she was being a nuisance, which she very definitely wasn't.

'I hope you're not too busy, but I've found something that might interest you.'

'I'm not busy right now.' It was a relief to have something else to think about. Anna may be secure for now but what about the future? She'd be safe enough in France but what about when she returned in the autumn? She couldn't spend the rest of her life worried about who was out there, always having to look over her shoulder. All because of a ring. He was tempted to say, 'Just give him the ring,' but doubted that was the answer. The ring had been valued at around ten thousand pounds. Bryson probably wouldn't turn his nose up at ten thousand pounds, but he was afraid there was much more to it than that. It came to him in a flash. It was Drumlychtoun he was really after.

He realised he was still holding his phone to his ear.

'Are you still there?' Elsa asked.

'Yes, sorry, got distracted for a moment. You've found something?'

'Yes. My sister and I are planning to expand the B&B and we thought we would look into converting the loft into a couple of bedrooms.'

'Very popular, loft conversions.'

'Yes, well, we've not been up there much. Just shoved in a few boxes of stuff we didn't know what to do with.'

That reminded him of his own two upstairs rooms. He should really sort them out some time.

'Anyway,' Elsa continued. 'We thought we'd better clear it out before we took the builder up there. You can't get any idea of the space if it's full of junk. We thought we'd got it all out when I noticed this shoebox tucked into the eaves.'

'Was it full of hidden treasure?'

She laughed. 'I'm afraid not, but it seems to be something the Brysons left behind. Nothing valuable. Some letters and a few photographs. I thought I should try and return it to one of them, but I don't have any details for Orlando and his mother isn't answering her phone. Then I remembered you were interested in them, so I wondered if you'd like to take a look.'

Was that ethical? Rummaging through personal papers. But if they'd been in Elsa's loft for five years they probably weren't important or valuable so it couldn't do any harm. Might even throw some light on the family. 'I'd like to very much. Should I call in and pick it up?'

'It's a bit of a shlep for you. I wondered if we might meet halfway. What about Stirling? I could buy you that drink.'

'Stirling's fine. But why don't we make it a meal?'

'Great idea. Tomorrow's my evening off. Would that suit you?'

'Perfect. Seven by the clock tower?'

He ended the call and clicked on the message. A photograph of Orlando Bryson with a message from Duncan. *If you see him call us at once.* He studied the photograph. He didn't know what he'd expected – a villainous looking thug, he supposed. With arms like tattoo covered meat cleavers. Perhaps a crooked, broken nose, cauliflower ears and a head like a football. But Orlando looked harmless, rather bland and ordinary. It was difficult to tell from a head and shoulders shot, but he looked fairly slight, even featured and with mousey coloured hair. There was nothing about him that suggested any similarity to Xander, or even to Sheila. He was just an ordinary looking middle-aged man. Someone unremarkable who spent his days sitting behind a desk. Which of course Bryson might well do – while issuing instructions for violent attacks.

He forwarded it to Anna and Adrian and repeated Duncan's instructions not to approach him.

Elsa arrived a few minutes late and breathless.

'So sorry,' she said. 'An awkward guest arguing about his bill.'

'No problem. It's a lovely evening and I haven't been here long.' She was carrying a large leather bag and wearing jeans with a dark green jumper, her hair loose over her shoulders. She must be in her late thirties, and he wondered why such an attractive woman was living with her sister and running a B&B. He wasn't going to be intrusive and ask. Anyway, what was wrong with that? It was a perfectly respectable and probably lucrative way of making a living. It was just

that she looked as if she should have been doing something more...
more what? Artistic maybe. Or something like a TV presenter.
Weather, he thought. He could imagine her standing in front of a
weather map, joking with presenters and issuing warnings of gales
and heavy snowfalls.

They found a quiet, rather old-fashioned pub similar to many
Scottish city pubs, where tired looking workers leaned on the bar for
drinks after a heavy day's work and probably lurched out onto the
pavement at closing time for a punch up. But this evening everything
was quiet and orderly. They ordered drinks and studied the menu.
All good traditional pub grub. Ian chose steak and ale pie with green
beans and Elsa opted for chicken Caesar salad.

'It'll be about fifteen minutes,' he was told. That was fine. It would
give him a chance to look at the contents of Elsa's box.

They found a table and sat down. Elsa reached into her bag and
took out the box – a cardboard shoebox with *MacBirnie's shoes*
stamped on it next to a picture of a hefty looking pair of brogues. His
grandfather had owned a pair. Polished them every day. 'Shoes like
that can last a lifetime,' Grandad always said.

Inside the box he found a bundle of letters in envelopes which
had been carefully slit open. The address, to White Lodge he noticed,
all written in the same hand and addressed to H. Bryson Esq. He was
no handwriting expert, but he thought the writing looked like a
woman's. Written with a fine pen and in curly letters.

There was also a collection of photographs held together with an
elastic band. He flicked through them quickly. They were in no
particular order, just a bunch of random pictures mostly of groups of
people.

Their food arrived and he put everything back in the box and set
it to one side.

'Interesting?' Elsa asked as they started eating.

'Fascinating, I think. I'll need to spend some time with them in a
good light.'

'It's a bit gloomy in here, isn't it?'

He agreed, peering at his fork trying to decide whether what he was going to eat was a piece of meat or a mushroom. 'I'll go through it all at home and then post it all back to Sheila. It's nosy of me, but it could help with a case I'm working on.'

'Private investigator sounds very glamorous.'

He laughed. He'd never been called that before. 'It can be quite boring,' he said, thinking of hours spent sitting in his car waiting for people, usually outside hotels. Not *quite* boring – *very* boring. 'I don't think I'd call it glamorous. But you should see me off duty when I'm wearing my kilt,' he laughed.

'I'd really like that. Nothing like a man in a kilt. Is there a Skair tartan?'

'Not as such, but we're an Aberdeen family and there are traditional local designs. The one I wear is red and grey.' He hadn't worn his own kilt for a while. Just the Ogilvie one that Bridget had lent him a couple of weeks ago. At Drumlychtoun it had felt entirely appropriate. At a pub in Stirling, it would get laughs. The last time he'd worn his kilt had been the day he met Rosalie at a party celebrating the one hundredth birthday of a friend of his grandfather. An afternoon tea party with traditional dancing. He'd meant to take up Scottish dancing again after he moved, but somehow hadn't had time. Which was good, he supposed. He'd not been short of work recently. But he was wandering off into a daydream and neglecting his companion. 'Curran isn't a Scottish name, is it?' he asked.

'Irish originally, but my sister and I were both born in Scotland. And our mother was a *Born Free* fan which explains why I'm called Elsa. She'd probably rather have had a lion cub than another little girl,' she laughed. 'She was all set to call me Hamish.'

'My mother was going to call me Cynthia. I'm really quite glad she didn't.'

'It wouldn't suit you,' Elsa agreed.

She was great company and Ian wanted to know more. 'You enjoy driving miles on your free evening to have meals with strange men?'

'I make sure of it whenever I have time off,' she laughed. 'And you're not that strange.'

'I'm relieved to hear it.'

She still seemed out of place cleaning a B&B, although her get-up had been rather fetching. She suited overalls and a headscarf. 'What made you and your sister start the B&B?' he wondered.

'It's in the family I suppose. Our parents ran a hotel near Loch Lomond. But I never thought I'd follow them. I studied at Glasgow School of Art, jewellery making, but somehow I never got going with a career.'

Now that was interesting. Very interesting. 'What kind of jewellery?'

'I liked working in silver, or gold if I could get it. I made necklaces and bracelets, that sort of thing. I just wasn't very good at selling them.'

'Did you ever make rings?' he asked hopefully, thinking she might have a useful insight into making fake jewellery.

'I have done, but it wasn't something I specialised in. Why?'

He got out his phone and swiped through his photos. He chose the close up of the bishop and showed it to her. 'It's a seventeenth-century bishop's ring. I'm working on a case at the moment which involves passing off a copy of this ring as genuine. I was wondering what kind of skills someone would need to do it.'

She studied the photo, enlarging it as much as she could. 'Do you know when it was copied?'

'Probably during the sixties.'

'It's not an elaborate piece. Quite an easy design to copy. Most students could probably do it. The problem would be making it look the right age. They would also have needed authentic materials. Amethysts are easy to get hold of. They're not valuable so it would be simple enough to take one from another setting. The gold would have been more of a problem.'

'So where would you go for authentic gold?'

'Seventeenth century? Now, almost impossible without going abroad to Turkey perhaps, or India. I'm not sure. But in the sixties, we were still importing precious metals from all kinds of sources. It would be frowned on these days because there would be accusations of plundering from other cultures.'

'Like the Elgin Marbles?'

'In a much smaller way, but yes, kind of.'

This was fascinating. If Bryson Remington were importing just after the war, they would have access to all kinds of treasure. Things people had stashed away and in the post war chaos, were not able to return to. 'So given the right materials you think a student would have been able to make a copy?'

'I could and I wasn't a particularly brilliant student. So yes.'

So, if his suspect had been a student at, for example Glasgow, and also happened to have a father in the precious metals import business, he might just have pushed Joshua Remington even further up the list of suspects.

It was late when Ian got back. They had chatted in the pub until it closed and then he had an hour's drive home. He'd enjoyed the evening and it had been very informative. Hadn't he thought that Elsa looked like an artistic type? He'd never have guessed that she was going to be exactly the kind of artist he needed. Why hadn't he thought of a student before? They would have access to the right kind of tools and materials and wouldn't have raised suspicion in the way taking the ring to a dealer to be copied would have done. It would have been easy for Joshua to show an interest in the ring on one of the occasions he and Ailish had sneaked into the castle. He'd have been able borrow it and return it the same way a few days later. He hadn't seen much in the way of security at the castle. It was likely that the old Laird had kept valuables in his bureau just as Xander did now. He wondered if Ailish had known about it. It was likely but not inevitable. She could have helped Joshua because she was angry with her father. Or she could have told him just enough to pique his interest. It would only have taken a second or two for Joshua to take the ring and smuggle it out in his pocket, then return it the same way. All Ian needed now was to find out if Joshua had been a student somewhere that gave him access to both tools and skills. Then he would have to work out how Pete got hold of it, when according to Anna he hadn't spoken to his parents since he joined the army.

He parked in his usual spot in the road and climbed up through the garden carrying the shoebox. He unlocked the door and waited for Lottie's usual ecstatic greeting. As he bent down to stroke her, he noticed a folded piece of paper on the doormat. He picked it up and put it in his pocket while he carried the box into his office. He'd left the door open so that Lottie could scamper round the garden and as it was a lovely evening, he strolled out to join her. He sat down on the doorstep looking across the estuary. One of his favourite views at any time of the day or night. He remembered the piece of paper, a note probably, and pulled it out of his pocket. There was a lamp above the door, put there by a previous resident. It was wrought iron and made to look like an old-fashioned carriage lamp. Ian didn't like it particularly, but it gave him enough light to read his note. It was from Lainie asking him if he could drive her to a hospital appointment next week. *Of course he could*, he thought, smiling. Lainie asked for very few favours and he was only too happy to help when he could. He put the note back into his pocket and called Lottie. It was time for bed. And then it hit him. Why hadn't he remembered that earlier? Pete had visited his father in hospital. Joshua had died a few days later. He remembered Anna's exact words about the visit: *My grandfather died not long after that and Mummy thought that he might have given Daddy the ring then.* Did Ailish know about that visit? Probably not. Contacting the CO and arranging a last-minute reconciliation visit smacked of secrecy. And if that was the case, then Ailish would be in the clear. Ian felt strangely relieved by the idea. As would Xander, he expected.

He went inside, poured himself a nightcap and gave Lottie a handful of dog biscuits. He glanced at the shoebox which was sitting on his desk but it was too late to go through its contents now. He would get a good night's sleep and spend time on it in the morning.

16

It had become a habit now for Ian to check Anna's blog first thing every morning for any new comments. There'd been nothing for days. There were new blogs and Anna's was beginning to retire into the background of blogging history. Ian had bookmarked it, but he noticed that without the bookmark, he'd have had to scroll through many pages of later entries. Was it all now a thing of the past? The lack of interest made him hope that Anna was safer. There had been no further sign of Bryson's henchmen and no more messages on *Forebears and More*. Students were out in force every evening enjoying the summer weather and the approaching summer vacation. In spite of this there were no reports from the police of any further attacks. The town was peaceful and safe. Did he need to be quite so vigilant? Probably not, but it was a difficult habit to break and if something *did* happen to Anna, he'd never forgive himself.

He logged in, opened the blog site and found a new comment. This was the first in days and he stared at it in surprise, unsure what to make of it. Should he be worried? He wasn't sure. Right now, *any* activity worried him. But this seemed innocent enough. It was from someone who claimed to be an authority on Scottish antique jewellery asking Anna to send him a photo of the ring with a view of adding it to a book he was writing. It could be genuine, but something didn't quite ring true, although he couldn't work out why. Perhaps it was the lack of information. This person used only a username. He, or she, didn't mention any qualifications or other publications. Better to be safe than sorry. He sent Anna a text advising her not to reply. He didn't want to frighten her, so he just suggested that as she now had the fake ring it was better not to circulate a photo of it. If this was a genuine request a picture of a fake would not be well received and could even lead to accusations of fraud. And if it wasn't genuine, well, that was obvious.

His next task, and again something he did every day, was to call Adrian and make sure all was well with Anna herself. Adrian had nothing to report. No strangers hanging around in the village. No uncalled-for barking from Hector. No suspicious phone calls. The police had driven past a few times, but not enough to arouse suspicion. Anna had been given a GPS panic alarm but was going out very little. She and Robin were supposed to be revising for exams, but Adrian suspected they were more interested the prospect of a long summer in France. 'But they're good kids,' he told Ian. 'They've both worked hard, and they'll be fine.'

'And the thought of France is a good distraction from what's been going on. Have they got their flights booked?'

'Yes, three days after the end of their exams. I couldn't persuade them to go any sooner. They want to celebrate with friends, which seems fair enough. I'll make sure they're driven everywhere, and security's pretty tight after exams. The powers that be are trying to curb excessive celebrating and encouraging students to push off as soon as possible. Most of them have run out of cash by then anyway.'

Ian would have felt happier if they'd gone straight away but there was not much he could do about it. 'Did you speak to Anna's mother?' he asked.

'Jeanette? Yes, I called her a couple of nights ago. I told her there'd been a bit of trouble in the town. I didn't go into detail. Just said that

Anna wanted somewhere quiet to work for her exams and she was welcome to stay here for as long as she wanted. Jeanette said she'd be delighted to have Robin for a few weeks in return.'

Adrian seemed to have it all under control and Ian felt that *he* had done all he could.

Now it was time to explore the shoebox. He opened the box and laid its contents out on his desk. He imagined they'd been in a drawer in an old-fashioned desk or bureau and tipped into the shoebox in a hurry. Why? A sudden house move, or furniture sale? A last-minute reprieve from a clear-out? Not valuable as such but too personal to throw away. Obviously not precious enough to sort into albums or tie up with pink ribbon. Did people still do that? Photo albums were a thing of the past. There was no longer the excitement of getting them back from the developer, sorting out the best and sticking them, carefully labelled, into an album. Now everyone took thousands of photographs and hefted them up to various virtual spaces probably never to be looked at again. The Cloud, or whatever it was called, must be pretty crowded by now. And letters tied up with pink ribbon had definitely had their day. Although thinking about it, Ian didn't think he'd ever done that. He'd never had many personal letters. Never had a love letter. How sad was that?

He looked at the photos first – a collection of family snaps. He thought they covered a period of around five to ten years. It was a family not unlike his own. He remembered family snaps being taken on holidays or at Christmas. Did his mother have a box of photos like these? No, she wouldn't. His grandmother might have had one, but not his mother. She and his father had their own IT company. They were definitely people who stored things in the cloud. Invented it, probably.

There were two boys who appeared regularly. They reminded Ian of himself and his brother, although these two looked the same age. Friends perhaps, rather than brothers. He arranged them in order, taking the size of the boys as an indication. In the photos on the left of his desk the boys looked about twelve. By the time he got to the right he thought they were probably in their late teens or early twenties. There were a couple of men who appeared regularly and seemed to be around the same age as each other. They rarely appeared in the same photo, so Ian assumed one or other of them was behind the camera. Two women also made regular appearances, although one of them had disappeared from the later photos. Then a baby appeared but disappeared again around the same time as the woman. He reached for some post-it notes and started to guess at possible dates. He labelled the early photos as late 1950s. The men were both in suits and ties even when sitting casually in the garden. The women had short tidy hair and dresses with full skirts. The boys were in shorts and long socks, sometimes wearing open-neck shirts, sometimes hand-knitted jumpers. The later photos he labelled as late 1960s. Hair was longer and clothes more casual. In some he thought he could identify White Lodge by its white walls and art deco style window frames. Likely enough as the box had been found there.

Could he assume that at least some of these people were Brysons? That seemed reasonable since it was their house in the background. One of the men could be Harold Bryson, one of the boys George. Could the baby be Sheila? And if so, why had she disappeared from the pictures? Was the woman who had disappeared her mother? Was it too much to guess that the other man was Gideon Remington and the boy Joshua? And, of course, the woman who hadn't disappeared could be Joshua's mother. The two men had been business partners, so it wasn't impossible that the two families were also friends.

He copied all the photographs onto his phone and turned to the letters. Letters and photographs had all been bundled together in the box so perhaps the letters would give him an idea who the people were.

As he had thought when he glanced through them quickly in the pub, they were all from the same sender. All in the same cream envelopes and, as he began to open them, all on the same headed notepaper. This in itself was interesting. They had been sent from The Briars Nursing Home, Newtonside. Nursing homes seemed to have gone out of fashion. Now there were care homes, mostly for the elderly. He knew quite a lot about those since his fight to keep his grandfather out of one of them. He googled The Briars but with no result except to discover that Newtonside was a village in Ayrshire. *Not that far from Glasgow,* he thought, wondering if that was significant.

He arranged the letters according the date on the postmarks and opened the earliest. It was a short note that began *Dear Harold* and ended *Your loving Joyce.* The few sentences in between told him that The Briars was satisfactory, and she was being well cared for. No clue as to why she needed caring for or how she was. If she was one of the women in the photos, she wouldn't be in a nursing home because of her age. Could she have been paralysed after an accident, or suffering from a long-term illness? He continued through the rest of the letters and discovered very little more. Joyce occasionally sent good wishes to George and hoped that the baby was doing well. The only glimmer that this could be in any way connected to his case was in one of the final letters when she wrote, *You must tell Gideon not to be concerned about his son. He's young and needs to stretch his wings.* Was she writing about Joshua?

He started making a list of the two families.

Brysons

Harold Bryson m Joyce (?)

Harold was joint chairman of Bryson Remington, later Bryson Holdings.

Two children – George and Sheila – both unmarried?

George took over the company after his father's death.

Sheila's son Orlando – father Alexander Lyton?

Remingtons

Gideon – wife's name not known

One son – Joshua lived with Ailish Lyton

Their son – Pete Lymington

Pete's daughter - Anna

Ian sat and looked at it. It was interesting but had it brought him any closer to solving the question about who took the ring? Or had he just wasted a whole morning? It was too soon to know that, and it had at least given him a bit more background. Bryson Remington were importers of precious metals, so if he could prove that Joshua was Gideon Remington's son and that he had been an art student, or had at least studied jewellery making, then yes, it added a bit of weight to his theory that Joshua was still his chief suspect. It was all guesswork on his part, but Xander might find it an interesting bit of family history. Particularly the way the two families connected to his own as well as to each other. He took copies of all the letters and saved them to a Remington/Bryson folder along with the photographs that he would share with Xander and Bridget.

By now his back was aching. It was time for some fresh air and something to eat. A walk down to the village for some lunch, then a long walk with Lottie. Tentsmuir, he decided, where she could scamper around in the sand dunes. It would give him a chance to think things through and decide what to do next. Xander still insisted that he wanted to know everything about the ring's disappearance. Was he just wasting his money? The ring had been found and was now in a safety deposit box. It was such a long time ago. What good would it do to rake over the past? He'd send Xander what he had found out and suggest that it was now time to draw a line under it. But first he needed time off and to have the evening out that he'd had to curtail after Anna was mugged. He'd kept an eye on the blog during the morning but there'd been no more messages posted. He needn't check in again until tomorrow morning.

He could take the evening off. Go to the pub for a pint and have an early night.

He packed the letters and photographs back into their shoebox, wrapped it in brown paper and addressed it to Sheila Bryson. On the back he added his own address, remembering that the woman at the post office insisted on it before she would give him a proof of postage slip.

Then he and Lottie walked to the village for something to eat, calling in at the post office on their way.

17

'I'd like to pay you to work for me for a day.'

The phone had woken Ian up and his first thought was that he was still dreaming.

'This is Ailish Lyton and I said I'd like—'

'Yes,' he said, rubbing his eyes and sitting up. 'What can I do for you?' Did this mean another trip to London? He was still checking Anna's blog, watching out for Bryson and considering the long list of prospective clients that sat in his inbox. He didn't need the extra work right now, particularly in London. 'I'm afraid London would be too far,' he said, hoping that would be the end of it.

'No, it wouldn't be in London,' Ailish said, giving him the impression that she considered this a particularly stupid idea. 'I have to come to Edinburgh for a funeral. And I need an escort for the day.'

An escort? That's one thing he'd never considered doing to make a living. He didn't think he was the right type. Not suave enough and his wardrobe definitely wouldn't be up to it.

'Hear me out,' she said. 'It's not what you think.'

Did he even know what he thought?

'I know you're still searching for information about that stupid ring. If you come with me to this funeral, I may be able to help you.'

He failed to see how, but he was intrigued.

'You will need to meet me at the airport at eleven thirty tomorrow morning.'

'Edinburgh Airport?' he asked.

'Yes, of course Edinburgh,' she said, impatiently. 'The funeral is at two forty-five at Morningside crematorium. We will take lunch at Donald of Drummond Hotel and I will explain more to you then. My flight back to London leaves at six-thirty so I shall need you to drive me back to the airport. I will pay you your daily rate plus reasonable expenses for petrol and car parking. Is that clear?'

'Do you know what my daily rate is?' he asked.

'I'm quite capable of checking a website. I also know you have an online contract which I will complete and submit to you today with a deposit.'

She hadn't asked if he was free tomorrow. He could claim to be working, but something had caught his attention. It was strange that just when he thought there was no more he could do about the ring, Ailish should pop up out of the blue and dangle this over him. No, he couldn't turn it down. Xander had been hoping to lure Ailish back to Scotland. He'd not had any thoughts about how to do it, but if he knew she'd been in Edinburgh and Ian had declined a meeting with her, Xander would probably never forgive him. 'Fine,' he said, hoping he didn't sound too reluctant. 'I'll see you tomorrow morning.'

He got up and took Lottie out for her morning walk. Then he made some breakfast and sat down at his desk to see if he could work out what it was all about.

He started by checking recent death notices for Edinburgh. There were several announcements about cremations in Edinburgh tomorrow. No names that jumped out at him but he'd find out soon enough. He turned his attention to car parking in central Edinburgh, hoping the hotel had a valet service. There was nothing on the website about it so he supposed he would have to drop Ailish off and then go and search for somewhere. At least he knew where Morningside crematorium was. He'd been there for his grandfather's funeral. And because of that funeral he was also the owner of a black tie.

He printed out the folder he had made the day before, hoping Ailish would be able to confirm some of the people in the photos. It seemed Ailish had now decided to be helpful by suggesting she might be able to fill in some gaps for him. He wondered what had changed her mind. A sudden glimpse of her own mortality perhaps? A need to revisit her roots and reconnect with family? Guilty conscience? She'd given the impression, when they'd met, that she had no guilty conscience, but things change.

He was glad he hadn't sent the folder to Xander and Bridget yesterday. If Ailish had more information, he could add it after he came home from the funeral. He printed out a copy, put it in a plastic folder and then into the bag he planned to take with him tomorrow. Then he ironed a white shirt, brushed his one and only dark jacket, and polished his shoes.

There was not much more he could do to prepare so he checked Anna's blog and found a new message. It was posted by the same person as before but it now sounded more threatening. It spoke about missed opportunities and time running out. He hoped Anna wouldn't respond and that she knew enough now to ignore it. Just in case, he sent her a warning text.

18

It was another early start. For a few minutes Ian chatted to Lainie, who was looking after Lottie for the day. It was lucky she and Lottie got on. There was no way he could manage without her. Life must be tough for people who had to organise childcare every day. As he drove through the village he passed a nursery, where parents were dropping off small children with backpacks before hurrying off to jobs in Dundee and Edinburgh. Dundee wouldn't be too bad. He'd done it himself for a week or two when he'd first arrived here. Just a quick drive over the bridge. A whole lot easier now they had the bridge. But of course the bridge was the reason Greyport was now populated mostly with commuters. Edinburgh was different. An hour's drive or train commute. He wouldn't fancy doing that every day. Once in a while was fine, but on the whole he was more than satisfied with a life that involved working mostly from home with occasional jaunts to more exciting places. Did many of these people own dogs? And if so, were there dog nurseries? He might try and find one. There were bound to be times when Lainie wouldn't be able to help him.

He pulled away out of the village and stopped to fill his car with petrol and himself with coffee. Then he headed south for a drive that his satnav told him would take him an hour and ten minutes. Longer than usual so he suspected a queue to cross the new Forth Bridge, not long opened and already a bottleneck. Sensible commuters, he supposed, took the train.

He arrived at the airport half an hour before Ailish's flight was due to land and found a space in the short stay car park, which was close to the arrivals hall. A quick look at the tariff told him it could well be cheaper to park further away and take a taxi, but it was too late to change his mind. He checked the board and found the flight from London was scheduled to land on time. He bought a Starbucks cappuccino and sprinkled it with chocolate. Then he perched on a stool, where he had a good view of arrivals, and looked around. He wondered if Ailish would recognise him. Their last meeting had been short, and he wasn't sure how much attention she had paid him. Perhaps he should have armed himself with a board with her name and stood with all the drivers who were waiting for arrivals. In his funeral get-up he could well be mistaken for a driver. But if she'd forgotten what he looked like, and he'd be the first to admit he wasn't that memorable, she would have seen his photo on his website. Her electronic contract had arrived minutes after he put the phone down, as had the deposit she made into his bank account.

He needn't have worried. A crowd of people came through the barrier, more commuters he supposed, and she spotted him before he saw her. She made her way purposefully towards him. He jumped off his stool and held out his hand.

She shook it and smiled at him. 'Good morning,' she said. 'I'm very pleased to meet you again.'

'A pleasant flight?' he asked.

'Pleasant enough, I suppose,' she said. 'When surrounded by people with laptops. But it's only an hour and a half.'

A lot less than the train. But not nearly as pleasant. One could walk around on trains or sit and watch the countryside go past. Planes didn't provide much opportunity for walking around and the

view was mostly of clouds. And then there was the tedious underground ride into the city. Nearly as long as the flight itself.

She must have read his thoughts. 'I took a minicab to Heathrow,'
she said. 'It's only half an hour from my flat.'

He was glad he'd made the effort to look funereal. Ailish was
dressed in a black trouser suit with a black silk shirt and high-heeled
black patent shoes. She was carrying a Burberry raincoat over her
arm and had a small leather shoulder bag. She had her hair in a bun
at the nape of her neck. She looked stylish and elegant. She could
pass for the director of a successful company. Perhaps she was. He'd
no idea how she passed her time. She was obviously well-off but he'd
assumed that was because Joshua had left her very well provided for.
But from what he knew of Ailish perhaps that was less likely. She was
fiercely independent and could very well be in charge of some huge
global company, never having relied on anyone else to support her.

'My car is quite close,' he said as he led her towards the entrance.
At four pounds for every ten minutes, it was just as well her flight was
on time. Although he didn't suppose she'd quibble over a few pounds
spent on car parking. He swiped his credit card into the machine and
stashed the receipt away in his wallet. He imagined Ailish would
expect an itemised bill with details of his expenses.

Just as well he had a new car. He couldn't imagine driving her
around in his old one. She'd have taken one look at it and demanded
a taxi.

She strapped herself in and looked around as he left the airport
and headed into the city centre. 'You know Edinburgh well,' she
commented as they drove into the city.

Yes, he was a confident driver and knew his way round Edinburgh. 'I lived here until a few months ago. In Morningside.'

'I was at school in Morningside. Hated it.'

He wasn't that keen on it either. He'd only moved there because it
was where Grandad had lived. 'Did you hate the school or Morningside?'

'Both,' she said firmly. 'The school was run by dried up spinsters and Morningside was full of people who looked as if they were permanently sucking lemons.'

He knew that look well. Although there were people who lived there that he liked. Grandad for a start. And Rosalie. Her grandmother had lived there as well. It was how they'd met. But on the whole, yes, he agreed with Ailish's summing up. There was definitely a Morningside type that looked down on the rest of Edinburgh.

She was looking around with interest. It must have changed since she was at school here. 'When were you last in Edinburgh?' he asked.

'1967. It's changed a lot since then. When did this tram thing arrive?' She was looking out of the window at a tram snaking along beside the road.

'It opened in 2014,' he said as they passed Haymarket Station. 'It runs from the airport to York Place. Right along Princes Street.'

'Good God,' she laughed. 'That would have given my father palpitations.' She seemed to quite like that idea. 'As far as he was concerned Princes Street was the heart of all that was Scottish. He'd be turning in his grave.' She thought for a moment. 'Perhaps I'll take the tram back to the airport,' she said.

Still trying to upset her father. He smiled at her. 'Whatever you like. But I won't have worked my full day unless I drive you there.'

'Think of it as a bonus,' she said. 'I'm sure your wife will be glad to see you home a little earlier than expected.'

'I'm not married,' he said. 'But I do have a dog who would be pleased to see me.'

Half an hour after leaving the airport, Ian pulled the car up under a wrought iron and glass awning at the entrance to the Donald of Drummond Hotel. It was a five-storey sandstone building complete with a clock tower, which reminded Ian of a prison. He had read Scott's *The Heart of Midlothian* at school and he carried an image of poor Effie incarcerated somewhere not a million miles away from the Donald of Drummond. He'd never been inside but imagined deep pile tartan carpets and dark mahogany furniture. A man in a top hat and red overcoat stepped out to open the door for Ailish.

'I'll just be a minute parking,' said Ian. 'I'll meet you inside. Won't be long.' Dressed as he was, he might very well be mistaken for the driver. He wanted to make it clear that he was Ailish's lunch guest before he was directed away to wherever it was drivers parked. Round the back somewhere probably. This was the kind of place where the workers were seen and not heard. There would be a separate, less ostentatious entrance for them where they could sneak in and out without being seen.

He needn't have worried. The man walked round to his window and said, 'If you'd care to leave your keys, I can get someone to park it for you. Just tell them at reception when you're ready to leave and they'll bring it back.'

He reached into the back for his bag, handed over the keys and followed Ailish inside. The entrance foyer was far less intimidating than the exterior, with helpful looking people in suits and tartan ties standing behind a reception desk. There was a bar and groups of comfortable chairs.

'It's a little early for lunch,' said Ailish. 'We'll sit here a while and have a chat. Perhaps you could get us a drink. I'll have a sparkling mineral water. Highland Spring if they have it, with a slice of lemon and no ice.' She looked around and spotted a pair of unoccupied chairs. 'I'll be over there,' she said, pointing to a table by the window.

Ian felt surprisingly nervous in Ailish's company and fancied a scotch. But it was probably better not to. It would give quite the wrong impression, although he wasn't too sure what kind of impression he wanted to give. Businesslike investigator was what he usually went for. But this wasn't his usual type of case. Should he go for sympathetic funeral guest, smooth escort or even friend of the family? He had no idea, but whatever role he decided on it was probably better to remain alcohol free. He settled for a tomato juice with extra Worcester sauce. He carried the drinks to the table with a menu under his arm.

Handing Ailish the menu he said, 'If you would like to order your lunch at the bar here, they'll tell us when it's ready. They already have a table reserved in the dining room.'

'Excellent,' she said, looking around. 'I've never been here before but I assumed somewhere like this would provide good service.'

Ian was sure that was something Ailish was familiar with. She had an air of well-heeled authority that demanded it without ever having to open her mouth. She ordered a vegetarian salad, and since this was on expenses he chose a ribeye steak.

'Right,' he said, sitting down. 'Are you going to tell me whose funeral we are going to?'

'Of course, but perhaps you could tell me what you have found out first. I assume it's about Joshua's family. That way I can see what needs filling in.'

How on earth did she know that? Last time they met, all he'd told her was that Xander had asked him to find *her*. But he wasn't going to argue with her. 'Fine,' he said, reaching for his bag and handing her his plastic folder.

She took her time looking through the folder, taking sips of her drink while turning the pages and nodding at some of the photographs. 'I'm impressed,' she said as she came to the final page. 'I didn't think you would have got this far.'

How far did she think he would have got? And why was she even interested in his research? 'The archive in Glasgow was very helpful,' he said. 'Then I had a stroke of luck after I visited the house in Beardsley.' He turned to a page with a photo and laid it on the table in front of Ailish. 'I'm hoping you can identify these people for me. I'm just guessing.'

She didn't ask why he wanted to know. She pointed to one of the two young men. It was one of the late photographs, taken, Ian had assumed, when the two of them would have been in their twenties. 'This is Joshua,' she said. 'The one next to him is George Bryson. They were at school together. George went straight into the family firm when he left school.'

'But not Joshua?'

'No, he went to Glasgow to study art. Much against his father's wishes, I have to say. That's one reason he left home when he did.' She pointed to the two men standing at the back. 'That's Joshua's father on the left. The other is Harold Bryson. They were in business together.'

That much he knew, but he was pleased to have their identity confirmed. 'And this woman?'

'That's Gideon's wife. I forget what she was called. I only met them once. Joshua didn't have a lot of time for his family.'

'Keen to escape?' Ian could relate to that, and the weight of family expectations was probably even worse during the sixties than it had been for him in the nineties. But he'd done well with his guesses. He pointed to another photo. 'This woman here. Is that Mrs Bryson?'

'Batty Joyce? I assume it is, although I never met her.'

'Batty?'

'One isn't allowed to say that these days. I imagine it was schizo-phrenia. In those days it was something to cover up. Poor Joyce spent her last years in an institution. A fairly upmarket one, I would imag-ine. Her baby was sent away to be cared for.'

'The baby being Sheila?'

'You have done your homework. I gather Sheila chummed up with my brother a few years later.'

Chummed up was one way of putting it. But how did she know? She hadn't seen Xander for fifty years and it didn't sound as if they'd kept up with Joshua's family either, never mind the Brysons. He still didn't see where today's funeral was going to fit in. Ailish must have read his thoughts.

'I can see you're puzzled,' she said. 'So before we get to the funeral, I need to tell you about a visit I had recently. From an unpleasant little man called Orlando Bryson. Sheila's son apparently.'

She'd met him? 'Yes,' he said. 'I know of him. From what my police contact tells me he's a lot more than unpleasant. He operates some kind of business that deals in contract violence. Beating up debtors and unwanted tenants. Why did he visit you?' How had he even found her?

'Same reason as you. He wanted to know where the ring was.'

'When was this?' he asked.

'A couple of weeks ago.'

After he had been to see her, but before the attack on Anna. Also before she published her blog. 'And what did you tell him?'

'I told him what I told you. That I hadn't got it.'

'And he believed you? He didn't...'

'Beat me up? Intimidate me? No. I just showed him the door.'

'And he left? Just like that without any fuss?'

'I made it pretty clear that I wouldn't stand for any nonsense.'

He could believe that. She was probably a head and shoulders taller than Bryson and certainly had a history of taking care of herself. Had Bryson found Ailish the same way he had? He would have seen Joshua's name on Anna's family tree, and also that of Pete Lymington. So he knew that Joshua had a son. How did he know that Ailish and Joshua were partners? They'd never married so there were no marriage records. But he could have found Pete's birth certificate. He felt a chill run down his spine. The same feeling he'd had at the museum. That someone was shadowing him. Just a few steps behind him and waiting to catch up.

'He did leave with one parting shot though,' Ailish continued. 'He told me he was my nephew. Does he have any reason to believe he might be?'

So that must be how she knew about Sheila and Xander. And that was why she was here. She wanted to know if there could be any truth in what he said. 'Sheila spent part of one summer at Drumlychtoun when she was studying botany,' he told her. 'And yes, she had an affair with your brother. Alexander confirms that but seems to think that he can't be Orlando's father. Even Sheila isn't sure. Apparently, there are other contenders. She seems to have spent a good many nights in sleeping bags with a number of different men.'

'Well, I suppose a DNA test would clear it up if Bryson starts any kind of claim over the ring, or Drumlychtoun. But to get back to the funeral...' At that moment they were told their table was ready. 'We'll take our drinks with us and I can tell you all about it over lunch.'

They were seated at a table with a view of the castle which towered above them on its rock. It was illegal to climb the rock. The thought of ever climbing it made Ian wince. It was a sheer cliff face of volcanic rock. It hardly needed to be illegal. Impossible was closer to the mark.

It was a good meal. They knew how to cook a steak here. He watched Ailish eating her salad and wondered if she was a vegetarian. It seemed likely. He hoped that having to watch him tucking into a slab of Angus beef wasn't upsetting her. But if it was, she was keeping tactfully silent.

'So,' said Ailish, as she put her fork down and took a sip of her drink. 'The funeral. I can see you're itching to ask me about it.'

'I'm interested to know why you want me there.' She certainly didn't need him. She was more than capable of finding her own way around Edinburgh. And she didn't seem too bereft and in need of a sympathetic shoulder to lean on. He couldn't imagine that was something she ever needed.

'I'm here to be with an old friend of mine,' she said. 'Her name is Janet Munro. Her mother, Mary, was a friend of Gideon's, widowed when Janet was a baby.'

Ah, he thought. A Remington connection.

'Mary was left with very little to live on,' Ailish continued. 'And it was at Gideon's suggestion that she fostered Sheila Bryson for a fee when Joyce was taken ill. Sheila stayed with them until her mother died a few years later and she returned to live with her father. That was around the time Joshua and I met. Joshua and Janet had been friends since they were children. Janet moved to London a year or two after we did and she and I became friends. She was very good to me when Joshua died and that's why I want to be with her now.'

Ailish looked at her watch. It was time to go. There was so much more that Ian wanted to talk about, but they couldn't be late for the funeral, so he went to reception and asked them to bring his car round to the door.

.   .   .

It was a simple funeral with only a handful of mourners. Ailish greeted Janet with a hug and they went into the chapel arm in arm. They sang a couple of hymns to a wheezy organ accompaniment in the rather embarrassed faltering way that small gatherings do. Then they listened to someone who had volunteered with Mary at a local charity shop. Janet read a poem about a small bird escaping from a cage. Then they all filed out to the strains of Nimrod, piped over a crackling PA system.

There was to be a small gathering for tea at a nearby house. Owned by a friend of Janet's, he supposed, or perhaps a friend of the deceased. Or perhaps people who lived near crematoria ran lucrative little businesses in providing afternoon teas for mourners.

Ailish introduced Ian to Janet as her companion, which amused him. He didn't think companion as a job existed any more. It made him think of plain, unmarried daughters from families who had fallen on hard times and who had no way of earning a living. They were condemned to sit around reading to irascible old ladies and writing letters for them. Not a career path he'd ever considered. But he was relieved she hadn't described him as an escort.

'Ailish tells me you want to know more about Sheila Bryson,' said Janet, sitting down next to Ian, who was now perching a cup of tea and a very small cucumber sandwich on his lap.

Had he said that? Sheila did have a way of popping up unexpect-edly during this case. 'I met her recently,' he said. 'It was an enquiry on behalf of a client who had known her when she was a student.'

'Poor Sheila,' said Janet. 'I always felt sorry for her. Even as a little girl. She'd been shunted off by her family when her mother was ill. No explanation and only very occasional visits from her father.'

'Did you keep in touch?'

'A little. Not so much once I'd moved to London. There was always this cloud hanging over her. A fear that mental illness could be inherited. It can't have been easy living with a father who was constantly looking out for some sign that she was going the same way as her mother. It became a little easier for her after her father died and it was just her and George. He was a lot older, but I think they were fond of each other. But she was always a bit unconventional. And then she got pregnant and wouldn't or couldn't say who the father was. But dear old George put up with all of that. Even gave the son a job when he left school.'

'That was Orlando?'

'Yes. God knows what happened to him. He soon ran the business into the ground. He's probably in prison by now.'

If only, thought Ian. He put his teacup down on a nearby table. 'I shouldn't be taking your time like this. I'm so sorry for your loss. My grandfather died recently so I know a little of what you must be feeling.'

She smiled sadly at him. 'Thank you,' she said. 'But I'm glad you could come. It was lovely to see Ailish again. And actually, talking about something other than funerals and wills was rather soothing.'

Ailish signalled to him that it was time to leave. She hugged Janet and made her promise that she would visit her in London soon.

'Do you still want to take the tram?' Ian asked as they walked to the car. 'There's a stop quite near.'

She looked at her watch. 'I think I'll leave the tram for another visit. If we drive to the airport now, we'll have time for a quick drink before my flight.'

She was thinking of visiting again? After a gap of more than fifty years that was interesting. Perhaps she would come for a longer stay next time. Janet hadn't said what her immediate plans were, but she'd miss her mother and would probably welcome visits from Ailish. He also hoped she had plans to visit Drumlychtoun and patch things up with her brother. It hadn't been Xander's fault that Ailish and her father didn't get on. Xander was probably nothing like his father and it would be sad if they didn't have a chance to get to know each other. And what about Anna? Wouldn't Ailish be proud of a feisty granddaughter? Her own flesh and blood and a link to her son. She'd not said a word about Pete, so he had no idea how she felt about him and his death. Was she really the type to bear lifelong grudges? It seemed she was, which he found sad.

Ailish studied the departure board. 'There's over an hour before we board,' she said. 'Can I buy you a drink? We can have a chat while I'm waiting.'

He bought her a gin and tonic and himself an orange juice. A gin and tonic would have been nice. But while all Ailish had to do was get on a plane, he had a long drive ahead of him and he would be getting caught up in the rush to escape over the bridge.

They found comfortable chairs by a window from where they could watch planes arriving. Ailish sat down with a sigh and took a gulp of her drink. 'Funerals are draining, aren't they?'

He agreed. He'd knocked back a few whiskeys after Grandad's funeral. Even after today's funeral he felt tired and he hadn't known anyone involved in it.

'I suppose they remind us that we're all mortal,' said Ailish. 'More so the nearer we get to our own deaths.'

He looked at her - tall and elegant and apparently in robust good health. 'You've got years to go yet,' he said. 'You're just a spring chicken.'

'More like an old boiler,' she said, laughing. 'I've had to live with loss and all the grief that goes with it, but today's made me aware that I have a family and I should start building bridges. And not just with my brother. You know I have a granddaughter?'

He nodded. 'I've met Anna. She came to find me after I visited you.'

'Did she? Why?'

'She thought you were one of my clients and she wanted to know why.' Ailish was looking puzzled. 'She'd seen my card in your flat,' he explained. 'I'm only a bus ride from St Andrews. She turned up on my doorstep the day after she got back from London.'

'Cheeky little monkey. What did you tell her?'

'At first nothing. I told her client information was confidential.'

'But I wasn't your client.'

'We discovered that. She saw the press cuttings I had about you and I had to tell her I was working for your brother, not for you. I'm sorry, I should be more careful not to have things like that where people can see them, but it's so rare that anyone just drops in like that, I didn't have time to think.'

Ailish shrugged. 'Not a problem, I've never kept any of the press stuff a secret.'

If anything, she was probably rather proud of it. 'Anna appointed herself my assistant for the day. We helped each other with some research. Anna's very into family history and I was able to fill in some Lyton details for her. And she...' He paused.

'Go on.'

'She told me about her father. You'd said very little about him. I thought he must have died when he was a baby.'

She nodded sadly. 'I thought it was none of your business,' she said. 'Although of course it was. My brother had asked you to find me. I'm guessing he's thinking about who inherits Drumlychtoun. And of course, it was news to me that he had no children. Pete would have been his heir but I couldn't bring myself to talk about that. It's all too raw. And when you saw me I didn't know about Anna.'

'Would that have made a difference?'

'I think so, although that was a bit of a shock. She's a lovely girl and I didn't give her the time she deserved.' She put her drink down. 'I must put that right,' she said firmly. 'I've spent far too many years being angry with my son. It's time to forgive. I only hope he would have forgiven me. And that Anna does as well.'

'I'm sure she will. She was thrilled to find she had a family – a connection to her father.'

'Has she met my brother?'

'Yes. She was a big hit with him and his wife.' How would that make Ailish feel? 'If you want to go to Drumlychtoun, I'd be happy to drive you there.'

'I need to think about that,' she said, draining her glass. 'I'm not ready yet.'

'Or we could go and see Anna. You could catch a later flight.'

She shook her head. 'It's been a long day and I need to get home.'
He could understand that. 'I'll write to Anna. Do you have her email?'

He ripped a page out of his notebook and wrote it down for her.
He wrote Adrian's address as well. 'She's staying with her boyfriend's
family right now,' he said.

'Lucky girl. Are they nice, the family? Have you met them?'

'I have and they're delightful.' Should he tell Ailish why Anna was
staying with them? He decided not to. They had no proof that Bryson
was behind it and he didn't want to worry her.

'She's lucky,' said Ailish. 'If Joshua and I'd been closer to our
families things could have turned out very differently. Not that I
regret any of it. We had a wonderful life together. But we cut
ourselves off and it wasn't good for any of us, least of all my son.' She
took a tissue out of her bag and dabbed at her eyes.

It was the first time she'd shown any kind of emotion. It must
have taken a lot to tell him that. He suspected this was the gin talking.
'Ailish, can I ask you something?'

She nodded.

'Did Joshua take the ring?'

She looked him in the eye. 'I honestly don't know. He could have
done. He knew about it of course. I think I even showed it to him one
time.'

'Morag told me the two of you used to sneak into the castle.'

'Morag? Good God, is she still alive?'

'Very much so. In her late nineties and still with a razor-sharp
memory. She told me you had a boyfriend who rode a motorbike. She
couldn't remember his name though. Only that it was biblical.' He
paused, wondering whether to ask his next question. 'Do you think
Joshua made the copy?'

'He had the opportunity and the skills. But if he did, he never told
me and I didn't find it after he died. He could have sold it, I suppose.
And if my brother has the fake, I don't suppose we'll ever know where
the original is.'

He took both her hands in his. 'Anna has it,' he said. 'Her father
left it to her with a letter. I can only assume that Joshua gave it to him.

Anna's mother told her about a meeting they had at the hospital shortly before he died.'

'I don't remember much about that time. I know that sometimes it got a bit much for me and Joshua would pack me off home to rest. There were times during his last few days when I wasn't with him. It would be so like Joshua to get in touch with Pete without telling me because he knew how hurt and guilty I felt.' She smiled at him. 'You really are a good detective,' she said.

'I had a lot of luck,' he said. And then he laughed. 'Seeing Anna with the ring nearly gave poor Alexander a heart attack.'

'If you see Alexander, tell him I'll be in touch soon.' Her flight was called. 'Thank you for today,' she said. 'And not just for today.' She gathered up her raincoat and walked to the departure gate. Turning at the last minute, she smiled and blew him a kiss.

Ian returned to his car and slapped another few pounds onto his credit card. Traffic was heavy and it took him longer than usual to reach Queensferry and cross into Fife. After just a few months it surprised him that Fife felt more like home than Edinburgh ever had.

It had been quite a day. Ailish was surprisingly good company. He wasn't sure that he had learnt a lot apart from confirming that Joshua was indeed a link to the Brysons. It was probably time he wound it all up and sent Xander his final report. He was still in doubt about Anna's safety but that was a problem for the police. He'd keep an eye on things but he'd do it because he was fond of Anna. There was no way he would bill Xander for that.

He'd been driving for an hour and was close to home when he reached a familiar junction. One road leading to Greyport, the other to Cupar. Lottie, he decided, would be fine with Lainie for an hour or two longer. What he needed now was a break from anything related to Drumlychtoun. He swung right and headed to Cupar, where Caroline lived.

'What a nice surprise,' said Caroline as she opened the door. 'Is Lottie with you?'

'Only me, I'm afraid. I wondered if you felt like going out for a meal or a drink. I've had a bit of a long day and could do with unwinding.'

'Me too. School's been hell today. How about phoning out for something and spending the evening here?'

'That sounds wonderful.' He had the very pleasant thought that he might call Lainie and ask her to keep Lottie overnight.

19

Perhaps he should offer his services as an escort more often. He could specialise in funerals, market himself as professional mourner. He could buy a black suit and provide a rock-like arm for grievers. That was pretty much all he'd done yesterday and he'd been paid by the hour for it. And he got a good lunch thrown in, not to mention a cup of tea and sandwiches. But he supposed it would all get rather repetitively dull after a while. And there were certainly worse ways of making a living than what he was doing now. The last few weeks had brought some fascinating people into his life: a charming laird and his down to earth, no nonsense wife, a lively student with an interest in genealogy and a passion for dogs, a founder member of women's lib and a potential rogues gallery of jewellery thieves and hitmen. He'd have a hard time finding a new case that had enthralled him as much as this one. Which reminded him that he needed to finish his report and email it off to Xander.

He tapped a key and his computer screen sprang to life with a portrait of Lottie proudly held up by its artist, a beaming (now seven-year-old) Jessie. Jessie's mother had taken the photo and emailed it to him. He was glad it was the picture of Lottie and not the one of him with one leg shorter than the other. He downloaded a few emails, none of which, disappointingly, offered him new and exciting cases. After Drumlychtoun any case was going to seem dull.

He opened the Drumlychtoun folder and copied in the notes he had made after his day in Edinburgh. The case was coming to an end and he wanted to sign off in a way that was more personal than just sending a report and his final invoice. He composed an email to Xander and Bridget. He wanted to tell them about Ailish's day in Edinburgh, but it didn't feel right putting that in a report. She wanted to build bridges, he told them. But left it there. He couldn't do more than that. It wasn't any of his business, but he hoped they would find a way to be a family again. If anyone could do it, Bridget was the one to get things moving.

He told them how much he had enjoyed the case. He hadn't been able to explain everything, but he thought he had done as much as he could. Remington had both the means and opportunity and they would probably never know for certain that he had taken the ring, but that seemed the most likely explanation. He added that he believed Ailish when she said she didn't know one way or the other.

Bryson was still a loose end, but the matter of his paternity was something between him and Xander should either of them want to pursue it further. The only certainty would be a DNA test and since Bryson and Xander didn't exactly mix in the same social circles, it seemed unlikely that it would ever happen.

He signed off a little sadly, hoping that one day they would meet again. Then he drew up a list of expenses and attached it, along with his bill, to the email. He clicked send and apart from an anticipated payment into his bank account, assumed this was the last he would hear from them.

He returned to his inbox. He needed work even if it did mean going back to the humdrum stuff he was used to. There were a few enquiries, and he was trying to decide between a background check for a slightly dodgy sounding job application for the post of after school activities assistant, and a man who suspected his daughter's boyfriend was, in his words, up to no good, when there was a knock at the door. Lottie started her usual yapping and skidding routine and he picked her up and went to see who it was. The postman, who usually slipped the mail through the letterbox and ran, had decided to brave Lottie and was standing on the doorstep with a parcel. It was the box he had posted to Sheila just the other day. It had been stamped *Recipient unknown. Return to sender - excess charge for non delivery £3.50.*

Ian paid the money and took it inside. Very strange. He knew the address was correct and he had seen Sheila there recently. He felt uneasy about it. She hadn't looked well and was obviously drinking too much. He tried unsuccessfully to find a number for the Elsbeth Mackay community. He had no urgent work this morning. He'd go there and check that Sheila was all right. It was a long drive but there didn't seem to be any alternative. And there was something that might make the drive worthwhile. He picked up his phone and called Elsa Curran.

'Hi,' she said. 'This is a nice surprise.'

He told her about the returned parcel. 'I'm a bit worried about Sheila. Do you fancy a drive to Balloch with me? We could get a spot of lunch up there. Or are you too busy with work?'

'I could get away for a bit,' she said. 'I was planning to descale the shower heads, but they can wait another day.'

'It's wall to wall fun running a B&B, isn't it?'

'It sure is, but I daresay I can tear myself away just this once.'

Ian looked at his watch. 'Can I pick you up in an hour and a half?'

'Sure. It'll give me time to glam up a bit.'

'Scrub the drain cleaner off your hands?'

'Something like that.'

'Do you mind if my dog comes too?' Poor Lottie hadn't had much attention from him recently.

'Not at all. We can take it for a walk by the loch.'

'She'd enjoy that,' he said. His day had suddenly brightened up. They'd probably find that Sheila was fine. That there had been some sort of mix up over the address, or the postman had been too lazy to climb the hill with it and marked it to be returned. Once he'd reassured himself, he'd treat the day as a holiday – an afternoon of good food and good company. He'd had quite a lot of that recently, he realised. Things were looking up.

Just like the last time he'd visited, the artists' community was still lacking in artists. It was a nice day. Why weren't they sitting outside their cabins with paints and easels enjoying the view and having deep discussions about perspectives and light, or whatever it was artists discussed? Surely the whole idea of living in a community like this was the like-minded company it provided. But here the residents seemed to communicate even less than the buttoned-up inhabitants of Morningside, who rarely did anything as normal as chatting over garden fences and regarded neighbours as more or less invisible.

Ian prised open the gate and he and Elsa trudged up to Sheila's cabin. Lottie strained at her lead. Fields usually meant freedom to run around and chase things, but Ian thought it safer not to let her. Who knew how many rottweilers were hidden away inside the cabins. Not likely. Artists probably went for more gentle pets, but he couldn't be sure, and it wasn't worth taking a risk. Lottie could have her freedom later.

Reaching Sheila's cabin, Ian knocked loudly but there was no reply. He left Elsa and Lottie at the door and wandered around peering through windows, but the place looked empty. He explored a small area of garden behind the cabin and noticed a man with some nails in his mouth repairing the fence behind Sheila's garden.

'She's gone,' said the man, removing the nails.

'Gone where?'

The man shrugged. 'Paid up to the end of the month and said she was leaving. A bloke came and took her in a car.'

A bloke? Could it have been Orlando? 'What did this bloke look like?'

'Regular sort of bloke.'

Not helpful, although if he'd had to describe Orlando, regular sort of bloke was probably what he would have said, so it could have been him. It seemed unlikely, but perhaps Orlando had suddenly discovered a streak of filial affection. Could Sheila be moving in with him? 'Did she have a lot of luggage?' he asked.

'Just her laptop bag. She said to clear out the cabin, help myself to what I wanted and burn the rest.'

Even stranger, but there wasn't much he could do about it. He wasn't going to track down a character of known violent disposition to return a box of old letters and photographs. And at least it sounded as if Sheila was okay. She wasn't lying on the floor of the cabin in a drunken stupor. He should feel relieved about that. Anything else Sheila did with her life was none of his business.

He returned to Elsa, who was sitting on the doorstep of the cabin with Lottie on her lap. 'I'm sorry,' he said. 'She's not here, but it sounds as if she's okay. It's all been a bit of a waste of time.'

'Not really. We can still get lunch. It's lovely down by the loch.'

'Bit of a poor substitute for descaling shower heads.'

She laughed. 'I can live with that. They'll still be there tomorrow.'

They returned to the car and drove back to the village where they found a pub. They ordered food and Ian tried to put Sheila out of his mind. He'd done what he could, hadn't he? More than most would have done, probably. All the same, he felt uneasy and when the food arrived, he stared at it wondering if he was actually hungry.

Elsa reached across and took his hand. 'You've done all you can,' she said, sympathetically. 'You'll not help her by picking at your food like that.'

She was right. And more importantly he didn't want to spoil what looked like being a very pleasant afternoon. He smiled at Elsa and tucked into his lunch.

It had been a grey, damp morning but as they finished eating the sun came out and the water of the loch sparkled. 'Come on,' said Elsa, jumping up and grabbing his hand. 'Time for a walk. We should make the most of this glorious weather.'

They walked along the shore of the loch and watched the boats coming and going. Elsa looked at her watch. 'I've to be home by five,' she said. 'We've new guests checking in. But there's time for a boat trip, isn't there? It's only an hour and it says dogs are welcome.'

. . .

When had he last been on a boat? he wondered, leaning on the rail and watching the far side of the loch as it came closer. Probably not since he was a kid. He didn't have particularly happy memories of boating. It usually involved family squabbles, damp clothes and stories of drownings. But this was quite different, standing shoulder to shoulder with Elsa, the warm sun on his back as they were rocked gently in the breeze and little waves slapped against the side of the boat. It was still early in the season but there were a few groups of tourists taking photographs, one little boy shouting that the log he'd seen on the far bank was a crocodile. Elsa handed her phone to one of the passengers who took a photograph of the two of them with Lottie sitting at their feet, posing like a famous model deigning to have her picture taken with the common herd. Ian held her lead firmly. Lottie loved the water and he didn't want her jumping overboard. The safety check hadn't mentioned dog rescue procedures and he didn't feel like finding out. And if she got wet the car would smell dreadful all the way back to Glasgow and Elsa would never want to go anywhere with him again.

He dropped Elsa off outside White Lodge at exactly five o'clock. She kissed him on the cheek. 'Lovely day,' she said. 'We must do it again some time.'

That would be something to look forward to, he thought as he pulled out of the drive and headed home.

They were home a little before seven. Lottie wolfed down a bowl of dog food and retired sleepily to her bed, where she snored loudly. She'd had a good day too. He wondered if she'd ever been on a boat before. Boats and Stephanie didn't seem a good fit, so probably not. He liked the idea that he was introducing Lottie to new experiences – and new people, although that was more for him than Lottie.

He turned on his computer and found an email from Bridget.

Dear Ian,

Thank you for everything and your final report. We've paid your bill. Money should be in your account very soon. Lovely news about Ailish. We will write to her, hoping she might come and visit soon.

Xander and I feel a little sad. You've done so much for us and now it's all over. With Anna heading back to France soon we thought we might have a celebration – a ceilidh here at Drumlychtoun a week on Saturday. All the trimmings – a band, dancing, hog roast, the lot. Do say you'll come. Dress up in your finery and dance the night away. You'll see the castle at its very best. Anna's going to love it and we gather she's now got a boyfriend – very exciting! And do bring someone yourself. I'm sure you have a lady friend hovering in the background somewhere. See you soon. Bridget.

Lady friend – that word again. Why was he too old for a girlfriend?

Wait a minute, he thought. A few short months ago he'd been a down at heel divorcé with a girlfriend who had ditched him for a singer from New Zealand. Now he had two rather beautiful women who actually liked spending time with him. Were they girlfriends or lady friends? And how the hell was he supposed to know the difference?

20

T hey could see that something special was happening the moment they left the village and drove over the bridge. Every window of the castle was lit. Someone, for some reason Ian thought it was likely to have been Sandy, the work experience girl, had rigged up coloured floodlights on the edge of the illuminated walls, which sent waves of colour across the water. The bridge itself was decorated with coloured lights and after crossing it they were directed to a car park behind the castle by two teenage boys with torches. A short walk brought them to the double doors at the back of the great hall.

'Wow,' said Caroline, as she and Ian stepped inside and looked around. It did look amazing. Always a spectacular room with its giant fireplace, wood panelling, huge heads of stags with antlers gazing down from the walls, giant oak table and chairs. Tonight it looked incredible. Lit by candles, the huge table pushed to one side and loaded with food: pewter dishes of cold ham and chicken, a poached salmon on a china platter, earthenware bowls of salad, fruit piled high on dishes, flagons of wine and glass jugs with iced water. And that wasn't all. There was a mouth-watering smell wafting in from a terrace where the hog was roasting over a spit. He'd expected it to be roasting in the open fireplace, but it was a warm evening, and the heat would be overpowering. Perhaps he would be invited back for Hogmanay or Burns Night when venison would be in season.

In the gallery three musicians were playing while people danced in the room below.

'How do they get up there?' Caroline asked. 'It's not a long way but I don't imagine they have to climb over the rail.'

She was right. The band were only a few feet above the dance floor. 'You see the curtains at the back?' he asked. 'They're hiding a couple of doors. One on each side. One has stairs down to the kitchen. The other leads straight into the hall. There's a door over there behind one of those curtains.' He pointed to the far side of the hall where a tartan curtain ran the length of the wall.

'How do you know?' she asked.

'Xander gave me the full tour the first time I came here.'

'Xander's the Laird?'

'Yes,' he said. 'Come and meet him.' He took her hand and edged round the room to where Xander and Bridget were standing watching the dancers and chatting to guests. He hadn't expected so many people. Everyone who worked on the estate, he assumed. He wondered if Anna was here yet. Robin was borrowing his father's car for the evening but Ian still worried about her safety. What if she was being watched? Could they have been followed? It would be easy enough to waylay them on a quiet stretch of road. Would Anna still be carrying her alarm? But then he spotted them and sighed with relief. They had arrived safely. Now he only needed to worry about them getting home again. He shouldn't let that stop him enjoying the evening, but there were so many people here.

'Ian,' said Bridget, suddenly noticing him and greeting him with a kiss. 'So lovely to see you. Both of you,' she said, extending a hand to Caroline.

'I've heard so much about you,' said Caroline. 'And about the castle and how beautiful it is. Ian's told me all about it, but seeing the real thing, well...' She poked him in the ribs. 'Ian, are you looking for someone?'

'Are you okay?' Bridget asked. 'You seem a bit distracted.'

'What? Yeah, sorry,' he said. 'It's just... Bridget, do you actually know all these people?'

'Most of them.'

'Most of them? Not all of them?'

'Well, some of the people who work on the estate have brought friends with them. A date, I suppose you'd call it. Why?'

'He can't forget what he does for a living,' said Caroline, laughing. 'Always on the lookout for lurking baddies.'

'Oh Ian, you're here to enjoy yourself.' said Bridget. 'Everyone here has had an invitation and I'm sure they can vouch for anyone they brought with them.'

Yeah, he should try and enjoy the evening. They were miles from anywhere, with locals who all knew each other. There'd been no threatening messages on websites. No lurking men in hoodies, no reason why this shouldn't be a lovely relaxed, safe evening. He just wished he didn't have that uneasy feeling, cold shivers running down his spine.

Xander bounded up to them looking every inch a laird; full highland dress tartan, velvet jacket, lace cravat and buckle brogues. 'Come and join the dancing,' he said, slapping Ian on the back. 'I can see you've come prepared.'

'He looks great, doesn't he?' said Caroline. 'Nothing like a good looking man in a kilt.' She took Ian's arm and led him onto the dance floor for the final bars of the Gay Gordons.

'You're rather good at that,' she said as the music stopped.

'Thanks. I think. I'd rather you hadn't sounded quite so surprised about it.'

She laughed and squeezed his arm. 'Sorry. I'm not surprised at all. You're good at all sorts of things. I was just worried your leg might have been a problem.'

That had surprised Rosalie as well. And that was the last time he'd danced, more than ten years ago. But he'd learnt to dance when he was a boy, and it wasn't something one forgot. It was like swimming and riding a bike. He'd not done those recently either and possibly his biking days were over. Swimming had been part of his therapy after the shooting; muscles work well in warm water and it took the weight off his leg. He should do more of that. There was a new pool in Dundee and an early morning swim a few times a week would do him good.

'My leg's fine as long as I don't do too much jumping,' he said. 'Exercise is supposed to help and it's nice doing it to music.'

'More Strathspey than sword dance, then?'

He nodded. 'Do you like swimming?' he asked.

'What?'

'Swimming.'

'Here in the lake? I didn't think it was that kind of party.'

He laughed. 'No, it's not. Although I'll throw you into the lake if you like.'

'I'd really rather you didn't. But why did you ask?'

'You were asking about my leg and it reminded me that one of the best ways to help it is swimming. I thought I might take it up again. We could go together.'

'As long as it's in a nice warm pool and not the sea.'

This was a stupid conversation. Why had he started it? He really should learn to keep himself on track. Here he was on a beautiful evening in a wonderful place with an attractive woman who actually seemed to enjoy his company. Well, she probably wouldn't for much longer if he kept wittering on like that. Luckily the band leader chose that moment to interrupt their conversation by announcing an eight-some reel. It was once of Ian's favourite dances, probably because it was a nice mixture of standing still, clapping and shouting, and a few bars of solo when each dancer in turn had their moment of glory and could be as energetic or gentle as they liked. He watched as well-ordered circles of eight emerged from apparent chaos. He spotted Anna and Robin and beckoned to them to join him.

'I don't know how to do it,' Anna said, laughing.

'It's not hard,' said Robin. 'Just follow us.'

. . .

Ian was quite sorry when the music finished, but then remembered that it was traditional for this dance to be followed by a supper break, and Xander and Bridget were nothing if not traditional. He was right. As the final chord sounded, Bridget snapped her fingers and four men appeared from the terrace carrying trays of roast pork. They marched through the crowd of guests towards the tables, which were already groaning with food, and set down their trays.

'Help yourselves,' Bridget said, glancing up to the gallery where the band had already put their instruments down and were looking hungrily down at the tables of food. 'There's a meal for the band in the kitchen. I need to show them the way.' She slipped behind the curtain, appearing a moment later in the gallery where she held the door open for the band to make their way down to the kitchen. Ian was sure a magnificent meal would be waiting for them. They definitely deserved it.

Ian and Caroline loaded plates with food and, following the majority of the other guests, wandered out onto the terrace where after all the dancing, it was refreshingly cool. *A perfect evening,* Ian thought as they perched on a small wall overlooking the lake. 'Glad you came?' he asked, smiling at Caroline. Not that there had been any doubt. She'd jumped at the chance to see Drumlychtoun and tonight she was seeing it at its glorious best.

Xander appeared carrying a bottle of wine. He topped up their glasses and sat on the wall next to them. 'Going well, I think,' he said, looking around at groups of people who were chatting and laughing.

'Do you have a lot of parties here?' Caroline asked.

'We always have one like this in the summer for the estate partners and their families.'

'And you've enlarged your family since last summer,' said Ian, looking at Anna and Robin who were with Sandy and another young man.

'We're so pleased to have Anna with us this year. The cherry on the cake, you might say. We did hope Ailish might come. Bridget sent her an invitation, but we've not heard from her.'

'She didn't say when she would be in touch,' said Ian. 'Perhaps she'd prefer to come when it's quieter.'

'Maybe,' said Xander. 'She knows she's welcome to come whenever she likes.' He stood up and picked up his bottle. 'I'd better keep going,' he said. 'More glasses to fill.'

He looked disappointed, Ian thought. Had he been counting on Ailish being here? Or was he thinking about Anna returning to her family in France? Reminded perhaps of the nephew he would never meet.

People were beginning to drift back into the hall.

'What happens next?' Caroline asked.

'More dancing, I suppose.' He drained the last of his drink. He was ready for more dancing. His leg felt nicely oiled and up for more.

They went back into the hall and Ian glanced up, expecting to see the band back in the gallery warming up their instruments.

That wasn't what he saw. And it took a moment to realise what he *was* seeing. There were no musicians. Only the figures of a man and a woman. Orlando Bryson, he realised in a horrified flash of recognition. Bryson had a gun, and with an even greater sense of horror Ian realised that the woman was Bridget and that Bryson was pointing the gun at her head. He had pushed her towards the rail at the edge of the gallery and pulled her arms behind her back. Ian had to do something. There was a high level of chatter in the hall and no one had noticed them yet. He needed some way of distracting Bryson before anyone saw the gun and started to panic. Ian tried to work out a plan. Bryson was staring down into the hall. Ian could edge his way to the curtain without being seen, climb the stairs and sneak into the gallery through the right hand door where Bryson would have his back to him. Would he be able to grab the gun? Or was it too risky?

He was just starting to move towards the curtain when the gun went off. The guests were suddenly silent. None of them looked particularly worried, he noticed, puzzled until he realised they probably thought this was some kind of surprise cabaret. Something like the murder mystery events that were quite popular in Scottish castles right now. He turned away from the curtain and looked up at the gallery, terrified of what he would see. But Bryson had fired up at the ceiling and now had the gun aimed once more at Bridget's head. It was attention he had wanted.

Everyone had edged to the back of the hall for a better view, except Xander who stood helplessly below the gallery, staring up. He was only a few inches away from Ian who had slipped back behind the curtain. 'Keep him talking,' Ian whispered to Xander, hoping he was not frozen into speechlessness with shock.

'What do you want?' Xander called up to Bryson in a voice that was surprisingly calm in the circumstances. Bryson looked down at him and smirked. This was Ian's chance. He noticed that Anna and Robin were standing quite close to him and signalled that he was going up to the gallery. It was lucky he'd remembered enough about the castle to know that there were two staircases. Explaining to Caroline just now had jogged his memory. Bryson must have slipped into the castle by the kitchen door and seen Bridget and the band come down from the gallery. He would have waited until they settled down to their meal, followed Bridget out of the kitchen, grabbed her and climbed back up to the gallery with her.

Ian didn't have much of a plan. He was armed only with his kilt pin, which wouldn't be much use against a man with a gun. But of the two doors the one he was using was tucked away at the back of the gallery and with any luck he could creep in behind Bryson without being noticed. He climbed the stairs and opened the door very slowly, hoping it wouldn't creak. He had a good view down to the hall. Xander had stopped talking and was staring speechlessly up at the gallery. Not surprising. It was a terrifying situation. But Ian needed him to keep Bryson talking.

Luckily at that moment Anna stepped forward. 'You're Orlando, aren't you?' she said.

He stared down at her and nodded. 'Ah, little miss perfect, the granddaughter.'

'Great-niece, actually,' said Anna.

Just go with granddaughter if that's what he wants. Ian tried not to feel impatient with her. She was bravely doing her best. And perhaps a discussion about family relationships would keep Bryson occupied.

'I know you want the ring,' Anna continued. 'You've been leaving me messages, haven't you?'

'Which you never answered.'

'I'm sorry. That was rude of me.'

'Yes, it was.'

'I'll give it to you if you let Bridget go.'

Ian watched as she slid her hand into her pocket. Clever girl. He knew she didn't have the ring in her pocket. He could see the chain round her neck, but she must have tucked the ring down inside her dress out of the way when she was dancing. What she did keep in her pocket was her panic alarm. How long would it take the police to get here? They were miles from anywhere. How long could they wait like this and how long could they keep him talking? What would they do if Bryson accepted Anna's offer? The ring was safely locked away in a bank in Edinburgh, but Bryson obviously didn't know that. Could they head him off with the fake? That could be very dangerous once he discovered the ring was not the original. But that was a discovery Xander hadn't made for fifty years. Could they take the chance that it would take Bryson just as long? Ian doubted it. Getting it authenticated would probably be the first thing he did. No, he'd have to work out a way of getting the gun off him before it came to that.

'Nah,' said Bryson. 'Keep your poxy ring.'

'So what do you want?' Anna asked.

'I want what you've got.'

Anna looked puzzled.

'I'm your cousin,' he said.

There was a gasp from the guests. This was turning out to be some cabaret.

'Didn't know that, did you? Thought you'd inherit all of this. Well, I've got news for you darlin'. That's my dad standing next to you.'

Another gasp from the riveted guests.

'What I want,' continued Bryson, 'is for him to acknowledge me. Sign this place over to me as his successor.'

Ian couldn't wait much longer. If only he could distract Bryson long enough to aim the gun away from Bridget, he could grab him from behind and wrestle him to the ground. But he couldn't risk it yet.

Something moved to his right. He turned slightly so that he could see the door while still not letting Bryson out of his sight. The door was opening. For a moment he thought he was hallucinating as he watched Ailish edge her way into the gallery – creeping very quietly and gradually towards Bryson. As she sidled into the room, Ian saw that she was carrying an iron grappling hook. It was one of a number of nasty looking weapons hanging on the walls of the staircase. She must have heard Bryson from the stairs and grabbed it to protect herself. It was a vicious looking thing. An iron bar with a sharpened barb on the end like an outsize fishing hook. Tackling an armed man, even with a thing like that, was not a good idea. He tried to wave her back but she either hadn't seen him or didn't intend to take any notice.

As he was wondering what to do, his attention was drawn to the double doors at the back of the hall, where two men in black hoodies had just entered. Bryson glanced towards them and nodded. 'Okay, lads,' he said.

One of them pulled out a knife and waved it at the crowd, who backed away in alarm.

Bryson waved the gun backwards and forwards between Xander and Bridget. 'So who's it to be? Daddy or wifey?' He turned and swung the gun towards Xander. 'Admit I'm your son and heir and I'll let her go.' He raised his arm and aimed at Xander.

'You're not his son.' Ailish stepped forward. Bryson turned his head and the gun went off. In the seconds of confusion that followed, she grabbed the grappling iron in both hands, swung it to her right and then forcefully left, catching Bryson with a powerful blow on the side of his head. Bryson dropped the gun and sank to the floor. Ian leapt forward and kicked it out of the way, kneeling down next to Bryson, who groaned. Thank God she hadn't killed him. There was no blood so she must have hit him with the flat side of the hook.

What would have happened if she'd gouged him with the sharp barb, he didn't like to imagine. He yanked off his sporran and used the chain to bind Bryson's wrists behind his back. Ailish took off her belt and tied his feet together.

Having successfully prevented him from escaping, Ian looked down into the hall, where things were no less dramatic. The bullet had thankfully missed Xander but had caught one of the henchmen on the shoulder. He was now on his knees whimpering with pain; his knife had skidded under one of the tables. Ian watched as Caroline tackled the other, wrestling him to the ground helped by two of the other guests. They then hogtied him with a selection of belts. She'd lost none of her self-defence skills, apparently.

With all three of the villains successfully disarmed, there was nothing to do except wait for the police. Ian was just feeling around for his phone, which he realised too late was still in his sporran, when the police stormed in, armed and dressed in full combat gear. They stopped open-mouthed in the doorway. Then one of them stepped forward and pulled off her helmet. She looked around, making the not unreasonable assumption that Xander was the host and shook his hand. 'Inspector Wallace, Montrose rapid response team,' she said, then added scowling, 'Seems we weren't quite rapid enough.'

'Better late than never,' said Xander, graciously. 'We're very pleased to see you.'

Xander, Ian supposed, had been drilled from childhood to be polite in all circumstances. Probably a necessary requirement among the Scottish aristocracy.

Wallace waved two of her team forward and pointed to the men on the floor. 'You know what to do. See to their injuries and get them back to Montrose. Process them and lock them up. And you two,' she said, pointing to two of the others with one hand and up to the gallery with the other. 'Get that man down and do the same with him. The rest of you stay here with me and start taking statements.'

Ian, Ailish and Bridget watched as Bryson, untied and then hand-cuffed, was carried downstairs and out to a police car. Ian picked up the gun gingerly and handed it to one of the police officers who politely returned his sporran to him. He was relieved to see the back of the gun. It had prompted some frightening memories for him. He was, however, very pleased about the return of his sporran.

Bridget peered over down into the hall. Seeing that Xander was unharmed, she brushed herself down and turned to Ailish. 'Thank you,' she said, sounding every bit as polite and gracious as Xander. 'I'm afraid I've no idea who you are but I'm very grateful to you.'

When the police arrived Ailish had discreetly kicked the grappling hook behind the door. Now she brushed some dust from her black velvet dress and rearranged her tartan sash. 'I'm Ailish,' she said, reaching for Bridget's hand and shaking it warmly. 'I assume you are married to my brother.'

Bridget reached out and gathered her into her arms. 'Ailish, it's so wonderful to meet you after all these years.'

It was a touching meeting, but they should probably join the rest of the family. Ian fastened his sporran, checked his phone and suggested that they should go downstairs.

The police had everything well organised, with groups of people sitting at tables giving names, addresses and witness statements. Xander, Anna and Robin were sitting with Inspector Wallace in Xander's sitting room. Seeing Ailish standing in the doorway, Xander stood up and stared at her open-mouthed. 'You came,' he said, once he'd got his breath back.

'It's been a long time, little brother,' she said, smiling. 'If I'd known you were having this much fun I'd have come a lot sooner.'

'Why didn't you let us know?' asked Xander. 'We could have come to meet you.'

'I thought of asking Ian to drive me from Edinburgh. He did offer but I decided to surprise you, so I booked a hire car from the airport.'

'Sorry to interrupt your reunion,' said Wallace impatiently. 'But I need to take statements from you both.' She turned to Bridget. 'You okay, ma'am? There's an ambulance outside. Would you like them to check you over?'

Bridget waved her away. 'I'm fine, thank you. I think we should make tea. All our poor guests…'

'Good idea,' said Wallace. 'And Miss Lymington, is it? Perhaps you would like to give her a hand. While I have a chat to the Laird and… I'm sorry,' she said to Ailish. 'I haven't quite worked out where you fit in.'

'She's my grandmother,' said Anna.

'Right,' said Wallace. 'Perhaps when you've got the tea sorted you could make me a plan of how you all relate to each other. You?' she said, turning to Ian.

'I'm Ian Skair.'

'Are you one of the family? If not, perhaps you could join the others in the hall.'

'He's a close friend,' said Xander. 'Near enough family.' Ailish nodded approvingly. 'And,' Xander continued, 'he's with the young woman who floored one of the thugs.'

'She'd better join us then. Is there anyone else closely connected to the family or can we send everyone else home? Once they've had their tea and left their contact details I don't see any need to detain them.' She looked around. 'You, young man,' she said to Robin. 'You are?'

'Robin Walter. I'm with Anna.'

'Perhaps you could go and tell one of my officers that we need Ms er…'

'Gillespie,' said Ian. 'Caroline.'

'That I need Ms Gillespie to join us.'

'Can I send the band home?' said Xander. 'I don't suppose there'll be any more dancing tonight.'

'Fairly unlikely, I'd say. In the circumstances.'

'Shall I tell them?' Robin offered.

Xander nodded. 'And give them this,' he said, handing Robin an envelope. 'It's their fee.'

Caroline joined them and sat on the sofa with Xander and Ailish. Wallace looked at them sternly.

'Are you going to arrest us?' Ailish asked. Ian thought she looked quite hopeful at the idea.

Wallace shook her head. 'You, sir, have done nothing wrong. Ms Gillespie? Let's say you assumed the man to be armed like his companion and were acting in self-defence. And in any case no injury was inflicted.' She turned to Ailish. 'Carrying some kind of climbing implement? Well, it's not a weapon as such so I'll give you the benefit of the doubt. Let's say you were merely showing an interest in one of the castle's artefacts and just happened to need it to make a citizen's arrest along with Mr Skair here. And as I said earlier my officers and I should have been on the scene sooner.'

'Actually I was surprised you came as soon as you did,' said Ian.

Anna and Bridget arrived with trays of tea, which they handed round. Wallace took a cup and looked at Anna. 'You are the young lady who was mugged in St Andrews?'

Anna nodded. 'They tried to steal my ring.'

'Well,' continued Wallace. 'The local force went through all the ANPR footage for that evening and spotted a couple of men who fitted the description driving a black Honda SUV out of the town at about the right time. An alert was sent out and this evening we picked it up on the Montrose bridge heading south. We tailed it for a few miles but then lost it when it turned off the main road. Then we got the GPS position from Anna's panic alarm, so we were already close. I'm sorry we weren't able to keep up with them, but you all seem to have responded very efficiently, if a little unconventionally. We've made three arrests – all villains we have been watching for some time.' She turned to Xander. 'Do I understand that one of them is your son?'

'Well,' said Xander. 'That's what he thinks.'

'You don't know?'

'I thought it was unlikely, but well, er, not actually impossible.'

'He's not yours,' said Ailish.

They all stared at her.

'We hope he's not,' said Bridget.

'I *know* he's not,' Ailish insisted.

'How can you possibly know?' asked Ian. Did Ailish know where Sheila Bryson was? Had Sheila had a sudden flash of memory and confessed all to her?

It was nothing so interesting. 'When he came to visit me in London I made him a cup of lemon tea,' said Ailish, looking at the cup she was holding and probably realising that she had let caffeine pass her lips for the first time in years. She took another swig. 'He didn't like it and spat some of it out. Very uncouth I thought. As he was leaving, he made that remark about being Xander's son, so I kept the glass and sent it off with some of my hair for a DNA test. The result came back yesterday. He's not related to me, even distantly so he can't be related to Xander either.'

Wallace sighed. 'I'll pretend I didn't hear that,' she said. 'Or I would know that you'd broken the law and I would then have to arrest you. But as I said, I didn't hear it so we'll say no more about it.'

She turned to Xander. 'Bryson's DNA will soon be on the police database. I suggest that you arrange another test but perhaps not mention your sister.' She finished her tea, rounded up her officers and left.

'Well,' said Xander. 'That was an evening to remember. But let's not end it there. There's plenty of food left and I have a few bottles of an excellent single malt. And don't even think of driving home tonight.'

'He's right,' said Bridget. 'We've plenty of bedrooms. Robin, you should call your father and let him know you and Anna are staying.'

'And tell him Bryson's been arrested,' said Ian. 'It'll set his mind at rest.'

'You and Caroline must stay as well,' said Xander.

Ian looked at Caroline and raised a questioning eyebrow. She nodded and smiled at him. 'We'd love to stay,' she said.

'What about Lottie?' asked Anna.

'She's fine,' said Ian. 'Staying the night with Lainie.'

'And I can call my neighbour to look after Angus,' said Caroline.

'Who's Angus?' asked Anna.

'He's Lottie's double,' said Ian.

'Another Lottie?' asked Anna. 'Oh, can I meet him? Please.'

'Of course you can,' said Caroline. 'I live in Cupar. Come and visit us any time you like.'

'Don't forget we're off to France the day after tomorrow,' said Robin. 'We might need to leave it until we're back in September.'

'Let's all go to the beach tomorrow,' said Anna. 'We'll help clear up here in the morning and we can be home by lunchtime. We can have a picnic in the afternoon with the dogs. There's Hector as well. Oh, please say yes.'

'What are your plans, Ailish?' Ian asked. 'Are you up for an afternoon on the beach?'

'I was hoping to stay for a few days if these two can put up with me.'

'Of course we can,' said Bridget. 'You can stay for as long as you like.'

'That's settled then,' said Xander, rubbing his hands. 'I haven't been to a picnic for years. Can we bring our dogs as well?'

'Of course,' said Anna. 'It's going to be perfect. We'll take lots of photos so I can show everyone in France all my lovely new friends and relations.'

Caroline slipped an arm round Ian's shoulder. 'You okay?' she asked. 'You look a bit serious. Has it all been a bit much?'

'It's not that,' he said. 'I was just wondering how Bryson knew about this evening. How did he know that he was going to be here the one night the whole family would be together?'

21

I an had taken a few days off. He deserved it after the weekend; the unexpected drama of the party and then a lively beach picnic with five dogs scampering around, plunging into the sea and then shaking themselves making sure everyone there, not to mention the food, was soaked. Funny how dogs came in such a variety of sizes. Hector was the size of a small pony, Xander's two were middle-sized Labradors, and Lottie and Angus were small – not much bigger than Hector's head. Cats, on the other hand, didn't vary very much. A large cat wasn't so much bigger than a small one. But it had been a fun day and a lovely way to say goodbye to Anna.

The next few days all seemed rather flat and dull. Anna and Robin were on their way to France, Xander and Bridget were catching up with Ailish, Caroline was busy with end of term stuff and Bryson was in prison.

So he'd taken time off. He could do some gardening, take Lottie for walks and Lainie to the shops. He had enough money in the bank for a week or two and no particularly interesting cases in his inbox. The weekend was, as they say on weather forecasts, fast approaching. Why did they say that? Surely weekends, most days in fact, all approached at the same speed. Whatever, he should do something with this weekend. Pack himself and Lottie into the car and head for the highlands perhaps. Find somewhere to stay before the tourist season kicked off in earnest. He did, of course, know of a very nice B&B in Beardsley. But that might not be his wisest decision. No, it would be just him and Lottie. He'd trawl the Internet for a nice, isolated cottage somewhere.

He'd just typed 'highland holiday cottage' into Google when his phone rang. He could ignore it. No one would need him urgently. Or perhaps they would. He wasn't good at ignoring phones, or emails and text messages, or people who called over garden fences or waylaid him in the pub. He glanced at the screen and saw that it was Duncan. Hopefully not phoning to tell him that Bryson had escaped and was heading in his direction for revenge.

He clicked to answer the call.

'Ian,' said Duncan. 'How are you? Recovered from your weekend?'

'I'm fine,' he said. 'Just planning a little holiday.'

'Good for you. But before you go, perhaps we could have a quick word. Kezia's with me. Do you fancy joining us for lunch?'

'Kezia?'

'Inspector Wallace. You met her on Saturday.'

Met didn't seem quite the right word. *Stormed* might be more appropriate. 'I didn't know she was Kezia. We didn't really get to first names. But, yeah, I could do lunch.'

'We'll come to Greyport,' said Duncan. 'See you down at the quayside in about twenty minutes?'

He wouldn't have recognised Kezia Wallace. On Saturday evening she had stormed into Drumlychtoun in full combat gear; full on black, padded sleeves and bullet proof vest, helmet, gloves and facemask. She had taken off her helmet, but her hair had been tied severely back. Now she was wearing jeans and a sweatshirt with a picture of a stag and the words 'deer lives matter' stamped below it. Her hair was loose around her shoulders, and she was wearing make-up. Quite a

change. She was obviously not expecting Greyport to need any kind of rapid response.

The café was quiet. They found a table and ordered toasted sandwiches. Duncan opened a folder. 'Just one or two loose ends we thought you might be able to help with.'

'Duncan told me that the two of you have worked together before,' said Wallace, 'and one or two issues have emerged. We're hoping you can help.'

'We thought lunch here would be less intimidating than an interview at the station,' Duncan added.

Always good to be kept in the loop, Ian thought. But why would he find the station intimidating? He was used to police stations. He used to work in one. 'How's it going with Bryson?' Ian asked.

'He's being extremely co-operative,' said Wallace. 'He's trying to wangle a deal.'

'Really? Does he have anything worth dealing?'

'He does. And it's something we discovered unexpectedly.'

'Interesting,' said Ian.

'It seems Mr Bryson had one redeeming feature,' Duncan added.

That was a surprise. Ian couldn't imagine that Bryson was anything other than a murderous thug.

'It seems he cared about his mother,' said Wallace.

Most people probably did, he supposed. But he couldn't see how that impacted on the case.

'The things is,' said Duncan, opening his folder, 'Bryson was involved with a lot more than having people beaten up.'

'Money laundering,' said Wallace. 'The Glasgow team suspected he might be but it's extremely difficult to find evidence. So many bank accounts involved, mostly overseas ones. Bryson's assets were frozen following his arrest. That's standard practice when fraud is a possibility. It seems that Bryson was paying his mother a monthly allowance and he was worried that with his account frozen these payments might not happen. His solicitor made a good case for allowing them through. Apparently his mother is a near invalid. But when we looked into it further, the account had already been cleared

out. Bryson insisted that there should be around fifty thousand in it, but it had all been filtered out over the last week or two in small payments to a bank in the Cayman Islands. Bryson immediately assumed it was his money laundering associates, an inner circle of four other people. He started naming names and handing over bank details.'

'And were his associates fleecing him?'

'It seems not. We brought them in and all their accounts have been cleared out. They're all furiously accusing each other. We don't know how many more were involved and there's a huge case building for the fraud squad. Bryson's information will certainly help with that. It could be enough to get him into witness protection, but that's out of my hands now.'

'But,' said Duncan, 'we did find something that might interest you.'

Ian couldn't imagine what.

'After Anna's mugging incident, Bryson became a person of interest and his passport was flagged up at all the possible departure points, airports, ferries, international trains, you get the idea. The new microchipped passports are excellent for netting persons of interest.'

'But Bryson's still in Scotland.'

'He is, but the system flags up people with similar names. They're not stopped, just noted. And a certain Sheila Bryson appeared on the departure list for a flight from Glasgow to London a couple of weeks ago. At the time there was no need to take that any further, but since Orlando Bryson was arrested and named his mother as Sheila, we've done a bit of searching and tracked her from London to Madrid. And then from Madrid to Tunisia. Then we lost the trail. The system doesn't work so well outside Europe. She could be anywhere in the world by now.'

'You have to hand it to her,' said Kezia. 'She's not been on our radar at all. All we've found out about her is that she lived on her own near Balloch. For all the world just a harmless, slightly eccentric lady of a certain age.'

'And she seems to have cheated a highly organised money laundering ring out of a very substantial amount of cash,' said Duncan.

Ian suddenly remembered the expensive laptop on Sheila's table. Had she single-handedly hacked her way into a money laundering ring? There must have been more to her than he thought. Was her helpless alcoholic haze just an act? If it was, it had certainly fooled him.

Wallace leaned across the table. 'Now,' she said. 'Does it not strike you as strange that an elderly woman, not by all accounts in the best of health, could pull off something like that without assistance?'

'You think Bryson was in it all along?' Ian asked.

'No,' said Wallace, sighing. 'We don't think that. He seemed as surprised as anyone about the missing money and if he was part of it, some escape fund that he and his mother had put together, why mention it at all?'

'Could she have known someone who was not part of the inner circle but still part of the organisation?'

'Possibly,' said Duncan. 'Obviously not everyone involved has been traced yet.'

'But,' said Wallace, staring at Ian in a way he considered threatening. 'We asked around Balloch hoping to find out more about her. We discovered something interesting – very interesting.'

'Oh yes?' Ian still couldn't work out why they were telling him this.

'Yes, it turns out the residents living near the art colony are not as unobservant as you might have expected. Several of them mentioned a car they had seen on at least two occasions. A man snooping round the cabins, they told us. A couple of them even noted down the registration number.' She took a slow swig of her drink. 'Turns out, Mr Skair, that it was your car.'

Surely they couldn't be thinking he had anything to do with Sheila's disappearance. He tried to remain cool and looked directly at Wallace. 'I don't deny that I was there,' he said. 'It was part of a case I was working on.'

'Ah yes, your work as an investigator,' she said with a decided sneer. 'We'll need access to your records. You do keep records, I suppose?'

'Of course,' he said coldly. 'Am I under suspicion?'

'Of course not,' said Duncan.

'Well...' said Wallace.

'Look, Inspector Wallace,' said Duncan, becoming formal. 'I know you're a brilliant and conscientious officer. But I've known Ian since he joined the force. He's as honest as anyone I've ever met, and I'd trust him with my life. There's no way he can be any part of this. I'd stake my career on it.'

'I'm not making any accusations,' she said, looking offended. 'I just need to tie up all the loose ends.'

'Then can I suggest,' said Duncan, 'that you do it a little more politely?'

'If I seemed impolite, then I apologise,' she said grudgingly.

'I'm happy to give you access to all the information I gathered in the course of a long and difficult investigation,' said Ian, thankful that Wallace and Duncan were the same rank. He hated to think what might happen if Wallace was in charge. 'I daresay that investigators like myself have the time to be more thorough than yourselves.' *That should put her in her place,* he thought, noticing Duncan's surreptitious wink in his direction.

'Then I'll be on my way,' said Wallace, slapping her folder shut and standing up. She crossed the road, climbed into her car and drove off.

'You didn't come together?' Ian asked.

'God, no. I wouldn't travel in the same bus as her, never mind share a car from Dundee.'

Ian laughed. 'Time for another drink?' he asked, as a waiter came to clear their table.

'Don't mind if I do. Actually I wasn't supposed to be here at all. I'm not part of the investigation into Bryson, but we have liaised over Anna's mugging attempt so when I heard she was planning to interview you I insisted I should come as well.'

'I'm glad you did.' The thought of being dragged into Wallace's car in handcuffs wasn't a pleasant one. 'She doesn't seriously believe I had anything to do with it, does she?'

Duncan shook his head. 'My guess is that she's still miffed that she arrived late and you got all the action at Drumlychtoun.' Their coffee arrived and Duncan stirred in two sachets of sugar.

'Not really my action,' Ian said. 'It was mostly Ailish and Caroline.'

'That wouldn't have helped. She likes to think she's the only feisty woman in the area. Look, don't worry about it. You're not even named as a person of interest. Email her a massive folder. Every little detail you can think of about Sheila Bryson. She'll be bored in minutes and I'll bet you never hear from her again.'

Ian wouldn't be sorry if he was right about that. 'Did you find out how Bryson knew about the party?' he asked.

'We think so. The estate works with some project in Glasgow. You know the sort of thing. Kid commits a minor crime and is sent off to do a spot of labouring somewhere as an alternative to a custodial sentence. They had one of them last week, went back to Glasgow a few days before the party. We questioned him and it seems Bryson got chatting to him in a bar in the city just after he got back. The lad thinks he may have talked about how he helped with the floodlights.'

'Is he in trouble?'

'No. He gave us some useful info and the estate manager told us he was a good worker. Says they'd consider having him back.'

'That's good,' said Ian. He had a lot of time for kids who turned their lives around.

'Caroline, eh?' said Duncan, winking. 'You two seem to make a habit of tying up ruthless criminals.'

'It's her girl guide training. I may have to take her into partnership.'

'That's what Jeanie thinks, although I think she has a different kind of partnership in mind. Well,' he said, finishing his coffee. 'I'd better get back to work. Enjoy your holiday.'

Ian waved to him as he drove off and then walked up the hill to his own house. *Yes*, he thought, *a holiday*.

When he arrived home to an excited Lottie, he sat down at his computer. He tapped a key and it sprang to life on the page he had found before he left an hour ago. The one about holiday cottages. There were still plenty available for the next week. He chose one that was dog friendly and a few minutes' walk from Loch Fyne. He was about to book it when his phone rang. He glanced at the screen and saw Rosalie's name. When had they last spoken? Not for a while. Certainly not since he'd left Edinburgh. He clicked to accept the call.

'Ian,' she said. 'How are you?'

'I'm really well,' he said. 'How are you? And Toby?'

'I'm well. Toby's just finished school and he's off to spend a few months with his father before he starts university.'

That was hard to believe. He'd known Toby when he was four. Now he was all grown up and off to New Zealand, or he supposed he was as Piers lived there. 'That's nice for him,' he said.

'We're doing an exchange,' said Rosalie. 'Toby's going to New Zealand for three months. And I get Piers' daughter Nicola for the summer. He's worried about her. Thinks Edinburgh might be a distraction. But that's not why I'm calling. Are you busy right now?'

'I'm about to go on holiday for a week. But tell me a bit more. I can always postpone it.'

'No, don't do that. We can catch up when you get back. It's about my friend Felix. Do you remember me telling you about him?'

'Vaguely. Concert pianist, wasn't he?'

'He's staying with me for a while. I'll explain more if you decide to take his case.'

'Case?'

'Yes, we need you to do some searching for us. Look, why don't you give me a call when you get back and I can tell you all about it?'

He'd be happy to work for Rosalie, or her friend. And he had nothing else lined up right now.

He'd miss Drumlychtoun and all the people he'd met and got to like. But others needed him. He'd enjoy his holiday and come back with energy and enthusiasm for whatever turned up next.

ACKNOWLEDGMENTS

I would like to thank you so much for reading **The Laird of Drumly-chtoun** I do hope you enjoyed it.

If you have a few moments to spare a short review would be very much appreciated. Reviews really help me and will help other people who might consider reading my books.

I would also like to thank my editor, Sally Silvester-Wood at *Black Sheep Books*, my cover designer, Anthony O'Brien and all my fellow writers at *Quite Write* who have patiently listened to extracts and offered suggestions.

ALSO BY HILARY PUGH

Meet Ian Skair in:

Finding Lottie

Sign up for a free copy here:

https://www.hilarypugh.com/ian-skair-private-investigator.html

Bagatelle - The Accompanist - free download included when you join my mailing list. Click the link below:

https://www.hilarypugh.com/romance-among-the-notes.html

Minuet and Trio - The Dancing Teacher

Buy the book

The River Street Family

Buy the book

ABOUT THE AUTHOR

Hilary Pugh has that elusive story telling talent that draws you in and makes you feel you are in the room with her characters.
Michelle Vernal

UK based author Hilary Pugh has spent her whole life reading and making up stories. She is currently writing a series of crime mysteries set in Scotland and featuring Private Investigator Ian Skair and his dog, Lottie.

Hilary has worked as a professional oboist and piano teacher and more recently as a creative writing tutor for the workers Educational Association.

She loves cats and makes excellent meringues.

Printed in Great Britain
by Amazon

43663380R00136